SAFE HARBOR

SAFE HARBOR
By Valerie Davisson
Copyright © 2019 Valerie Davisson

SAFE HARBOR is a work of fiction. Names, characters, places, and incidents are the product of the author's imagination or are used fictitiously. Any resemblance to actual events, locales, businesses, or persons, living or dead, is coincidental.

Published by Vaughn House Publishing, Depoe Bay, OR
Second Edition

Print ISBN - 978-1-7340119-1-3
Ebook ISBN - 978-1-7340119-2-0

Cover and Interior Design by Kimberly Peticolas, www.kimpeticolas.com

Library of Congress Control Number: 2019917333

10   9   8   7   6   5   4   3   2   1

SAFE HARBOR

A Logan McKenna Novel

VALERIE DAVISSON

To our children and grandchildren—Clif, Dave, Danielle, Ashley, Johnna, Mack, Calvin, Cooper, Casey, Sadie, and Sawyer—may you all find safe harbors of your own and then provide them for those that follow.

PROLOGUE

August 15, 2018

Man Found Dead on Fishing Boat

By Samantha Badger

Newport, Ore—The body of a 45-year-old man was discovered on the deck of a charter fishing boat early Tuesday morning in Depoe Bay Harbor by local man, Eric Udall of Newport, Oregon.

Employed as a deckhand on the boat for the last two seasons, Udall spotted the body when he arrived to work that morning.

"I still can't believe it," Udall said. "I've never seen anything like that."

Police are not releasing the victim's name pending notification of relatives. The area has been cordoned off until the investigation is complete.

1

Logan put her phone on speaker, squeezed her eyes shut a few times, and refocused on the calendar in front of her. This trip was turning out to be a major pain in the butt.

"What about the first?" Logan asked. "That's a Wednesday—should have cheaper fares."

"Let me see . . ." said Amy. "Mine looks good. Let me take a look at Liam's."

Logan waited while her daughter finished checking her husband's work schedule. She'd been trying since the beginning of summer to find two weeks that worked for everyone. Rita Wolfe, the director of the New School she worked with up in Oregon, told her about a friend's house that was available for rent. The Wagners were 'summering in Spain'. The house would be empty until September.

Must be nice.

Rita had offered her own home again—where Logan stayed last time—but it was too small for the whole gang. Besides, Rita's house held some scary memories. Two years ago,

Logan's idyllic mini-vacation there had been interrupted by a murderous, uninvited guest.

That experience hadn't turned her off to Rita's neighborhood, though. A jewel on the Oregon coast, Little Whale Cove (LWC), a community of about two hundred homes, was tucked into an old-growth cedar forest, halfway between Lincoln City and Newport, Oregon, just off Highway 101. It boasted miles of paths and a five-minute walk to a spectacular rocky bluff overlooking the ocean. Breathtaking views included migrating whales who passed by each autumn on the way to Baja, then back up again in the spring, hugging the coast on their way to nutrient-rich waters in the north. A whale-watching excursion was definitely on their to-do list.

The whole gang whose schedules she was attempting to coordinate for this trip consisted of Amy, Liam, herself, Ben, and Benjamin Liam Buchanan—a mouthful of a name for a fifteen-month-old toddler.

With all good intentions, he'd been named after his father and Logan's significant other, Ben Halvard, her landscape architect neighbor. Ben had become part of the family, even recently walking Amy down the aisle. But no matter which name they tried to use, it became unwieldy to call him Little Ben or Little Liam, and Liam was dead set against calling him Junior.

Their neighbor's little girl, Shannon, came to the rescue inadvertently. When she tried to say *Liam*, it came out *Ian*, so Ian it was! Simple solution and they all loved the name. His elementary school teachers would just have to figure it out.

She watched Ben and Ian through her studio window—two towheads bent intently over some flowers. People always assumed Ben was the little boy's biological grandfather. He got such a kick out of it, Logan never corrected them. She loved seeing them together. The two were inseparable.

SAFE HARBOR

She and Ben often watched Ian on the weekends so Liam and Amy could fit in a date night, or on days when they both had to work. During the week, Amy ran the school education and fieldtrip programs at the Sea Otter Center just north of town and Liam, a botanist, recently took over the kelp management and restoration program that stretched from La Jolla to Huntington Beach. Although technically employed by the Scripps Aquarium an hour and a half south of Jasper, California, his current projects were all local. He only had to drive south for bi-monthly meetings.

"Yep, I think it's all clear!" Amy said. "I don't see any conferences or trips that week. I'll double check when he gets home, but I think we're good."

Logan wished she could tell her right now. She had the flights pulled up on her computer and wanted to click 'buy tickets' and get it over with, but she agreed Amy better check with Liam to make sure. It would be more of a pain to have to reschedule than wait a few hours and do it right the first time.

Ending the call, she laid her cell phone on her desk and stood up to stretch. Nothing that couldn't wait 'til Monday. Between writing grants and handling the paperwork to keep everything running smoothly, there was always work she could do, but Logan had gotten better at balancing her work and personal life, usually keeping weekends free.

She glanced at her phone and then back out at the two men in her life. Too nice a day to be inside. Logan flipped her laptop shut, tucked it under her arm, and trotted down the stairs. She made the fifty-foot commute across the gravel driveway to her front door in under three minutes. A few years ago, when she was first developing the Fractals Music/Math program for the school district, Ben had helped her convert her 1940s single-car garage into a two-story workspace.

The downstairs was turned into a recording studio, mostly

used for student projects. A narrow set of stairs led to the addition he'd designed for her, stacked directly over the studio. An open, airy space, the top half of the west wall was all windows, allowing her a sweeping view of Main Beach and the ocean. Lucky for her, her home perched on the side of Killer Hill, a street that rose from Pacific Coast Highway at a 45-degree angle, so she had an unobstructed view of the ocean from both her home's rooftop deck and her studio office windows.

That wasn't the only reason she loved her at-home workspace. The other had to do with not having to work out of a claustrophobic cubbyhole at the school district offices, a twisting warren in more ways than one. The halls were lined with school politics, which she'd never been good at, even during the very short time she was a classroom teacher. Working from home helped her stay at least somewhat independent of all that.

Dimebox, her five-year old tortoiseshell rescue cat, languidly stood up and stretched at her approach. In from his nightly rounds, he'd been dozing on the slate stepping stones leading up to the front door. He wound around her ankles, now, purring loudly.

"Time for lunch," Logan said.

Twenty minutes later, after feeding Dimebox, Logan assembled some sandwiches—peanut butter and jelly for her grandson, tuna for her and Ben—lots of dill relish and chopped celery. Ben, the consummate cook, had taught her a few culinary tricks. Tuna salad sandwiches really did taste better with some crunchy stuff in there. She even toasted the bread. Occasionally, she got wild and threw in some caraway seeds.

Reaching into the small, domed refrigerator that came with her hobbit-hole beach cottage, Logan retrieved a pitcher of freshly-squeezed lemonade and some leftovers from last night's

BBQ. Her best friend, Bonnie, had a Meyer's lemon tree in her backyard that way over-produced, so she was blessed with fresh citrus all year long.

Bonnie and her husband, Mike, had taken Logan in after the car accident that left her a widow seven years ago. Her recovery included dealing with the later discovery that Jack had been unfaithful during their marriage. She'd never told Amy, and, for the most part, had let that go.

For the most part. Maybe that's why she and Ben hadn't moved forward any further than 'being in a relationship'. She didn't know if she could ever trust someone enough to marry again.

Logan added a scoop of Ben's red potato salad and some black olives onto each plate, tucked in some paper towels and spoons, put everything on a tray, and headed outside.

"Come and get it!"

2

Ben had a full outdoor kitchen and dining area in his yard, but they decided to rough it today and settled around the small, round cafe table in Logan's. Ben brought Ian's booster seat from inside and strapped him in while Logan filled his sippy cup with lemonade. He soon had peanut butter smeared on every reachable surface.

She was just popping some black olives on Ian's fat little fingers, then eating them off one by one, which always made him laugh, when she heard her doorbell ring faintly from inside the house. Passing olive-nibbling duty over to Ben, Logan pushed her chair back and went inside.

Wiping her hands on a dishtowel she grabbed on the way through the kitchen, she opened the front door and stopped dead in her tracks.

There, on the doorstep, stood a woman. Fashionably dressed. Older. Crisp, white blouse, calfskin belt, linen skirt, bare legs, and expensive looking, sensible heels. Business-like, salon-styled hair, a shade lighter than Logan remembered. It complimented her olive skin. Minimal makeup—skillfully applied.

Louis Vitton purse on her arm, she hesitantly held a set of car keys in her hand, as if expecting to be turned away. Logan saw a white Lexus pulled up behind her car in the driveway. A single word involuntarily rose to Logan's mind and almost escaped out of her mouth.

Mom.

Instead, she blurted out, "What are you doing here?"

The woman glanced back at the cars. "I see you still have Lola," she said.

Lola was Logan's sapphire blue '58 Corvette. A graduation gift from her father, seeing the car always brought back a flood of memories—all good ones. Camping trips, science experiments, popcorn-fueled scary movie nights with their father—the parent who stayed.

Her father had died several years ago, and she missed him every day. She thought of all the things he'd missed. Walking Amy down the aisle, holding his great-grandson, Ian.

Logan dragged her mind back to the present. She was at a loss for words. She wasn't going to have a casual chitchat with the woman who'd abandoned her family thirty-some odd years ago. She'd only been thirteen and Rick was what, nine when she left? She'd have to do the math to figure out how old their father had been. Parents didn't come with numbers. Dad was always just Dad—and he'd been a great one—before and after his wife up and left. No explanation, no nothing. Just gone one morning when they woke up.

Logan decided to stick with the tried and true. "Why are you here?" she asked, keeping her voice even. "What do you want?"

"I'm not sure exactly. I'd like to talk to you if you'll let me," her mother said.

Her mother's face had more lines and she was thinner.

Ben appeared at her shoulder, Ian on his hip. He sensed the tension and looked questioningly at Logan.

Ian had no such qualms. After first burying his face in Ben's shoulder coyly, he whipped his head around and turned on the charm, blessing the woman standing before him with a huge smile and outstretched, somewhat sticky arms. Logan automatically reached up with the dishtowel to wipe at the remaining peanut butter on his hands in case he launched himself into his great-grandmother's arms.

Great-grandmother. Wow. Several lifetimes had slipped by.

"Hello," the woman said, reaching out a perfectly manicured hand to Ben, whose right hand was free, "I'm . . . Sofia."

Realizing he was in way over his head, he shook the proffered hand briefly and said, "Nice to meet you. I'm Ben."

Apparently, no one was going to tell him what was going on, so he shifted Ian to his other hip. "I'll just go get things cleaned up now," he said, returning swiftly to the safety of the kitchen, the toddler wailing his disappointment at not being allowed to greet the new visitor properly.

Logan waited until Ben was hopefully out of earshot.

"I don't know that we have anything to talk about," she said quietly. "Why now? Why after all this time?"

"Look, I'm sorry to spring this on you—just show up here unannounced—but I couldn't think of any other way. I figured if I called you'd just hang up on me."

You got that right, "Mom."

"If it helps, I'm not expecting or even looking for forgiveness, but there are some things you should know," Sophie looked awkwardly around her, as if she'd misplaced something.

"I'm staying in a hotel nearby. They have a nice restaurant. I can meet you there, we can talk over dinner—my treat—or anywhere else you'd prefer. I saw a coffee shop at the end of the street there as I was turning in. Tava-something with a lot of vowels. That's fine, too. I don't know if they're open for dinner . . ." her voice trailed.

She looked down at her shoes, waiting for Logan to speak. When she didn't, Sofia unclasped her purse, took a card out, and handed it to her. Not a business card, but a personal calling card—a throwback from some genteel era. Not a CPA anymore, then?

"I'll be in town for a few days. I hope you'll call. And if this time isn't good, I don't live far. I have a flexible schedule. I can be here on short notice. We can do dinner, lunch, or whatever time works for you," she said. "I really just want to talk. If after you hear what I have to say you want nothing more to do with me, I'll go away. You won't hear from me again."

"Like last time, Mom?"

3

Shaking slightly, Logan closed the door and walked carefully back down the short hallway to the living room, where Ben was playing on the floor with his namesake, stacking and knocking down wooden blocks. Logan loved the softly ringing sound they made as they tumbled. Reminded her of playing with Amy. Vaguely she registered the Lexus' engine starting up, transporting her mother to whatever hotel she was staying at. She'd neglected to ask.

Complicated Lego sets and video games were in her grandson's future, but for now, she was glad he was satisfied by these simple toys—wooden blocks, Tupperware bowls, wooden spoons, and ersatz percussion instruments made of Illy coffee cans partially filled with rice or beans. Everything delighted him. The afternoon sun streamed in the kitchen window and warmed the room. Ben had opened the kitchen window and the French doors leading from the living room into the garden for a soft breeze.

Grateful for a moment of normalcy, Logan sank to the floor, building and demolishing a variety of edifices to Ian's delighted shrieks. Ben started to ask her what happened, but she shook her head.

Knowing she'd tell him when she was ready, Ben wisely let it go. Amy and Liam were due to pick Ian up at 5:00 p.m. He'd just have to wait until tonight to find out who in the hell this woman was and why Logan not only didn't invite her in, but shut the door in her face. He had never seen Logan be rude to anyone. Obviously, there was a history there, but what could the mystery woman have done? It must have been something awful to cause the grim set of Logan's jaw and the fury in her eyes.

It took a while for her to calm down enough to talk about it, but later that night, Logan filled Ben in.

"What about Rick? Are you going to tell him?"

With a stab of guilt, Logan realized she hadn't even thought about Rick. How would he take it that his mother was back in town? How much did he even remember of her?

Of the two of them, Rick looked more like his mother than Logan did, inheriting her Sicilian features: black hair, smooth, olive skin that didn't require sunscreen, and a shorter, thicker build. Until he started lifting weights for the wrestling team in high school and carb loading, Rick couldn't push the needle on the bathroom scale past 145 pounds.

Logan took after their father's Scotch/Irish side: taller, tomboy build, fair skin, high cheekbones sprinkled with freckles, green eyes and thick, auburn waves.

"I don't know. I haven't even decided what I'm going to do," she said.

"Do you think she contacted him, too? If she found you, she must know where Rick is," Ben said.

"I don't know. He hasn't called and I think he would have if she showed up at the station or his house."

Ben pulled her closer and the blanket up over her shoulders. Logan's 5' 8" fit nicely against Ben's 6'2", her head comfortably resting on his shoulder, one leg and arm slung over his body—sideways spooning. Ben was always on a diet, but was solid due to his job, and she liked his heft. She snugged her body closer. Ben made her feel warm in more ways than one—and when she allowed herself to feel it, safe and secure.

Summer nights cooled off along the coast. Up here on the rooftop deck, there was just enough chill to warrant sharing one of the sturdy, teak lounge chairs. They usually each sat in their own, but she was glad they were big enough to share when the mood struck.

After Liam and Amy had picked up their son, she and Ben had had dinner, and then came up here to catch the sunset. There was something calming about watching Jasper's Main Beach close down for the day, volleyball players wiping their sweaty faces with a towel after a tough game, sunbathers packing up coolers and kids—everything bathed in golden light. Tourists returned to their hotel rooms, inland visitors who'd driven in to cool off with a beach break loaded up their cars, then fought the bumper to bumper traffic back to the suburbs.

Then it was just the locals. Jasper didn't allow bonfires on the beach anymore, so summer beer bashes had moved north to Huntington Beach to annoy the neighbors and give the police someone to arrest for drunk and disorderly.

Jasper kept a low party profile, which was one of the reasons Logan loved it. Almost every night, even in winter, she and Ben mounted the stairs that ran along the south side of her house from the yard to the roof for some sea gazing. When she moved in, some of the first items she bought were the two heavy-duty teak lounge chairs and a small table, which held ocean-watching essentials: corkscrew, wool blankets, and a pair of binoculars to check out the occasional dolphins that surfed the waves.

Right now, she allowed her eyelids to close and just listen to the sound of the shushing waves drifting up Killer Hill.

"I'll think about that tomorrow, at Tara," Logan mumbled into Ben's chest, in her best Scarlett O'Hara high, southern drawl, referencing one of her favorite movies, *Gone with the Wind*. "Tomorrow is another day!"

Ben smiled and kissed the top of Logan's head.

4

Tomorrow started with one of Logan's favorite activities, her Sunday morning beach run. For the most part, her knee had recovered from a torn meniscus and a sprained ankle she got two years ago. She had to wrap them occasionally, but more for prevention than cure. She wasn't going to be entering any marathons, but as long as she could still pound the sand for a few miles, she wasn't complaining. Much. Before exiting her house, she slipped on her flip flops by the door. What was the point of running on the beach if you couldn't splash in the water and feel the sand between your toes?

Ben and his dog, Purgatory, used to join her, but almost ten years old now, the gentle, Greater Swiss Mountain dog was starting to slow down. Leisurely late afternoon strolls suited his aging joints better than beach runs. But he could still romp with Ben's nephews, Calvin and Cooper, and regularly did—at least for short spurts—whenever they came to visit.

Purgatory earned his moniker. He was known for his lethal farts after ingesting his favorite food, grilled Polish sausages. You didn't want to ever feed Purgatory inside.

Ben had a big job Monday, so he'd left to pick up some

supplies. Purgatory almost always accompanied him, sleeping in the cab of his truck, or in whatever shade was available while his master played in the dirt. Although Ben was a successful landscape architect, that's how he usually described what he did for a living when asked. Another thing she loved about him—his dry sense of humor. Ben kept it real.

Making sure Dimebox had fresh water inside and out, Logan turned left out of her driveway, adjusted her ponytail and pulled her baseball cap lower to shield her eyes. A white, ribbed tank top hugged modest breasts and contrasted nicely with toned, tan arms. She loved the feel of sun on her skin.

It was going to be a beautiful day for a run. Light breeze, not too hot yet. September was usually almost unbearably hot, but late July was still manageable. Another perfect day in paradise.

Just as she started to pick up speed on the sidewalk, a blur of white, barking, puppy energy came barreling toward her, leash trailing wildly behind him. Her neighbor, Lori, came flying off the porch after him.

Two years ago, Lori came to Jasper to escape an abusive spouse. But he found her, put her in the hospital, kidnapped her preschool daughter, Shannon, and almost killed Logan. The guy got what he deserved. Lori and Shannon were now safe. Shannon had always wanted a puppy and had received this one, an English Cream Golden Retriever, for her birthday that year.

"Marmo! Marmo! Come!" Lori shouted.

Completely ignoring her, Marmo already had both front paws on Logan's shoulders and was proceeding to lick her face and neck, tail wagging furiously, wriggling with delight between bouts of jumping off and then back up again. He knew she could be counted on for treats and loves.

Logan saw him coming, so was able to brace herself. And slip him a few cubes of cheese.

"I thought his name was Matoskan, for White Bear," Logan laughed, ruffling his fur.

"Yes, that's his registered name, but Marmo's what's sticking," Lori said, "Marmo is Shannon's version of 'Marshmallow', which is what she's been calling him."

"Where is Shannon?"

"She's at school already," Lori said. "I'm just the designated dogsitter."

The eleven-month-old puppy tipped the scales at eighty-four pounds already and had huge, polar-bear paws, so Matoskan/White Bear, was the perfect name for him. But he was Shannon's dog, and if she wanted to call him Marmo, so be it. Besides, Marmo fit the dog's sweet, goofy personality.

Lori looked great. Her new life suited her.

After promising to stop by for a visit before she left, Logan waved and continued on her way. Waiting at the light at the bottom of Killer Hill, she saw Tava'e's was already buzzing. Actually, she smelled the mouthwatering aromas a block before she got there.

Epiphany, the ever-efficient, multiple-pierced and tattooed barista, was handling the line at the counter. No one knew Epiphany's whole story, but the girl's mother had a sense of humor. She once explained to Logan that her hippie mom saddled her with her unusual name because she liked telling people she *'had* an Epiphany'.

Weird or not, at least her mom was there for her, unlike mine. Or maybe not—who knew?

Pushing thoughts of mothers aside when the walk light flashed, Logan crossed the street, picked her way down the boardwalk steps onto the sand. Taking off her flip-flops, she tucked them behind one of the posts. She nodded at the lifeguard coming on duty. She wouldn't be gone long and not many people were here yet. Hopefully they'd still be there when she got back.

The beach here wasn't very wide. She did some stretches, then started jogging along the shore, splashing in and out of the waves as they slid up the sand and back out again. The lifeguard watched, admiring her form. Then, lengthening her stride, finding her rhythm, Logan ran.

What she was running from, only she could tell.

5

By the time she was done, she'd worked up a sweat. She stopped for a quick rinse off in the outdoor shower before retrieving her flip-flops and heading up to Tava'e's for breakfast. Sun blazing now, she was dry before she hit the front door. The bells jingled as she pushed it open and walked in.

"*Talofa*, Little One!" Round face beaming, the owner of the shop, a large Samoan woman named Tava'e, lumbered over and enveloped Logan in a massive hug.

"You too skinny!" she said.

Taking Logan's elbow, she maneuvered her to her booth, located in farthest corner of the cafe, next to a wall of windows overlooking Main Beach across from PCH. It had been specially made to accommodate her generous proportions, and where she held chess court each morning, taking on all comers.

As she sat down, Tava'e called back over her shoulder, "Epiphan . . ."

Epiphany beat her to it. She'd already materialized at the table, delivering a delicate, gold-rimmed espresso cup to her boss, sliding a plate of frosted, cinnamon heaven in front of Logan, next to a steaming white mug of coffee. She left as quickly as she came, attending to other duties behind the counter. The young woman was amazing.

Tava'e motioned for Logan to eat while sipping her coffee and setting up the chess pieces. She'd insisted Logan learn the game and although she couldn't yet beat Tava'e, she'd come to find the mental challenge strangely relaxing. Ben had a plastic set with a rollup mat he kept in his truck. They were more evenly matched, so picnics almost always included a game.

Owner of this establishment, mother to many, and friend to all she deemed worthy, Tava'e was one of Logan's favorite people. It didn't hurt that her husband, Jean, the silent French baker in the back no one ever saw, made the best cinnamon rolls in town. They were legendary and almost as large as dinner plates.

It was Tava'e who'd organized the search parties when Amy was lost in a storm at sea three years ago, attempting to rescue a baby sea otter and escape a killer. Tava'e who somehow found jobs and counseling for the homeless, old and young, that found their way to her door. Her coffee shop anchored not only this corner, but the whole community. She and Jean even hosted and catered Amy and Liam's wedding, offering their beautiful, oceanside home for the ceremony.

Once they'd covered how Amy, Liam and Ian were doing, Tava'e paused, looking at her.

What?

"I heard you had a visitor yesterday," she said.

How had she heard about that? Logan knew Ben wouldn't have said anything. He respected her privacy. But not much got past Tava'e. She knew pretty much everything that happened in Jasper.

SAFE HARBOR

"Uh, yes," Logan said, not elaborating.

Tava'e let the silence deepen.

Logan didn't rise to the bait.

"Well, if I'm going to get anything done today, I'd better get going," she finally said, pushing back her chair. She walked up to the counter and paid Epiphany. She almost made it out the door, which Tava'e was holding open for her.

"Talking costs you nothing. Listening is even cheaper," Tava'e said quietly, as she caught Logan in a hug.

Closing her mind to her friend's wisdom, wishing the whole world didn't know about her business, Logan scooted past a couple coming in the door and all but fled up the hill.

Back in her studio office, Logan didn't waste any time. A woman on a mission, verifying the dates once more with Amy, she pulled up the Alaska Air site, with the flights she'd saved yesterday, selected their seats and hit Buy Tickets with more force than necessary.

Ten days. In ten days she'd be a thousand miles away, whale watching, cruising the shops, eating caramel corn in front of the fire, sitting around the table, passing Ian around from lap to lap, BBQing on the deck, trying to beat Liam at Monopoly. So far, he remained the undefeated champ.

Dimebox jumped up onto her lap. Pressing against her hand until she started scratching the top of his head, he rumbled contentedly. Logan wished she could be pleased so easily. Hands occupied, her mind wandered, the problem of the day pushing front and center, not to be ignored.

She picked up the card her mother handed to her yesterday.

Sofia Landers

Must have married again, or maybe that was her maiden name. No, she was Italian. Landers didn't sound very Italian. From Sicily. Second generation. How weird was it that she didn't even know her mother's maiden name. Growing up, she'd just always been Mrs. McKenna.

What was she doing here? Why had she come back? Logan's mind ticked through the possible reasons she could think of: dying of cancer or some other terminal illness and wanted to make amends before she died? No, the woman looked healthier than she'd ever seen her. After rejecting a few more scenarios, Logan's mind came up blank. Sitting her wondering about it wasn't going to answer her questions.

And she should find out what her mother wanted before contacting Rick. He and Paula were getting married next year. The last thing he needed was a wrench thrown into the happy couple's plans.

As his big sister, it was her obligation to protect him. Whatever their mother's reasons, it was selfish of her to want to pop back into their lives now, after all these years. Her desertion blew a big hole into their family, with wounds that may have healed over, but who knew how deep they ran underneath. Rick was happy. He was settled. She wasn't about to knock off that scab.

Logan remembered the first few months after their mom left, holding her little brother when he woke up with nightmares, checking under his bed endless times for monsters, washing his sheets when he started wetting the bed again, staying with him until he drifted back to sleep, and worst of all, listening helplessly some nights as their father sobbed quietly in his room, trying not to wake them. Logan was the only one of them that didn't cry.

Letting out a huff of air, Logan abruptly stood, depriving Dimebox of his comfortable lap. Landing on his feet, shaking off the insult, he stalked off, tail in the air.

Great.

SAFE HARBOR

Her mom was already ruining things! She stared out the window to the ocean. The only way she was going to fix this was to face it head on. No amount of caramel corn or whale watching in Oregon was going to take her mind of this one.

Sighing, she reached for the phone.

6

TUESDAY, AUGUST 7, 2018

DEPOE BAY, OR

11:30 P.M.

"What? So you're just going to ignore me, now?"

The woman's voice was low, but voices carry on the water. Unlike during the day, when the dock bustled with activity, except for the rhythmic bumps of the boats against the dock, it was usually quiet at night here.

Karen Monahan rubbed her eyes and blinked them wide a few times. As far as she could tell, the voice came from a boat a few finger docks away from the boat she was sleeping on. She thought it might be the *Mary Ann*. She'd noticed someone had been staying on their boat the last few nights. It was just one guy and she'd made sure he was asleep before she came down. Whoever was arguing with him must have come by after that.

Technically, there were no live-aboards allowed down here, but Karen wasn't in any position to turn the guy in. She didn't care what anyone did as long as they didn't bother her. She didn't sleep on the same boat every night, rotating was safer. And when she did come down here, she waited until it was completely dark, and made sure all traces of her camping out were removed long before the first deckhand arrived. She minded her own business.

Still, she couldn't help being a little curious. There was no TV to watch and she'd have trouble going back to sleep. Might as well let these two yahoos entertain her. She couldn't leave or they might hear her. She was afraid to even sit up all the way, so she peeked around the tip of the bow of the boat she was on and saw the man, silhouetted against the wheelhouse, facing a woman, who was almost as tall as he was.

"Look, Deb, I don't have anything left to say," the man said. "Go home. Who's watching the girls, anyway?"

The woman folded her arms and shifted her stance on deck.

"Don't even go there, Adam," she growled, "They're fine. Ariel's almost eleven—I was taking care of all four of my brothers at that age. They're asleep."

She took a breath, then said, "This is payback, isn't it?"

"Of course not, it's not like that. I told you," he said. "I was angry, yes, but I got over it. You had a right, in a way. I wasn't giving you what you needed."

He put his hands in his back pockets, rocked on his heels and looked down at his feet, "You just wanted to be loved. You deserve that . . . and so do I."

"But I do love you! We have three kids, Adam! What about them? What am I supposed to tell them?" she said, her voice rising. "I left him. I gave up Byron for us, for our family. Doesn't that count? That should count for something!"

"Yes, of course, but it's not about that anymore," he said. "Look, I'm selling the business . . ."

"You're what?!" she shouted.

Two boats away, Karen hunkered down in her sleeping bag and listened. This was getting good.

"Don't worry, as soon as it sells, I'll split the profit with you. You'll have enough to start over, take care of the girls."

"The hell you will! I put my blood, sweat, and tears into getting this business going and you're not going to sell it out from under me, from under us! This is our home, Adam. Where, exactly, am I supposed to go?"

Karen held her breath in the silence, not wanting to breathe, in case she missed anything. This was better than *Game of Thrones.*

"I don't know, Deb. I don't know," he said. "All I know is that I love Meiling and I'm leaving. You deserve more than I can give."

The woman's foot shot out to kick the man in the shin, but missed and she almost lost her balance.

"You bastard! Don't make this sound like you're doing me a favor! I'll make sure you never see us again, that the girls never speak to you again. You think it's easy to get a no-fault divorce in Oregon so you can run off with your little Chinese, geisha doll? Think again!"

Chinese geisha doll? Didn't the woman know geishas were Japanese, not Chinese?

"This isn't California. I'll get the best damn lawyer I can find if you so much as think about it. Statute of limitations in Oregon for rape is twelve years, Adam. I was only sixteen when we met—remember? And only seventeen when we got married."

"But you lied, Debbie!"

"That won't matter. I'll dredge it all up if I have to, Adam. I'll tell it all! But you will *not* leave our family!"

"I'm leaving you, not the girls," he said quietly.

This last statement must have been too much. The woman, presumably the man's wife, started swinging at her husband, hitting and punching his chest. He easily moved out of her reach. Finally, he stood still, holding his arms up in front of his face, absorbing her blows, but didn't try to defend himself. The guy looked fit. He could easily have decked her.

When she showed no signs of letting up, he grabbed her arms and held them by her sides and looked her in the eyes.

"You kicked *me* out, remember?" he said.

There were a few more back-and-forths, but the argument wound down after that. Didn't sound like there was much left to say.

Karen watched as the woman ran up the dock, yanked open the door to a blue Kia and threw herself in. Seconds later the engine revved and gravel sprayed as she floored it out of the parking lot. She watched the car turn left at the light, speeding south down 101. Hopefully, the woman would make it back to her daughters without killing herself on the way.

When she looked back, the *Mary Ann* was dark again. The man must have turned in. It made Karen never want to get married. Rape, cheating, three kids, and no easy way out. Fun. Made her problems seem small by comparison. At least she hadn't screwed her life up yet. Not irreversibly, anyway.

She wasn't really homeless. Her mom lived in Newport. Theoretically, she could go home anytime, but a few months ago her mom had started drinking again and lost another job, which led to more drinking. It was a cycle Karen was all too familiar with. She may be broke and sleeping on the streets, but she was safer and more in control of her environment than she would be at home. Finals were in two weeks. After that, she was transferring to University of Oregon in Eugene.

SAFE HARBOR

Her grades were decent, so she got into the computer science program without too much effort. She had a couple scholarships lined up and wasn't afraid of working. Karen had waited tables at the Horn on weekends ever since she was old enough to get a job. Most of the cooks were nice. They let her take some of the send-backs when the owner wasn't around and the manager wasn't looking. She'd get by.

And getting by meant not getting involved in other people's problems.

7

Shocking everyone, the flight to Portland wasn't full and Ben was able to upgrade them to first class. One of his wealthier clients had just given him a bonus. Once everyone was settled in, Logan looked out the window and thought about her almost meeting with her mother.

She'd made the call and agreed to meet her at the restaurant she suggested. She waited for an hour, but dear old mom never showed. Angered at putting herself in the position to be left again, Logan refused her mother's calls the next morning then blocked her numbers, ripped up her card, and shoved her out of her mind. At least she hadn't gotten Rick's hopes up. She was glad now she never told him their mom was in town.

Ben's namesake slept for most of the flight to Portland, but went into a full wail upon landing. The change in air pressure must have hurt his ears. Amy was able to distract him into muffled sobs on the way to pick up their rental car, but Logan hoped they wouldn't have two and a half hours of fussy baby on the drive to the coast. She'd forgotten how tough it was to travel with young children. She loved her grandson, but there was a reason people had kids when they were young.

They'd rented an SUV with lots of room for people and luggage, but she was surprised at how much equipment and other paraphernalia accompanied children these days. The car seat and stroller were larger than her and Jack's first apartment. Diapers, bottles, and blankets she expected, but there was an entire array of things a toddler apparently couldn't live without anymore, supplied mainly by the wealthy grandparents in Scotland. Three different baby monitors, some kind of jumper thing, special battery-operated mobiles, an iPad—the technology alone took up an entire suitcase.

Things were much simpler when she had Amy. Good thing she and Ben were light packers or someone would be strapped on the roof.

Once you got out of the snarled suburbs, the country opened up onto green fields and golden, rolling hills. She lowered the window a bit and took a deep breath, inhaling the newly washed air.

The car ride and fresh air must have had a relaxing effect on Ian, too, because just as they were passing the turn off she usually took to the New School, he conked out. Logan pulled down her visor and glanced into the back seat to see how everyone was doing. Amy was asleep on Liam's shoulder. Liam was scrolling through something on his cell phone.

All quiet on the western front.

Logan squeezed Ben's hand and handed him a bottle of iced tea she'd picked up in the airport, then settled back into her seat. Mentally, she went through her checklist, making sure she hadn't forgotten anything. Coffee pot unplugged, doors locked, key left with the neighbor. Lori always kept an eye on the place and took care of Dimebox when she was away. Ben's sister was dogsitting Purgatory.

She wished she could have resolved things with her mother, but it's not like she hadn't tried. Logan put her firmly out of her mind. All she had to do now was keep her there.

Ben had moved a lot of his jobs around in order to make this trip, and Amy and Liam both took time off work. She owed it to all of them to be fully present for the next twelve days. Besides, she hadn't taken a real vacation since Jack died. She was determined to enjoy this one.

They stopped at the Thriftway on the way into Depoe Bay to pick up food for the next few days. They'd do a major shopping trip in Newport at Fred Meyers tomorrow. Logan hadn't tried any of the local restaurants while she was there, but Lincoln County had quite a few. Rita recommended a Mexican place and a Chinese restaurant within a half-mile of their rental where the food was good and kids were welcome.

The sun was still bright when they drove through Depoe Bay late in the afternoon, Logan watching for the wooden entry sign for Little Whale Cove. In keeping with the low key, natural style of the place, it blended in with the trees and was easy to miss. She spotted it just in time and Ben turned right in front of it and pulled up to the gate.

They punched in the code and as they drove through were immediately surrounded by forest. Logan was gratified to see everyone had the same reaction she did her first time here. It felt like driving into a fairy tale or a national park.

"Wow! This is amazing!" Amy said.

"Yeah, I know. Isn't it beautiful? Rita said when they developed this place, they decided to leave everything as natural as possible," Logan said. "No lawns—only native vegetation—and they only cut down enough trees to build the house, but the rest are left unless they're diseased or something."

"Rita's house is down that street," she said, pointing left.

She checked the map the Wagners sent and started watching for their street.

"Here it is. Hemlock, fourth house on the left, at the end of the cul de sac. She said it was right on the water . . ."

They all held their breaths waiting to see if the house they'd be spending the next two weeks in was as nice as it looked in the pictures they were sent. You never knew with a rental, but when Ben pulled into the driveway, Amy squealed, "Awesome!"

And it was. Strongly built, with two and a half stories to take advantage of the view, the large, modern home's exterior was weathered cedar shingles and solid, white-framed windows. A gnarled shore pine, nestled against a boulder covered in moss, graced the front yard. Bark chip and a few small hillocks of ice plant lined the driveway.

The homes at this end of Little Whale Cove were strung along a winding, ocean path, perched above a dramatic, rocky coastline. Even from the car they could hear the crashing waves and seagulls calling.

Getting out to take a look before unpacking the car, they trooped around to the back patio, which boasted a panoramic view of the ocean from the edge of Depoe Bay to the right, where they just were, to a trio of rock formations jutting into the ocean about a mile south, hinting at small coves. Logan was familiar with one of them, Little Whale Cove, for which the community was named.

Whoever designed the house knew what they were doing. When you walked in the front door, the first thing you saw was a floor-to-ceiling ocean view from the huge, trapezoid window in the living room. Open kitchen and dining areas were off to the right. The master bedroom, which had plenty of room for Amy, Liam, and Ian's crib, was down a short hallway on the left and there were decks and balconies off each floor. Ben and

Logan took one of the smaller, upstairs rooms.

To top it off, the downstairs game room came complete with a very nice pool table. They'd planned on playing a game, but after dinner, everyone was so tired from the trip, they decided to go to bed early and begin their vacation tomorrow.

The next few days would be do your own thing. Logan wanted to do one of the Shop the Dock tours and Ben wanted to do a fishing trip. She didn't care where they got it, but Logan wanted to boil up some fresh crab, then sit around cracking them open, dipping the crab meat into butter, making a mess on the picnic table out back on the deck. She saw it in a movie once. It was on her bucket list.

The only firm event on the calendar was one Rita had lined up for them: two tickets to an in-home classical music concert at the neighbor's house next week. She'd explained a little of the background when she emailed her the receipt and directions.

For the last fifteen years, Vivi and Stan Hosteler had provided the venue for visiting musicians from all over the world in their home as part of the Siletz Bay Music Festival. Vivi was a retired human resources director for a Silicon Valley tech company, and Stan was former military.

Three or four times a year, they set up several rows of folding chairs in their great room for the intimate venue. The reasonable ticket price of only thirty dollars bought you an evening of high-quality music, up close and personal, performed by internationally renowned musicians. The whole evening was catered by the local culinary school. It was a win/win all around.

The concerts were always sold out, but one of the guests fell and broke both her wrist and arm last week, so had turned their tickets back in. Rita had snapped them up as soon as she heard and gave them to Logan.

"Rita told us you're a musician yourself, Logan," Vivi said

when she came over earlier to give them their tickets. "You'll really appreciate the performance. They are so popular we've had them back several times. It's a brother and sister duo, Meiling and Jian Zhang. She's a violinist and her brother accompanies her on the piano."

Not exactly the bluegrass fiddling tunes Logan had been playing all summer with her friends at the Otter Festival, but good music was good music, no matter the genre. She hoped Ben would enjoy it.

8

In the morning, Ben frowned at the bowls of cold cereal, but was reassured he'd be able to buy real food in Newport this afternoon after they went to the aquarium. A town of a few thousand residents, Newport was about thirty minutes south on Highway 101. Highway 101 was the only game in town, Rita warned, so if there was an accident on it, they'd be sitting in bumper to bumper traffic until it was cleared. Or you could get out and hike through the forest on the east side or swim along the ocean on the west. Those were your options.

Good to be forewarned. Logan made sure they packed some extra snacks and water bottles along with sufficient diapers for Ian.

On this vacation, everyone was free to do their own thing, from sitting on the deck sipping a Chardonnay or tackling an all-day hike on one of the tougher trails inland. And there were some things they'd want to do together. They decided over breakfast to take turns selecting various group activities, and Amy picked today's outing. She heard they had a southern sea otter along with two northern ones at The Oregon Coast Aquarium.

Logan didn't think such a small venue would amount to much, but it turned out to offer more than she expected. It was also in the middle of fundraising for a major facelift and ambitious expansion of educational programs and marine animal exhibits.

At the entrance, someone took their picture and then asked for an email address to send it to should they decide to order any. Logan scribbled hers down and they went in.

In the Coastal Waters area, Ian was mesmerized by a group of transparent, pale Moon Jellies gracefully pulsing up and down in slow motion through the column of water in their well-lit eight-foot, cylindrical tank. In the Rocky Shores area, one of the volunteers showed him how to touch the myriad and colorful starfish—correction, sea stars—and anemones so as not to harm them. While talking with the man, they learned the majority of the docents manning the exhibits were volunteers from the community.

When they got to the sea otter exhibit, Amy was in seventh heaven. She asked so many questions, Molly Gorman, the woman in charge of the education and school field trips who was passing by at the time, took them back behind the scenes to meet the trainers. Logan invited her to join them for lunch. Molly and Amy had a great time comparing notes and exchanging ideas.

After loading up the car with groceries at Fred Meyers, they headed back home. They'd been too tired to swing by the docks for fresh crab, so had to settle for steaks.

Darn.

9

Logan rolled over, lifted herself up on an elbow, and pried open an eye. Cheerful, male, whistling sounds emanated from the shower in the bathroom. A ribbon of light and steam curled over the door. The bedroom was still dark. She flopped back down, pulling her pillow over her head and quietly groaned. Logan wasn't against mornings *per se*, just ones that started before dawn.

Yesterday, sitting outside on the deck, sated and relaxed, watching the lovely setting sun, Ben's suggestion of going on a half-day fishing trip sounded like a great idea.

Not so much, now. But she'd agreed to go, so kicked herself out of bed and stripped off her pajamas. She padded barefoot across the hardwood floor and joined Ben in the shower. Might as well get some benefit out of getting up this early. Ben was a great back scrubber.

Among his other talents.

Dried, dressed, and fed by 5:00 a.m. Logan and Ben hit the road and were queued up with the other fishing trip customers at Dockside Charters in Depoe Bay by 5:30 a.m. Most warmed their hands on cups of coffee provided in the lobby. It was a mixed group. Some families, some singles—mostly men and boys. Logan loved the directions they'd been given yesterday when she called to reserve their spots.

"Turn right at the only stoplight in town. Can't miss us."

Small towns were the best.

Ben signed them in while Logan scanned the harbor for their boat. They'd signed on for a half-day trip on the *Mary Ann,* they later learned was named after the wholesome, girl-next-door on *Gilligan's Island.* Delores, the woman behind the counter, said the current owner of the boat was too young to have watched the show, but kept the name when he bought her because everyone knows it's bad luck to change the name of a boat.

Advertised as the world's smallest harbor, Depoe Bay fit the bill. No more than twenty or thirty boats were tied up at the docks. She could almost throw a rock across the harbor to the concrete, arched bridge spanning the short, rock-lined entrance to the harbor. The narrow passage couldn't have been more than a couple hundred feet wide. She wondered if there was a height limit on the bridge like there was on tunnels and parking garages.

"Mrs. McKenna?" a young man's voice called out to her from one of the boats.

Logan located him standing next to a compact, freshly painted, green and white boat bobbing in the water, clipboard in hand. *Mary Ann* was painted in neat script along the bow, bright white against teal green. She wondered how he knew her name, then realized she must be the only woman going on this trip. Seeing how small the boat was, and how it bobbed in the water, she was glad she'd put on a seasick patch before she left the house.

"Hi," she said, reaching out to shake his hand, "That's me, but just Logan is fine, nice to meet you."

"Well, hello, Logan. I'm Eric. I'm the deckhand. Captain will be down with the others in just a minute. In the meantime," he reached out his hand and smiled broadly, "Welcome aboard! You're first, so you get the tour."

Nice kid.

Tall and gangly, with a thick wave of stiff, red hair swooping off his forehead, Eric helped her step onto the boat. He had a nice face, tan and sprinkled with freckles. Starting a stream of chatter, he showed her around, explaining that this was the best boat in the harbor and that his boss, Captain Adam, the best captain to work for.

"I was lucky to get hired on the *Mary Ann*. Technically, he doesn't have to hire a deckhand for just a six pack, but he does."

"What's a six pack?" Logan asked.

"Oh, it's what the smaller boats like this are called. It means he can take out up to six paying customers for each trip by himself, and not have to pay a deckhand, but Captain Adam's big on training the young guys. He's trained half the skippers out here. I want to have my own charter boat someday. Get my masters license. You got on a good boat. Everybody respects Captain Adam."

Stuffed into her jacket pocket were two baggies of ginger cookies as backup, in case the seasick patch didn't work. Bonnie, who took her students on a whale-watching trip every year near Catalina Island, swore by Trader Joe's Triple Gingers.

"Save my butt every year!" she laughed. "Without those cookies, I'd be tossing mine over the side within two minutes of leaving shore."

Logan spent the next few minutes people watching as customers like her located and boarded their boats. She heard a few foreign accents and saw a lot of sunscreen and sandals. She felt for the women wearing skimpy shorts and tank tops. This wasn't Florida or the Bahamas. It looked like several of them were regretting their wardrobe choices already.

"Here they come," Eric said.

Ben's blonde head could easily be seen over a small group of Japanese tourists as they made their way down the dock. Bringing up the rear was a dark-haired man, as tall as Ben, about their age. Solid. Like Ben, he looked fit from working outdoors.

Dark, brown eyes under straight brows, he sported what could have been the beginnings of a beard, or yesterday's 5:00 shadow. He waited until everyone was on board before introducing himself and Eric Udall, their deckhand. He gave a brief safety speech, indicating where the lifejackets were stowed and the raft located should they be needed.

"Once everyone's ready, we can head out. We like to get under the bridge by 6:00," Adam said.

When they were all safely seated or hanging onto something, Eric gave the thumbs up.

Adam took his place at the wheel and called out, "Let's go get some fish!"

"Woohoo!" Eric crowed.

Their enthusiasm was catching and as the captain skillfully maneuvered the boat through the rocks and out onto the open ocean, Logan found herself getting excited about actually catching something she could eat that night for dinner. The cold, morning air was fresh and clean and she didn't feel seasick at all! Of course, they'd only been on the water about five minutes. But still . . .

10

The coastline was on their right, so she knew they were heading north toward Lincoln City.

"How do you know where to go—where the fish are?" Logan asked, trying to speak up over the roar of the engine. Eric had set her up just outside of the wheelhouse where the captain was piloting the boat. Ben took the next spot up from hers. Logan knew there were probably better, more precise nautical terms for all this, but she didn't know any. She thought starboard was right, but she wasn't sure.

Adam pushed his hair out of his eyes, then replaced his cap, looking ahead. Even though he'd probably answered the same questions hundreds of times, he didn't seem to mind explaining it again.

"Well, we know where the reefs are—rocky reefs for rock fish. We use GPS. We have a chart plotter on the boat. If we catch fish, we can find it again."

"Do you guys share your favorite fishing spots?" Logan asked, wondering how competitive this business was.

Adam looked over at her and smiled, "We have our friends."

Logan laughed. Human nature was the same in every field.

For the next few minutes, she kept her eyes on the horizon ahead of her. The sun was up and the seas relatively calm, but she wasn't taking any chances.

When they arrived at a spot that looked like every other spot on the ocean as far as she could tell, Eric and Adam helped everyone bait their hooks, make sure their poles were secure, and begin 'jigging for fish'. One of the Japanese gentlemen snagged the first one, a bright orange rockfish and quickly caught three more. For sustainability reasons, the limit was five. Logan lost her first one, but Ben was having fun. After a long wrestle with a scary looking lingcod, he finally landed it on board.

"They're ugly, but they're good eating," Adam assured them.

Near the end of the trip, with a little help from Eric, Logan brought in her own rockfish, so she at least wasn't going back empty handed.

Depoe Bay's rocky harbor looked even more dangerous on the way in than on the way out this morning. The swells were higher for one thing. But the captain delivered them safely back to the dock without incident, although Logan couldn't help shutting her eyes when they shot through.

Exiting the boat, she almost lost her balance.

"Watch your step, you'll be a little wobbly for a while," Eric instructed.

They were just about to head up to the stainless steel sinks where Adam said they could get their fish filleted and vacuum packed, when a man, not much bigger than Logan, pushed past them, almost knocking Logan down. Ben caught her elbow to steady her.

Not stopping to apologize, the man plowed past, and when he reached the *Mary Ann*, started to jump onto the deck, but Adam saw him coming and stiff-armed him in the chest, knocking him back onto the dock before jumping down easily himself to face him. Ben started to come forward to help, but Adam looked like he could handle it himself.

The guy staggered a bit, then caught himself. His back was to Logan, but she could see he was wearing clothes he probably slept in—flannel shirt over a tee and baggy Carhartts. Greasy black hair curled at his collar, and he clenched a piece of paper in his right fist. For some reason, she noticed he was balding at the crown.

At least a head shorter than Adam and slender, his body language was in turns threatening and beseeching, as if he couldn't decide which approach would be more effective. Logan was impressed that Adam didn't move.

"Why, man?" the man finally said, waving the piece of paper in Adam's face.

"Not here," Adam said.

"Yes, right here! You can't do this. I need to work!"

"You knew what the rules were, Chris," Adam said.

Now the man's tone went to full-on begging. They could see both men in profile now.

"Come on, man," he whisper pleaded, "give me another chance."

"I already did," Adam said. "The lab results came back positive. Again. And look at yourself, you're drunk *and* high."

"Fuck you, man!" Chris shouted, exploding into Adam's face, shoving him against the boat, then stomped up the dock past Logan and Ben, who stayed as far back as they could without falling into the water.

He'd only gone a few feet when he turned back and growled, "You'd better watch your back, man. This isn't over! You can't do this to me! Nobody fires Chris Larsen! I'm the best guy down here and everybody knows it!"

Eric busied himself on board the boat, cleaning up, doing boat things, trying to look invisible. Seeing that they saw the outburst, Adam just shrugged his shoulders and apologized for the man, saying, "Chris has had some problems."

Yeah . . . I guess so.

Without elaborating further, he helped them carry their gear and fish up to the filleting station, leaving Eric to finish scrubbing the *Mary Ann* down as all the other deck hands were doing on their boats.

Logan admired him for not trashing the guy, or even badmouthing him, when it seemed he had every right to do so.

11

When they got home, Vivi Hosteler, the woman next door, was out in her front yard, watering an azalea. Ben nodded hello, then took the packages of fish inside while Logan went over to say hello.

"I didn't think anyone had to water up here with all the rain," Logan said.

"Not in the winter, but the flowering plants need a little help in the summer," she said, "How was your day? Did you make it up to the shopping outlets yet?"

Logan said no, she hadn't been up there yet, then started to tell Vivi about their fishing trip. To her surprise, she discovered that their captain, Adam, was Vivi and Stan's son.

"Oh, yes, he's had the business here for over ten years, now," she said proudly. "We bought this house before that, when Adam was little, as a second home for family vacations. We're from back east, but my brother married into a fishing family here and ran a charter boat out of Depoe Bay for many years. Adam learned the business by working with him in the summers," she said.

"Did he move here after high school, then, when he turned eighteen?" Logan asked.

"No, not right away. He went to school—Princeton, where Stan and I went—got his MBA, worked in the financial industry for a few years. Married a New Yorker. Unfortunately, they divorced not long after, so he decided to take a loss on everything and move back here to do what he really loved. He worked commercial crabbing in the winters for a few years before his charter business became self-supporting. He's been happy as a clam—pardon the pun. Loves the water."

"Did he ever remarry?" Logan asked.

"Yes, he married a local girl, Debra. They have three girls," she said.

"All named after Disney princesses," she added with a tight smile and an eye roll.

Vivi may have disapproved of her daughter-in-law's naming protocol, but was obviously proud of her grandchildren, pulling out her phone and scrolling until she found a picture of the three girls on the deck of their dad's boat.

"This one's Ariel. She's eleven, going on thirty, wants to be a scientist. Jasmine's nine and loves to draw, and Cindy just finished her first year of kindergarten. Smart as a whip, that one."

She put her phone back in her pocket and resumed watering, moving on to a large rhododendron.

"We sold our home back east and moved here full time once I retired. Do you have any grandchildren?"

"Just the one, Ian, the toddler you may have seen—or probably heard—already."

"Oh yes, the little blonde boy—he's adorable. We don't have children at the concerts, though," she added, with a slightly alarmed look on her face.

"No worries," Logan reassured her, "Seven is past his bedtime and he'll be staying home with his mom and dad."

SAFE HARBOR

While Liam helped Ben with the BBQ, Logan decided to take a short run before dinner. With the boat leaving at its god-awful early hour this morning, she'd missed her usual exercise.

Pulling her hair back into a loose braid, she put her hat on and stepped out onto the porch. Her phone buzzed in her pocket, but with a determined grimace, she ignored it. Probably just her mother again.

She supposed it was possible she had a reasonable explanation for standing her up, but based on past history, it wasn't likely. Even if she did, Logan wasn't in the mood to hear it. Working up a sweat seemed the best way to purge her mom from her mind. Movement was how Logan usually handled stress.

She decided to take advantage of a little-used gate Rita had told her about at the back of the community. It led to a road that ran through a residential section into Depoe Bay. That way she wouldn't have to run along the highway. She went back in and grabbed the key from its hook in the laundry room. It was the only one with a round tag attached that said GATE. It shouldn't take her more than an hour to get there on surface streets, run to the end, power up some hills, then come back down and around the harbor. She'd be home by dinner.

The first half-mile had some gnarly inclines, but nothing as steep as Killer Hill back home. Once she got across the bridge and into town, it was easier going. She resisted a stop at Ainslee's Taffy. Taffy was Amy's favorite candy and Logan had discovered their caramel corn on her last trip.

Following the rough map in her head, she headed toward a logging road she'd spotted the other day. Half an hour later, she was headed home, blood pumping, sweaty, and full of fresh air. On her run she thought about all she had. Ben, Amy, Liam, and her new grandson. Good friends. Her brother, Rick. Life itself.

She hadn't missed her mom for years, no sense starting now.

While they set the table and sat down for dinner, Logan filled Amy and Liam in on the day's adventures, ending with the man's outburst at the end of the trip. She'd already told them Adam was Vivi and Stan's son.

"Even though the guy was a scary jerk, you've got to feel sorry for him. Chris, I think his name is. Vivi said he used to be a nice guy, hard worker, until drugs got their claws into him. Adam took him on as a deckhand three years ago, but he got injured two winters ago working on a commercial crabber."

"Yeah," Ben said, "I talked to him for a few minutes while you went inside to get Ian his t-shirt. Adam said he took him back even though he physically had trouble getting around. Within a pretty short time, he said Chris got addicted to the pain killers the doctors gave him. When the prescriptions ran out, he said he started buying heroin and meth, whatever he could get, and he's gone downhill from there."

"Yeah, it's just like that documentary we saw the other night," Liam said.

"It's happening all over. But no matter how nice he is or was, you can't expect people to hire a drug addict," Amy said.

"Yeah, I know," Logan said. "At least Adam gave him at least one other chance. I just wonder what kind of help he got. Maybe if he had gotten the right help earlier he wouldn't have spiraled down like that. Vivi says none of the good boats will hire him anymore."

12

Jian Zhang took his coffee outside and set the mug down on the railing. His bedroom was on the ground floor and had a separate deck that overlooked the harbor.

He reached in his pocket for his cigarettes, lit one, took a deep drag and scratched his smooth chin. He blew on the coffee, then took a chance on a small sip. Too hot, he burned his lip. This was pretty much how his day was going so far.

No one was up yet. Their host family, the Andersons, set their coffee maker the night before, knowing their guests often suffered from jet lag.

Although the house was humble by American standards, being straight up the hill from the harbor, it had an amazing view. The sun was just rising behind him, bathing the white boats bobbing at their docks in a rose-colored wash, carelessly strewing crystals across the ocean beyond.

None of this registered with Jian. He needed to think. There had to be a way out of all this. He got another text this morning. They'd given him four more days. As if that helped.

And now he had another problem. Meiling. Oblivious to the trouble she was causing him on top of everything else, she was still in bed. She'd always been a late sleeper, even more so now that she was spending some nights on that man's boat. That could not continue. She should know better. Still, she was his sister and it was his job to take care of her and fix her mistakes.

He hadn't confronted her yet. Hopefully he wouldn't need to. He doubted she would listen to him, anyway. He would just have to handle it himself.

When they were young, Meiling adored and looked up to him. He was her little brother by a year and a half, but he was male, and even in modern China, that still carried a lot of weight in families, particularly theirs.

Needing a son to care for them in this life and the next, their parents, after their first child turned out to be a relatively useless girl, risked having a second, defying the 1979 one-child-only policy. Jian was treasured from the day he was born, and Meiling, being sweet in nature, simply loved him.

All that changed, though, when the government became aware of Meiling's blossoming musical talent. Suddenly she became of value to the government and therefore, their mother and father. His parents soon began reaping the benefits. Their housing improved, as did many other aspects of their lives. Jian's importance and status in the family went down as his sister's star rose. It's not that she took advantage of this, he admitted, it was just a natural turn of events. Still, it rankled.

But not enough for him to mind too much. As her accompanist, Jian enjoyed the same perks his parents enjoyed, plus, he got to travel—and in recent years, that travel included the American tours. He loved it here. Or at least he had.

SAFE HARBOR

He remembered he and Meiling's first visit to San Francisco. Walking through the city was such a delicious luxury, but what most surprised him was how people could say anything they wanted to about the government and were not arrested! From late night TV to news shows to newspapers he read in the morning at the hotel, anyone could say anything it seemed. Still, it took almost a year for Jian to taste any of these freedoms for himself.

He allowed himself to indulge in things here in America that he would never have thought of doing back in China. Knowing he was on a tight travel and performance schedule, he stayed away from serious drugs, but two years ago, on his first visit to Chinatown, Jian discovered *Pai Gow* Poker.

He couldn't get a line of credit at the casinos, but a man sitting next to him said quietly that he knew of a place that would advance him some gambling cash. A quick cab ride away and they landed at the San Francisco Jockey Club, where they would loan a fellow compatriot some money to play. His new friend, who introduced himself as Li Wei, was very helpful. He also introduced him to the track.

It was a glorious night! Wine flowed! There were beautiful women and expensive bottles of champagne. He kept winning! It was a night to remember.

This last visit, two weeks ago, was memorable in a very different way. Li Wei picked him up at his hotel as usual, greeting him like an old friend. For the first couple of hours, everything went as before. But then his luck did a one-eighty.

No matter what game he played or what race he bet on, he lost. At some point during the early morning hours, stumbling back to his hotel room, Jian realized he was in way over his head. He wasn't even sure how much he owed, but someone knew. Why they let him leave without trying to collect, he didn't know.

When he woke up, it seemed his head had just hit the pillow. Nursing a splitting headache and an increasing sense of dread, Jian expected a knock on the door at any minute. But nothing happened. No one came to his hotel room. No one showed up at their breakfast table. No one stopped them from getting in the taxi taking them to the airport.

Maybe it wasn't that bad. Maybe Li Wei convinced his friends at the social club to write it off. Fellow Chinese to fellow Chinese. All part of the family. He had been tempted by America's evil ways, but he swore to himself it would never happen again.

The ride to the airport was uneventful and Jian had started to feel slightly optimistic that everything was going to be okay after all. He got in line while Meiling used the restroom one more time. Women were so much trouble. He'd have to push her bag as well as his along the roped off path snaking to the security check area.

Suddenly, someone was there. He felt it more than saw him. Turning his head slightly, he saw a man standing behind him, just a little too close. Short, squat, bulging biceps. Not Li Wei, but Jian knew instinctively that's who sent him. The man said nothing. Just tapped something into his phone, nodded at Jian, and left, walking calmly toward the nearest exit.

Before the man was out the revolving door, Jian's phone alerted him he had a message. He did not want to read it, but needed to before Meiling got back. There were two messages.

$27,000. Now. Double if not paid by Friday. When you have it, text YES. Wait for instructions. Do not think of not paying.

Your sister is beautiful. Enjoy your stay in Oregon.

Jian felt the gorge rise in his throat. In an instant, his world had changed. Obviously, these people knew a lot more about him than he thought.

SAFE HARBOR

Where was he going to get that kind of money? He had only a small amount of cash left in his hotel room when he got back last night. The Chinese government arranged their travel, their expenses. He couldn't turn to them for help and he would rather die than ask his parents. Even if he did, he doubted his parents had that kind of cash.

What was he going to do?

This was the question he'd been asking himself ever since they got here. They arrived in Portland and took the shuttle out to Depoe Bay without incident, but last Friday's deadline had come and gone and now they told him he owed these thugs almost fifty-five thousand dollars! It might as well be a fifty million. And in two more days they were going to double that. He didn't remember signing any loan papers, but then laughed at the thought. These guys weren't from any bank. They wouldn't leave a paper trail, and normal interest rates didn't apply.

He didn't know if they would kill him or just hurt him if he didn't pay, but he didn't want to find out. And he didn't like that they had singled out Meiling. That really worried him.

There had to be a way out of this mess. He just had to find a way to get his hands on $54,000. Until then, he'd just have to keep pretending everything was okay. If their sponsors in the government ever got wind that anything was wrong, they'd cancel their tour and never let them come back, and Jian wanted to come back.

Yes, he'd made a mistake, but he'd learned his lesson and would never make that mistake again. He'd just had an unlucky day, that's all. Next time he went he'd change his betting strategy at the *Pai Gow* tables.

In spite of this setback, he liked America. He had four days. He'd just have to figure something out.

13

Stan kissed his wife on the cheek on his way out the door to pick up tonight's musicians. She was fluttering around the kitchen, talking on the phone.

This was their fifteenth year doing these home concerts and they had it down to a science. Each had their assigned roles. He was furniture mover and chair setter-upper and she handled the program, catering, and people stuff. He was proud of her. He would have been happy to not do anymore of these, but Vivi enjoyed it. He hoped she would be willing to pass the baton on to someone else to host these concerts soon, but for now, he was happy to let her do her thing, as long as he could stay in the background.

He had a couple of errands to run while he was out, but he didn't think the Chinese kids would mind. They were good sports. They'd already rehearsed yesterday, so they should be okay with taking a thirty-minute detour while he ran up to Lincoln City. Lamont had called him this morning and told him to come on by. Lamont Clairview didn't open the place every day, so you needed to nail him down to a specific time if you wanted to do business with him. And Stan did. He'd done business with Lamont for years. Lamont helped him fill the holes in his collections and always got a fair price for his coins when he wanted to sell one.

He and Vivi were comfortable, but lived within their means. Their fiftieth wedding anniversary was coming up, and he wanted to surprise his love with a trip of a lifetime—a trans-Atlantic cruise followed by a month of luxury touring to all the major capitals of art and culture in Europe. The tour guide had recommended all of the usual stops like Paris, Florence, and Rome, but also added a few surprises, like Cambridge and Granada.

It was something they'd always talked about, but never got around to doing. Selling the Morgan would pay for it, plus maybe some paintings or small sculptures along the way. The 1904 O MS-65 Grade DMPL silver dollar was one of his favorites, but Vivi was worth it. Fifty years. That was worth celebrating.

As predicted, Meiling and Jian didn't complain about the unplanned stop along the way. Jian seemed distracted, anyway, spending most of the drive up to Lincoln City staring out the car window glumly. Meiling sat in the front seat, happily keeping up her brother's end of the conversation, wanting to know all about his coin collecting. She was always a sweet girl, but today she was absolutely glowing.

They arrived on the outskirts of Lincoln City around two o'clock. Perched atop a minuscule, gravel parking lot, L & M Coins didn't look like much, but Stan told them they did a booming business, handling everything from gold bars to coins of every shape, age, and size. The wobbly wooden stairs leading up to the only door didn't instill confidence, but the prominently mounted camera, steel bars and double-locked entrance let them know this was a serious, secure business. After identifying themselves, the three of them were buzzed in.

A gray-haired man in a Hawaiian shirt rolled his wheel chair up behind the counter to greet the new arrivals.

"Hey there, Stan. Did you bring her?" he asked, smiling.

"Got her right there, Lamont," Stan said, patting his pocket.

"You sure you want to sell her?" Lamont said, "You just picked her up last year. She hasn't grown that much in value."

"Yeah, I'm sure," Stan said.

Winking at Meiling, he added, "None of us know how long we've got, and Vivi's wanted to take this trip forever. Vivi's worth it."

Meiling beamed. This was the kind of family she would be marrying into. She hoped Adam would feel this way toward her on their fiftieth wedding anniversary someday.

Lamont wheeled his chair around, reached back to a shelf, and hauled something that looked like an oversized, old-school phone book onto the counter.

"That's okay, Lamont," Stan said, getting the coin, encased in a clear plastic cover, out of his wallet, laying it on the counter. "I trust you."

Lamont ignored him and thumbed through the catalog until he found the page he wanted, then stabbed at an entry half way down the page.

"I know," he said, "but this is a big one. Best you see it for yourself that I'm not skimming any off the top. I'll just take my normal markup off and that's what I'll give you for it."

Somewhere in this process, Jian had moved up until he was standing a foot or two behind Stan, without showing any interest, of course. But he heard every word. And the words that caught his attention were *seventy-five thousand, two hundred, and seventeen cents.*

Stan looked at the entry and put out his hand to shake, "You've got yourself a deal, Lamont!"

Lamont's face broke out in a grin. "Excellent. They picked up my cash already today. And you don't want to carry around that much cash anyway. How soon do you need it? Can you come back tomorrow? I'll stop by the bank in the morning. I can get you a cashier's check by noon."

"Perfect! I've got to pick up some things for the deck in town tomorrow. I'll stop by after that."

Stan didn't get the kids to the house until six, and the concert started at seven. Vivi wasn't pleased, but she was too busy herself to do more than raise her eyebrows at him disapprovingly. After going upstairs to hang his jacket up, he went to offer his services to his wife. The culinary arts students were here and it looked like they might need help hauling bags of ice in. Heavy lifting was his specialty.

Jian and Meiling went up to their rooms to change into their formal clothes and rest up for the performance. Yesterday, Stan had put Meiling's gown and shoes in the guest room and her brother's tux in Adam's old room. It saved time and made sure the inevitable wrinkles from travel were hung out before performances.

No one noticed when Jian made his way into Stan and Vivi's room. He checked Stan's inside jacket pocket first, but then realized of course the man wouldn't have left such a valuable coin there. Jian cursed silently. It could be anywhere. It was probably securely tucked away inside a wall safe. But Stan hadn't been upstairs long . . . maybe they didn't have a wall safe.

As quietly as he could, Jian began searching. He tried to put himself in Stan's place. Where would he put the coin if he only had a few minutes?

The bed. Pushing his hand between the mattress and box springs, he reached in as far as his arm would go but felt nothing. He straightened up the bedspread so it would not appear to have been disturbed, then continued to search the room. He checked both nightstands and even looked inside a pair of Stan's slippers by the bed. Nothing. Maybe the dresser.

Bingo! It was in the first drawer he pulled open. Right between a stack of boxer shorts and a row of neatly rolled socks. Breathing a huge sigh of relief, Jian tiptoed out and returned to his room.

Once there, Jian hadn't lost any time Googling Cash-for-Gold places in Portland. Now that he knew what the coin was worth, even if he had to take a hit on the price because he was in a hurry, it would more than cover his debt. He couldn't wait to pay these guys off. They weren't expecting a skinny Chinese guy with no connections to come up with that kind of money.

The thought of slapping that cash into their hands—well, it would have to be in a briefcase or something, he supposed— he didn't know how much space $60,000 would take up in bills, but whatever it was, it would be satisfying!

Taking the stairs by twos on the way up, Jian was almost looking forward to Friday now. He may even have enough left over to try out his new betting strategies when they got back to San Francisco. Of course, he'd find a new place to play. He wasn't stupid.

14

Amy and Liam offered to clean up after dinner while Logan and Ben went to get ready for the concert.

Vivi said the dress was coastal casual, so Logan took her at her word, pulling on her usual combo of jeans, black t-shirt, and boots. An afternoon onshore breeze kicked in and the temperature started dropping with the sun, so Logan grabbed a khaki jacket at the last minute. Not knowing how warm the Hosteler's kept their home, she could always take it off if it got too hot.

Since it was a date, she brushed on mascara and bronzer, and added a pair of emerald earrings Ben bought her for her birthday because they brought out her eyes. Even her long hair couldn't hide their deep sparkle.

Ben was wearing casual slacks and one of Logan's favorite shirts, a soft, chambray rolled up at his wrists. Logan was a sucker for sexy wrists. Deck shoes. No socks. Fit and tan from his landscape work, he looked great. And the blue stripes in his shirt brought out *his* eyes.

"Wow, you guys look great!" Amy said.

"Very nice," Liam agreed.

Snuggled on the couch in front of the TV, they were settling in with the remainder of their caramel corn for a JAWS marathon. Ian was already down for the night.

Not wanting to arrive too early, but still get good seats, Ben and Logan meandered over to the Hosteler's around a quarter to seven. Someone handed them a program at the door, which featured a black and white photo of the violinist, Meiling Zhang, on the cover. The young woman's pale face and clothing, in sharp contrast to a solid black background, made a striking portrait. Probably still in her twenties, she had a Mona Lisa smile set in a delicate face framed by smooth, glossy, chin-length black hair. Delicate drop pearl earrings. Scoop neck dress or top. Thin sweater just covering her shoulders, showing off her collar bones. Very little makeup. None was needed.

Tucking the program under her arm, Logan took Ben's hand and they followed another guest up a narrow staircase into an open room with baby grand up front, a fireplace on one side and a great view of the ocean on the other. They placed their programs on two vacant seats in the second row. Vivi stood near the piano, talking intently to a young, slender, Chinese man in a tux. Must be one of the performers. Vivi looked upset, but when she spotted Logan she put on a welcoming smile and waved them over. The consummate hostess.

"Logan!" she said, "and you must be Ben, so glad you could both make it."

Turning to the young man next to her, she added, "I'd like you to meet Jian, one of our guest musicians. He'll be playing the piano this evening."

Logan wondered why his picture wasn't also on the program.

Jian nodded and shook hands, then, telling Vivi he needed to go prepare, he nodded curtly and left the room.

"Is everything okay?" Logan asked.

"Oh no, everything's fine. There's just been a last minute change in the program. Why don't you two get a glass of wine—we also have coffee and some cucumber water at a station in the back," she said, pointing to a small table near the stairs. "You go ahead and get your drinks and get settled. We'll be starting soon," she said brightly, hustling off after her pianist.

"That's interesting," Logan said in a low voice to Ben.

"They'll work it out, whatever it is. Or not," Ben said. "Either way, I'm getting a glass of red. You want one?"

"Sure, if I do coffee I'll be up all night," she said.

While she waited for her wine, Logan did a little people watching, her favorite pastime. It was quite an eclectic group. White hair and silver jewelry dominated, but beyond that the concert attendees ran the gamut. There was an aging hippie couple replete in tie-dye. They probably had a VW van out on the street. Or maybe a camper. In the front row sat a group of women she overheard had driven down from Lincoln City for dinner and a night out. A large portion of the crowd was well-heeled, older couples, probably retired, with the women wrapped in silk and artsy jewelry. They reminded Logan of the women in Orange County who had season tickets to everything and frequented charity galas. Then there were a few regular people and students, who had probably saved up for tickets—even thirty dollars was a lot for a student.

One woman in the back, along the outside edge of the grid of chairs, looked out of place. Unlike everyone else, who were chatting with friends or reading their program, the woman leaned against the wall, arms folded, staring straight ahead, frowning, not inviting conversation. Mid-thirties maybe—younger than most of the retirees filling the seats, anyway. Frowsy blonde hair, dark roots. Logan had seen her earlier, in the kitchen with the culinary students. Logan wondered if she was a music lover. Good for her if she was. You didn't have to wear silk and silver to enjoy classical music.

Promptly at 7:15 p.m., Vivi floated back up the stairs and went directly to the front of the room, waiting for everyone to take their seats. She nodded briefly at the woman in back. The piano was several feet behind her and to the left, next to a music stand. The sun slanting in the large windows caught the sparkle in her beaded bolero jacket. She looked very stylish.

"Welcome, everyone, and thank you for coming. And don't worry, Stan's going to take care of those blinds right now, so you'll be able to see.

"There's been a slight change in tonight's program. One of our featured musicians, violinist Meiling Zhang, has taken ill and won't be able to perform tonight."

15

Ben raised his eyebrows. Logan shrugged. These things happened.

"In her stead, Sharon Rochelle, well-known to many of you already as the talented, first chair with our own Newport Symphony Orchestra, has agreed to step in. There will be a few changes in the numbers performed as well, but I'm sure you're in for a stellar evening of music here on the coast!"

Vivi then gave brief background information on both the performers and the music they were going to play, before turning to the musicians who had just arrived.

"And now, without further ado, let's give a warm welcome to Sharon Rochelle and Jian Zhang!

There were a few sounds of disappointment, but by and large the audience took the change in stride. There was a round of applause as the two musicians entered the room, bowed and took their places.

Rochelle didn't disappoint. Jian's playing was good, but not as powerful. It was clear he was not as gifted. Logan admired Rochelle's instrument, but still preferred the sound of her own violin, handed down to her from her great-grandmother.

But then, she was prejudiced. Bella had been lovingly crafted by a talented, young, Italian violin maker named Giovanni de Mantua for her Appalachian great grandmother, Norah McKenna. Their love story, as well as Bella, held pride of place in the family.

When intermission was over, Logan noticed the woman she'd seen earlier hadn't returned to her seat. She wondered if the change in the program had anything to do with it. Maybe she was a fan of Meiling's and when she couldn't see her perform, decided to leave. Or maybe she just worked nights or needed to get home to her kids. Several late arrivals took the remaining empty seats or stood in the back for the second half. These concerts must be really popular.

Logan looked around. So many stories. She knew each person in this room had at least one.

When the musicians had taken their final bows, Logan and Ben followed the crowd downstairs, but not before Logan grabbed a few leftover oatmeal cookies from a side table on the way and stuffed them into her purse.

"What?" she asked innocently. "I'm hungry. It's the ocean air."

An informal reception line formed at the bottom of the stair. Vivi, Jian, and Sharon were shaking hands, answering questions, and saying good night as people filed past on their way to the front door and to their cars. On their way out, a student was handing out flyers for the next concert, encouraging people to attend.

Logan was sure the musicians would just as soon go to their rooms, strip off their tuxes and flop into bed, but she supposed it was all part of their social, if not contractual, obligations. People were always envious of the lives performers lead, but in reality, every job came with its dull bits. And with what air travel had turned into, the flying alone would kill Logan off.

Even first class was subject to long lines, delays, and security checks.

"Hello, neighbors!" Vivi said, grasping Logan's hand with both of hers. "How did you enjoy the concert?"

"It was lovely. I've always had a soft spot for Bartok. Such a great venue and very generous of you to offer your home for these events," Logan said.

"Really enjoyed it," Ben said, steering Logan toward the piano player to get her to move more quickly toward the door.

They made it through the rest of the line, expressing their thanks to both musicians. Ms. Rochelle, the violinist, was relaxed, accepting praise and answering questions as if each person were a VIP guest. Jian, on the other hand, gave limp half-handshakes and monosyllabic answers, and by both body language and tone of voice clearly wanted to be anywhere but there.

What a jerk.

Ben was helping Logan on with her jacket when she spotted the other half of their hosting couple, the husband, Stan Hosteler, off to their left, in the back of the kitchen, standing just inside the doorway, trying to hand a man some cash. On closer inspection she saw it was Adam, their charter boat captain this morning. Adam was shaking his head and stepping back, open hands held up to refuse the money.

"No way, Dad. Keep your money," Logan heard him say, "The clients didn't want to take their catch. I'm glad the kids could put them to good use," he added, nodding toward the culinary students cleaning up in the kitchen.

Logan remembered the delicious crab cakes they served at intermission. Adam must have donated some of the fresh seafood. Generous. It was nice to see a family that was able to live near each other and got along. She would have gone over to say hello and tell him what a great time they had fishing on his boat that day, but even though it was only a few feet away, the kitchen was in the more private part of the family's home, so she decided against it.

After a few more attempts to pay his son for the seafood, Stan put his wallet back in his pocket, clapped Adam on the back, pride all over his face.

Just then, the woman Logan had noticed upstairs earlier poked her head inside the back door and said something to Adam. Not smiling, he said he'd be right there. Must be his wife? Stan nodded at her. He didn't seem happy to see her.

Logan couldn't hear the rest of what they said, because Ben was nudging her toward the door, eager to get home. One of those cheerful, early morning people, Ben was in bed, lights out, before nine or ten most nights. Logan was the night owl, but tonight she turned in with Ben. She wanted plenty of time to dream about the Eggs Benedict he'd promised to make in the morning. He made hollandaise sauce in the blender and it was perfect every time.

TUESDAY MORNING
AUGUST 14

Breakfast was all that and more. As was last night's dessert. Ben was a keeper.

Amy and Liam were still in their pajamas when she and Ben left to go on a beach run. Amy was curled up on the couch with an oversized mug of coffee, watching Liam play with Ian on the thick, blue-and-cream colored rug that lay across the glossy hardwood floor. They'd wisely added a baby-proof blanket on top. The rug looked like it cost more than their house back home.

SAFE HARBOR

Logan looked out of the living room windows on the way out. She still couldn't get over the view. This morning, a royal blue ocean, only gently ruffled with a breeze, gleamed under a bright, cloudless sky.

She was glad she could give her daughter and son-in-law this gift of unstructured time in such a spectacular setting. And a little privacy. They made a point of letting them know they'd be gone at least an hour or two.

Vivi had said she'd print off some information on local hiking trails and beaches for them, so they stopped by her and Stan's place first.

According to Vivi's map, Beverly Beach was perfect for a morning run and only a few minutes away. She said they used to take their black lab, Zeke, there for exercise when Adam was young. The dog passed away many years ago.

"We travel too much now to get another one," she said.

Pointing out the access points on a map, she said, "The beach goes a long way in both directions—just miles and miles of mostly empty sand. Even in the summer you'll often have the place all to yourself if you go early enough."

Stan came in from the garage with a miter saw on his way out back to his deck project and said hello.

"Be sure and check the tide tables, watch for the incoming tide. You don't want to get stuck out there."

"And watch for sneaker waves," he added, "Almost every year somebody gets taken out by one. Never turn your back on the ocean."

Vivi asked Logan if she could still make it for lunch later and Logan assured her she'd be back in plenty of time.

"That's great! You'll get to meet Meiling and you two can talk music. I just spoke with her on the phone, she says she's feeling much better this morning."

16

MONDAY, AUGUST 13/TUESDAY, EARLY A.M.

Karen had already showered at school this morning, so her hair was almost dry. At home, she had a blow dryer, a curling iron and drawers stuffed with tubes of all kinds of different hair products she used to think she couldn't live without.

It's amazing how simple her life had become since she left. Twisting her hair quickly into a braid, she exited the public bathroom. Ambling along the sidewalk, looking into the windows of shops fronting the highway across from the whale-watching center, for the next few hours she blended in with the tourists.

Right now she was nursing a coffee—black. Cheaper and she could always doctor it with cream and sugar—up the calories. No sense paying for a 'Double Half-Caf Mocha Latte' or whatever it was people ordered when she could make it herself from the free stuff on the side. Except the chocolate. She'd get some tonight at work. They had those little green, foil-wrapped mint chocolates. Pop two of those into hot coffee. Excellent.

Her last class finished at two this afternoon, so she hitched a ride with Mona, a friend who also waited tables at the Horn. Well, friend was a strong word. Karen was friendly enough with her coworkers and classmates, but she had learned to keep her distance and not spend too much time with anyone. Even as a kid, it was easier that way. No need to explain the condition of the house—or her mother—on any particular day if she never invited anyone over.

Mona knew she lived in Newport, so Karen would make up some excuse to not get a ride back when their shift was over. Tell Mona she had a hot date or something, and he was going to give her a ride home. Mona would believe that. All she thought about was boys. If she only had morning classes, she hitched in. So far, it had all worked.

Stations wiped and condiments filled, she was waving good night to Mona in the parking lot by nine o'clock. She told her she was meeting 'Michael', her fictional date, an electrician from Lincoln City, at the Tide Pool Pub later and wanted to walk. As expected, Mona bought the whole story.

A crow flew across the parking lot, cawing at her half-heartedly, then settled in the slender, top branches of a Douglas Fir, ruffling its feathers, near a smaller one, probably roosting for the night. The pair must have a nest nearby. The air was warm and soft. Well, warm for the Oregon coast, anyway. She checked her phone—59 degrees.

Her feet hurt, but once Mona was out of sight, Karen threaded her arms through the straps of her backpack and hoisted it up. Tucking her thumbs under to keep the weight high on her shoulders, she trudged up Bay Street until she reached an area of thick brush, unlit by any street lights, where she'd stashed her sleeping bag early this morning. Making sure no one was watching her first, she lifted some branches and looked. It was still there.

SAFE HARBOR

This was one of three safe places she'd found to stash her stuff during the day. Surrounded on three sides by stickery blackberry vines, most homeless and kids looked for other, easier places to crash or party.

Sometimes she slept here, but a nearby dumpster made this spot a bit more aromatic than she liked. She preferred being on the water in the harbor. She hadn't been down in a few nights, so tonight would be a good night to rotate.

The sun was already down, but true dark would take a while, so she pushed farther in and lay her head down on her backpack, drifting into lazy half-sleep for the next hour. At 10:00, she gathered her gear and headed south along side streets toward the harbor. If anyone asked her where she was going, she'd just tell them she was headed to Beverly Beach, meeting her parents at the campgrounds there. As if she had a normal family that went camping.

But she wasn't complaining. She had rolls, butter packets, and a leftover cheeseburger for breakfast from the Horn, along with a Pepsi and a package of peanut butter crackers from the Shell station she picked up earlier. All set.

The dock area was open from the Coast Guard station to the fuel dock. There was a park beyond that with trees, but she wasn't going that far. Standing for a few minutes in the shadow of the Dockside Charters building, she surveyed the scene. She checked out the *Miss Behavin'*, a boat she had camped on before, on the south side of Dock 2. She didn't think the owners used it often and the angles were good. Once she lay down, no one could see her from the parking lot or most of the other boats, if she kept her phone dark.

She paid particular attention to the *Mary Ann*, on the same dock, but a couple of slips down on the north side. Looked like he and his old lady were going at it again. Same blue Kia in the parking lot. Couldn't go down yet.

Let him go, woman. Have some pride.

Everyone else had gone home, so it was a long shot anyone would see her, but if they did, they'd wonder what she was doing here, crouched up against the building. She decided to take another loop around the block and try again in a few minutes.

Karen wandered around town until almost midnight, but she was starting to feel her long day. All she wanted to do was get some sleep. Finally, she went back. The *Mary Ann* was dark. The man and his wife had either made up or the woman had left without him, because the car was gone. Hoisting her backpack up, Karen gave it a shake to make sure nothing jingled or rattled to give her away. Nothing did, so she started down.

With practiced movements, she made her way quietly down the dock, softly jumping on board the *Miss Behavin'*. Lowering her sleeping bag carefully to the deck, she rolled it out and got in. She pulled it up under her chin—it was colder now—and settled in to enjoy the blanket of stars overhead.

As one of her general education requirements, Karen had taken a basic astronomy class and learned some constellations. It was pretty cool. She could only remember a few though. She saw the Big Dipper, tilted, as if spilling its contents, and used it to find Polaris, the North Star. She thought she saw Orion's belt, but she wasn't sure. She remembered the ones that didn't twinkle were planets, but didn't know which ones they were.

Eventually, her eyelids grew heavy, the slight rise and fall of the boat rocked her, and she drifted off to sleep.

Something jarred her awake. She wasn't sure how long she'd slept. She blinked a couple of times and tried to orient herself. Parts of the dock were lit, but the clouds had rolled in and most of it was pretty dark. She couldn't see much. Holding her body still, she listened, straining to hear.

SAFE HARBOR

Voices. Coming from the direction of the *Mary Ann*. Maybe the wife was back. She couldn't stand up to see what was going on without giving away her location, so she crouched, tense, on the port side of the wheelhouse, breathing rapidly, rolling up her sleeping bag as fast as she could, securing the bungee cords tightly.

Then there was a shout, followed by a clanking metal sound, a dull crack, and a heavy thud. Then someone running. Coming right at her.

17

Unable to sleep, Jian kept thinking of all the things that could go wrong. Things were finally falling into place, but nothing was for sure yet. If everything went as planned, by Friday afternoon, he'd have his life back. Four more days. A week from now, he and Meiling would be back on tour and his life would return to normal.

If everything went as planned. That was a big if. He knew he was cutting it close. So much had to go right. He had to find an excuse not to do the workshop at the high school Friday morning. Meiling didn't need him, anyway. She could do these in her sleep. The kids just wanted to see her, anyway.

As soon as Meiling got picked up at the house, he would sneak out the back and hustle down Highway 101 to the Caravan Transportation shuttle stop about a mile away. He had to get there before the van left for their only run of the day to Portland. That'd get him there just before noon.

From there, he'd already mapped out a route on the Max line to the cash-for-gold shop that would buy Stan's coin. That was assuming they didn't haggle him down too much from the price they'd given over the phone. They'd seemed anxious to get their hands on it, though. Apparently it was a rare one. He was taking a duffel bag along to put the money in.

The shop wasn't far from the shuttle stop, but he'd have to get there, conduct his business and get back to the pickup location by one-thirty. When he called to make the reservation, they made a point of reminding him the driver left promptly at two o'clock, so be there on time. That would get him home by five at the latest. That's when he said he'd meet them—somewhere away from the house, he didn't want to have to explain this to Meiling. She would never understand.

He couldn't be sure the shuttle would get him there by five o'clock. It would depend on how full the van was and how many stops they had to make along the way.

At first, Li Wei wanted him to meet them at noon, but surprisingly, they didn't seem to mind pushing it back a few hours. Technically, the loan wasn't due until midnight. There was no way he couldn't pay it by then. He had no intention of allowing these criminals to double his loan again.

Jian took some satisfaction in having a plan. He doubted Li Wei himself would show up to collect. He'd send some of his men. They probably weren't expecting him to have the money, so he couldn't wait to calmly hand them the duffel bag, heavy with cash, like this was nothing for him. Just like Clint Eastwood or James Bond in the American movies. He hoped they would tell Li Wei how cool he was under pressure.

Only one more obstacle to overcome. Adam. Jian had been putting it off, but time was running out. He could tell things were getting more and more serious between his sister and this man. He suspected before, but this trip confirmed it. He'd seen her sneak down to Adam's charter boat in Depoe Bay Harbor a few times.

He had followed her, but hung back, waiting for the right time to confront her. If they were back in China, his status as her older brother had more authority. He would just sit her down and get her to see reason, but here in America, he had a feeling she would simply refuse to stop seeing this American she thought she loved.

12:15 A.M.

You on boat?

Who is this?

Me, Meiling.

New phone? Don't recognize this number.

Borrowed. Mine charging. Can I come over?

Jian hesitated before typing more, in case Adam became suspicious, but he needed to know.

U alone? I can come down now.

Yes, course. Miss you, need you.

Jian cringed, but kept in character.

See you soon.

Jian pressed send to end the conversation, then decided to turn the phone all the way off. Less was more. He wasn't sure how Meiling and Adam usually signed off, but it seemed as if Adam believed he was texting Meiling. He'd find out soon enough if his impersonation had worked.

He slipped the phone into his pocket. He might need it again and when he got to Portland, he could always sell it for extra cash. If not, he could just dump it. Finding it on Bay Street yesterday had been a stroke of luck. Some tourist must have dropped it. So even if someone saw the text, they'd have no way of tracing it to him.

His own phone was on the dresser. He didn't think Adam had any way of recognizing his number, but he wasn't taking any chances. He laughed at how easy it had been to pretend to be Meiling. Americans were so gullible. It never occurred to them someone might not be who they said they were.

Jian thought about what he would say to Adam when he got there. He had his arguments ready. If Adam wanted what was best for Meiling, her career, her happiness, he would give her up. He didn't think an American would understand how things worked in China, but he'd try to make him see that Chinese couldn't just up and leave. If Meiling did, life for their family in China could change, in ways both subtle and drastic, depending on the mood of their handlers.

Jian also knew that the government would hold him, her brother, most responsible for his sister's behavior if she did not fulfill her obligations. Meiling was becoming a well-known, international artist. News of her choosing America over China—and that's how they would see it—would not go unnoticed. Jian was supposed to be managing her as well as protecting her on these tours. He had failed. He knew that. The consequences would be harsh.

This American would just have to understand.

18

God damn bastard! Who the hell does Adam think he is?

As soon as he realized Adam wasn't going to budge, Chris Larsen pushed past the good-looking woman and her man again and then almost plowed into a group of fishing trip clients from another boat at the end of the gangplank, shoving a young father aside who didn't move fast enough.

"Get the fuck out of my way!"

The man started to go for him, then thought better of it and stayed put. Instinctively, he put his arm protectively around his son's shoulders. No point arguing with idiots. The pair watched until the angry man got to the parking lot before continuing up the ramp toward Dockside Charters.

Chris yanked open the door of his truck, got in, and gripped the wheel. The truck wasn't even his. It was Lana's. His was repossessed six months ago. She knew he couldn't afford a work truck, so let him use hers. He'd been making the payments when he could, which hadn't been very often, lately.

Why couldn't Adam just give him another chance? He was such an asshole! And that skinny kid, Eric, who took his job. What a chicken shit. He could work rings around that kid. Well, it was Adam's loss.

Gunning the engine, he shoved the truck into gear and backed out of the space. Driving back to Newport, a wave of fatigue hit him and he could hardly stay on the road. His skin felt clammy. It had already started. Sharp pains began shooting up his spine and now his joints felt like they were on fire.

Chris grimaced and tears welled up in his eyes. It would only get worse. Only one thing would stop the train wreck he felt coming. He didn't want to, but nothing else would work. He thought about how much money he had. Lana'd given him money for cigarettes and he'd lifted another twenty out of her wallet this morning. That'd be enough.

He promised he would be home for dinner. She'd been letting him stay there since he lost his place. Just until he could get back on his feet.

She'd been pressuring him to move in together for the last two years anyway. So, really, he was doing her a favor. With all the work he did around the house—when he felt well enough—he more than paid his way. He'd get this under control. It was all going to be fine.

She was making chicken parmesan. Said she wanted to spend time together before she went to work. He couldn't let her see him like this. He could fool some people, but Lana was getting good at spotting the signs.

Lana worked at the Mystic Mermaid, a bar just north of town off Highway 101. Salary sucked, but she made good tips, especially during the summer. She was closing tonight, so didn't get off 'til two. She'd sold her Toyota, so for now, they had to share the truck. Work was close enough for her to walk, but driving was safer. It was one of the few shreds of manhood he had left—making sure she got home okay. Lana was a looker and guys were always offering her rides home. He made sure she had her own wheels so she could turn them down.

This afternoon before work, she was going over to her grandma's place, so he needed to get the truck back early. She had to take her grandma to the store and help her cut her cat's claws. Chris had no idea why Lana offered to perform this dangerous task, or how she did it. Murphy was the cat from hell.

"Come on, guys. Green means go in this country," Chris tapped the steering wheel and muttered at a car he felt was taking too long to turn right at the Walmart turnoff.

He was trying to keep it together, but felt like he was crawling out of his skin. He'd never be able to sit through dinner. He couldn't sit still five seconds now and it would only get worse. And he needed a bathroom. Meth either plugged you up or gave you the Hershey squirts. He felt the latter coming on.

Lana's was on First Street. Two streets before, he turned left on Olive. Short stop at Shane's. He didn't like worrying Lana. Stopping at Shane's would help him be able to stay in his seat through dinner, carry on a conversation, keep the chicken parmesan down, and send Lana on her way to work none the wiser. Really, he was doing it for her. For them.

Thinking about Lana, he decided to stop at Thriftways after Shane's and get her some flowers. Bet no other boyfriends were getting their girl flowers in the middle of the week for no special occasion.

10:20 P.M.

Chris couldn't sleep, but that was to be expected, and he didn't care. The trip to Shane's was successful and got him through dinner. If Lana suspected anything, she hadn't let on. He hadn't taken enough to feel great, just good enough to pass for normal.

He didn't have enough money left to buy flowers, but on his way out of the floral department at Thriftway, he spotted a vase full of little teddy bears on sticks near the register. They were really cute. They each held a little, stuffed, red heart and a card with room for a message. When the cashier wasn't looking, he stuck one into the inside pocket of his jacket and exited the store.

He found a pen in the cab of the truck and scribbled "To Lana, My Angel! Chris" on the card.

She loved it.

Lana was happy. Life was good. He had a few hours. Time to celebrate! He could walk down to the Mermaid, take the truck down to the Chinese place in Depoe Bay, have a few brewskies with the boys and be back before she got off work. In fact, he'd time it so he showed up right when she got off shift. He'd say he walked down just to give his angel a ride home. Tell her he'd made the extra effort. Just for her. Yep, he was the best damn boyfriend ever!

1:10 A.M.

TUESDAY, AUGUST 14

Pagoda Palace, located on Highway 101, just south of the bridge, overlooking the harbor, served lunch and dinner to locals, tourists and retirees. After dinner, a younger, locals crowd trickled in, eventually filling the bar stools. A jukebox played Johnny Cash and everything popular in the nineties, with a few current tunes in there. One beer turned into two, then three. Kevin just got his disability check and was sharing, so the beers were followed by some shots. It was now one o'clock in the morning. The bartender just escorted the last citizen out the front door, locking it behind him.

Everyone else vacated the lot. Chris sat in his car with the windows down, rubbing his face, hoping the cold air would help sober him up. He shouldn't have stayed so long.

He remembered this morning's confrontation with Adam. He'd made a fool of himself. If he was ever going to get his job back, he needed to apologize. He looked down at the harbor until he located the *Mary Ann*. To his surprise, there was a faint light on board. What was Adam doing on his boat this time of night? Must have gotten into a fight with the old lady.

Guess even Captain Adam, Mr. Perfect, screws up sometimes.

Maybe this was a good thing. Maybe if he talked to him alone, he'd have a better chance of getting his job back. Man to man. Without a bunch of people around. Without that deckhand to show off for, he was sure Adam would see reason. Chris knew he may have to eat some crow, but he was a big enough man to admit he'd screwed up. He made a mistake. He could change. He would change.

Chris looked at the dashboard. 1:20 a.m. He didn't have to pick up Lana for another hour. Getting his job back from Adam shouldn't take too long and it was only a twenty-minute drive back. Besides, if he came bearing good news, that he was fully employed again, Lana would forgive him even if he was a few minutes late.

He started up the truck.

19

Chris stumbled down the dock, trying to get as far away from the *Mary Ann* as he could. Rushing to the edge, he heaved what was left of his crab fried rice into the harbor. If it hadn't been for the cleat he was able to grab onto, he'd have followed his dinner right into the water. The copious amounts of beer and tequila shots he'd consumed earlier didn't help.

He should never have come down here.

Another wave of nausea hit. After several more trips to the side, he was down to dry heaving. Bent at the waist, he placed his hands on his knees until his head cleared somewhat.

Why hadn't he left well enough alone? Why was he continually making one bad choice after another?

The little hit he'd taken earlier, on the way home, had long since worn off, and the rest was back at the house. Sweat poured off him. He knew he stank. He couldn't go home like this. It'd be the last straw. Lana'd never take him back if she saw him like this. He fumbled and pulled his phone out of his pocket, squinting at the home screen.

Fuck.

Lana had probably already called Stuart for a ride home. Stuart just wanted to get into Lana's pants. He'd come running, especially if it meant rescuing her from one of Chris's screw ups.

Even if by some miracle she was still there, waiting for him, she'd see him driving down from the north, not coming up from Newport. She'd know he took her truck out. She'd never buy the lie that he walked down just to give her a ride home. Even if by some chance she'd gone back inside to wait, the engine would be warm. She'd know it hadn't been sitting there all during her shift.

Chris looked back over his shoulder at the *Mary Ann* and shuddered.

Back in Lana's truck, Chris rested his forehead on the steering wheel. He didn't start the engine. There was nowhere to go. He stared out the windshield for a few minutes, not really registering the dark shapes of houses and shops across the road, the empty, asphalt parking lot, boats in the harbor, or the ocean beyond. An owl hooted. His brain wasn't working. He couldn't decide what to do, so he curled up on the bench seat. Eventually, a ragged sleep took him.

Some time later, he opened his eyes and sat up. His eyes were drawn back down to the harbor, to the boat. Luckily, it was still dark and he couldn't see the deck from here. There were several boats in the way. Nothing he could do about that now.

Cold in the early morning hour, Chris reached for his jacket in the back seat and pulled it on. Making no effort to exit the truck, he thought through his options. There weren't many.

As he sat there, his gaze focused vaguely on the dashboard, but not really seeing it, an inexplicable calm descended over him. There was one place to go, after all. He pulled out his phone, found the message he'd stored there a few months ago, and made the call.

When his ride arrived, he told him he had to return the truck. The driver must have heard stranger things, because he just nodded and followed him to the Mystic Mermaid. Chris got out, locked the truck and left the keys in the wheel well, where he knew Lana would find them. No sense getting her involved in that mess back there. Then he lowered himself into the guy's car and buckled up for the ride. He was suddenly in a hurry to get there, to get as far away from his old life as possible.

Twenty minutes later, just as the sky was brightening from gray to salmon pink, the driver turned onto a narrow, gravel road off the Siletz River Road. A large, restored Craftsman, painted in forest greens with burgundy trim, sat well back from the road, tucked into alders, salal, and blackberry bushes. Beyond the house the river ran lazily by.

The driver parked, let Chris out, then drove away, leaving Chris to walk up the steps onto the front porch by himself, past a copper sign that read:

Safe Harbor
Private Recovery Center

The receptionist looked up from her station behind a long, polished, wooden admissions counter. It reminded Chris of a bar. Her nameplate read Thalia Khoury.

Handing him a clipboard with ballpoint pen attached to the top by a chain, she smiled up at him warmly.

"Welcome, Mr. Larsen! The nurse will be out in a few minutes to take you back to the intake room. So glad you decided to stay with us. You'll be feeling better soon."

To his surprise, she came around the barrier and gave Chris

a hug. He knew what he must look and smell like, but she didn't seem phased at all. Noting his expression, she explained.

"I've been through the program myself and can promise you there's light on the other side. It will be tough, but you've made the right decision."

The fact that this opportunity was available to him at all was a miracle in itself. Insurance didn't cover it, he sure as hell couldn't afford it. He'd burned through most of his friends-and-family bridges. One by one he'd run through their money, their patience, and in most cases, even their sympathy. Whether out of exasperation or tough love, they wouldn't even let him couch surf anymore.

But a few months ago, one of his mom's brothers, Uncle Arnold, threw him one last lifeline. A retired truck driver, he didn't have much in the way of savings, but still had good credit.

Having had his own troubles with alcohol after the war, he wouldn't give him any cash, but with a clear condition that this would be a one-time opportunity, he pulled some money off a card and put a deposit down for him at Safe Harbor. He'd heard about it through a friend, who said this place saved his daughter's life. The family agreed if he stayed with their program, they'd pitch in and help share the monthly costs.

All the other places they'd tried only kept people for ten days, because that's all insurance would cover. When the ten days were up they dumped them back on the street. Still sick and with nowhere to go and often drugs still in their systems, within hours, months, or days, most of them relapsed.

The last time he relapsed, he went through one of the ten-day programs and when he got out, thought he was fine. He didn't need meetings or any of that stuff. He wasn't like a real drug addict he told his uncle. He appreciated his offer, but he could do this on his own.

SAFE HARBOR

Arnold reserved a spot for him anyway.

"The road to hell is paved with good intentions, Chris," he told him bluntly, "What you need is real help. Use it when you're ready."

Safe Harbor was founded by a father who'd lost his son to opioid addiction. A commercial fisherman from Newport, he wasn't a wealthy man, but through sheer determination he'd raised enough money to start the foundation and defray ongoing costs. Through the continuing generosity and support of local families, Safe Harbor provided supervised, medical detox not just for the ten days insurance companies covered, but until the person was safely and completely off of whatever they were on. The scaffolded program then lead through true rehabilitation: counseling, nutritious food, sober living housing, with psychological and social support the whole way.

Since so many people got into drugs through a work injury and couldn't return to their old jobs, once they were clean and sober, Safe Harbor also worked with the local college to help retrain a lot of local people for clean-energy jobs and offered internships and scholarships.

When Arnold called Chris's mom and told her Chris had checked into Safe Harbor that morning, she broke down and cried. It was the first time she'd been able to in a long time.

Because for the first time, there was hope.

20

Seamen Apprentice Sean Pettigrew was tired and wired. Tired because of last night's emergency drill and a trailer sailor rescue the day before, wired because he was on his fourth cup of coffee. He could have gotten relieved of duty or switched schedules with someone, but this was a new posting. He didn't want to complain. In a few hours, he'd be able to crawl into his bunk and catch some sleep.

Pettigrew didn't mind. He loved night duty. His folks owned a truck-stop diner in Needles, CA. He'd worked plenty of graveyard shifts. You got used to it. And he was thrilled to be stationed on the Oregon coast. What he loved about this place was not just being right on the water, but the fact that it never got hot here. Not like back home. Back home in Needles, they started breaking 100 degree temps in May. Everybody had air conditioning, but you were still drenched in sweat just walking from your front door to your car. He did not miss that.

From his area at the front of the station, he had a pretty good view of the harbor and what he couldn't see from the window, got picked up on the CCTV screen behind him. He swiveled his chair around and flipped the view to camera seven, at the end of the dock.

Taking a small sip of his coffee—it was still pretty hot—he scanned the screen. Nothing happening. Just boats suspended serenely in the silky, dark water.

Swiveling back, he looked out the window again and saw movement at the end of the dock, out of CCTV camera range. He squinted.

He stayed put. No need to get up. He knew this one. He could make out the top of her head and shoulders in the dark as someone shook out a sleeping bag and laid it out on the deck of the *Miss Behavin'*, on the port side, away from the dock. He wasn't alarmed. Looked like that homeless chick he'd seen before. All she did was catch some sleep for a few hours, then move on.

It was a good place to hide. He was surprised more homeless didn't camp down here. It would be relatively safe. No one kept anything of value on their boats, so other than occasional vandalism at the fuel dock, they didn't have a lot of crime, so it wasn't a highly patrolled area.

Pettigrew knew he should report her—it was against the law to sleep on your boat, but he hadn't yet. She wasn't there every night. Or if she was, she slept where he couldn't see her—either from the station window or on the screen. Video coverage was spotty along the docks. He doubted she was aware there was any video, though, or she wouldn't be there. You couldn't really see the cameras unless you knew where to look.

She probably had a regular rotation schedule between here and wherever else she slept at night. Didn't bother anyone, cleaned up after herself. Must use the Porta Potties dotted here and there at the construction sites around town, or held it until the public bathrooms in Depoe Bay opened up in the morning. It was all boats, buildings and parking lot around here. No place to do her business. The thought embarrassed him. He had sisters.

There was just something about her. She didn't act like the homeless camped outside his parents' diner in Needles. For one thing, they took a dump wherever they pleased. Most were half out of their minds, ranting and raving, filthy. Mostly men, probably wackos or on drugs. This girl was about his age and looked pretty normal and clean.

He didn't know very many people here yet. The station was all guys and he had no way to meet girls. It's not like he could just go up and introduce himself. Didn't want to scare her away or think he was some creep.

The rest of the night was long, but passed without incident. The guy who was supposed to take second dog watch got sick, so he offered to do his stretch. He was already awake. A few more hours wouldn't matter.

5:35 A.M.

DEPOE BAY HARBOR

"911, what is the nature of your emergency?"

A young man's panicked voice said, "It's my boss. He's dead. At least, I think he's dead. He wasn't moving, I couldn't feel a pulse or anything, but I don't know! I'm so sorry, but I stepped in some of the blood. I tried not to, but it was everywhere. I probably messed things up. There was so much blood. Can you send an ambulance or something? He might be alive, I just don't know."

"Sir, what is your location?"

"Oh, right. I'm at the docks. Depoe Bay Harbor. I came in to work and found him just laying here . . . I usually get in first, but he's been sleeping here, so he was already here . . ."

"Okay, do you feel safe in your location? Are you or anyone else at the scene injured? What is your name?"

"Eric, Eric Udall. I'm up at the Coast Guard station right now. I just reported it to the officer on duty here."

"Seaman Apprentice Pettigrew," the young Coast Guard man on duty said, leaning toward the phone so he would be heard by the dispatcher, on his way out the door to put a barrier up on that dock. More deckhands were showing up for work now and he knew the sheriff's office wouldn't want anyone touching anything.

"I didn't know where else to go," Eric continued, "so I came here first. Figured they'd know what to do. He's going down there right now to make sure nobody goes on the boat. Jeez . . . everybody's coming into work now . . ."

"Good. That's good, Eric. You're doing fine. Can you tell me which boat and describe the exact location of the boat in the harbor and what it looks like?"

The emergency dispatcher, of Western Valley Communications Center in Salem, was already initiating a call to Lincoln County sheriff's office, but knew from experience to keep the caller calm and talking to get the most accurate information for the patrol officer.

"It's a six-pack, a small, green and white boat, second finger dock in off dock two. The *Mary Ann*. It's his boat—the *Mary Ann* is Captain Adam's boat. Or was . . ."

SAFE HARBOR

The sheriff's office had an officer there within minutes. When he saw what he had, he activated the Lincoln County Major Crimes Team. With a bloody fishing gaff laying next to the body, there wasn't much doubt this was a major crime.

With the help of the Coast Guard guy, the officer finished cordoning off the scene until the medical examiner, crime scene techs, and detectives could arrive.

21

TUESDAY, AUGUST 14

Meiling smoothed the covers on her bed and sat back down, straightening her skirt so it wouldn't wrinkle. She didn't want to arrive too early at Adam's parents' house.

Mrs. Hosteler had invited her to lunch. Meiling planned on taking the opportunity to apologize again for backing out of her performance at the last minute the other night. She couldn't tell her the real reason she had been so upset, that Adam's wife had gone down to his boat that day again, threatening to make everything really difficult—even keep him from seeing his kids. There was more, but he said he'd handle it and not to worry.

There was no way she could have played last night. She'd been so afraid he would change his mind, so was very relieved when he texted her late that night. Told her not to worry—he loved her and to get some sleep. He must have been able to reason with his wife and work things out, because he said he wanted to tell his parents sooner rather than later. He was going to join them for lunch today.

Meiling didn't understand how divorce worked in America, but she trusted Adam. They would face whatever it was together.

The Hostelers were such nice people. They'd been so good to her, and now that they would be her in-laws some day. She couldn't believe she'd had to cancel a performance so Mrs. Hosteler had to scramble for another violinist at the last minute. What if she thought she was irresponsible, not good enough for her son?

Her stomach twisted. She got up to use the hall bathroom. The Anderson's house was a small, three-bedroom home, conveniently located two blocks up from the harbor in Depoe Bay. She and Jian each had their own rooms and it was only a half a mile from the Hosteler's. They appreciated the free room and board.

Without people volunteering their spare bedrooms to visiting musicians, these tours wouldn't be possible. In addition, several generous donors helped keep the home concert ticket prices low so anyone could attend, and allowed her and Jian to offer free music workshops at the schools in the area the week they were there. She'd finished one up this morning.

She looked around the room. Their schedule was jammed full until the last minute, but luckily it wouldn't take her long to pack after the last workshop next week. She had her luggage down to her violin case and one carry on. With so many cities on the tour, she and Jian traveled light.

Mrs. Hosteler always insisted on driving them to the airport in Portland. She offered to take the shuttle next Friday, but Adam's mother wouldn't hear of it.

'I'm happy to take you, Meiling. Besides, I need my Nordstrom's fix!' she laughed.

Meiling looked at the clock. She didn't want to arrive early. While she waited, she thought back on the musical career she was about to abandon. Winning the Beijing International Music Competition when she was ten, attendance at the Central Conservatory of Music, every waking minute spent practicing her violin. Somewhere along the line, the party had taken notice of her talent and used her as a shining example of what communism could produce. They controlled her time even more tightly.

She hadn't minded. She knew she was lucky. After graduating from the Conservatory, the government supported her. When the subject of setting up a three-month tour in America came up, her only condition was that she be allowed to take Jian as her accompanist. The government agreed. They felt comfortable having her brother fill the roles of accompanist and chaperone. With all the temptations in the West, a young Chinese woman obviously couldn't travel alone. With the government's stamp of approval, travel visas arrived promptly.

This was their third United States tour and the second year since she met and had been seeing Adam. Well, seeing was an overstatement. They only had the one week a year to be together in person, but they talked every night they could while she was in America. She couldn't text, phone, or send letters from China. They'd never make it past the monitors, and she didn't dare try to send any to his home even here, but she wrote them, then gave them to him in person when they met. He read every one.

Early on, the Chinese government had provided private tutoring for both her and Jian to improve their English language skills. Image was important—they represented China abroad. Language lessons were all part of that training. Some sounds in the English language, such as Rs and Ls, were still a challenge, but for the most part, she no longer dropped verbs or used numbers in front of words to make them plural— and she understood the most common American phrases and slang. She knew she would never sound like a native speaker, but Meiling wanted to get as close as possible, so she would fit in as Adam's wife.

She wasn't sure when it happened, but it suddenly became intolerable to be apart. When she and Adam talked on the boat last night, he told her he couldn't wait. He wanted to get everything out in the open with his wife, his parents, and of course, his children. Last year he brought the two older girls to one of her concerts and she adored them instantly. They, in turn, seemed to be in awe of her. Adam said his oldest daughter wanted to learn to play the piano.

And he planned on telling his mother today. His wife knew already, of course.

Meiling hoped the girls wouldn't hate her. Adam assured her they wouldn't and that everything would be okay. They would fall in love with her as he had.

She hadn't told Jian yet. Of course, living and working so closely together, he was already aware of their mutual attraction, but he would not have approved if he had known how far it had gone. Like all brothers, he was overprotective. She would tell him last, at the end of their tour.

When they got to Chicago, after she talked with Jian, she'd write a letter to the authorities in Beijing so they would not blame him for her actions. It wasn't like the old days where families were punished if one member defected. At least she didn't think so. Jian was a loyal citizen. But still, she'd make double sure they knew she took full responsibility for her own actions and that Jian knew nothing about it.

After Jian flew back home, she would fly on to Portland, and Adam would pick her up there. The tour was only six more weeks. She momentarily felt a pang of sorrow at probably never being able to see her parents again if she stayed in America to be with Adam, but she had been living in Beijing, focused on her studies, for many years and had only been allowed to travel home for Chinese New Years or *Qinming* a few times, anyway. Qinming, known as the Pure Brightness or Tomb Sweeping festival that welcomed spring, was her favorite. Her parents would understand. Besides, maybe someday the travel restrictions would loosen and they would be able to come and visit or even live with her and Adam. But for now, she just needed to focus on getting to Portland in six weeks.

It would all work out.

22

Just thinking about it sent a happy shiver up Meiling's spine. She had grown tired of the grueling performance schedule and just wanted to enjoy music on her own terms, and her new life with Adam. He would have his business sold soon and they would find a place to live in Newport, Oregon, near his children and not far from his parents in Depoe Bay. He had already started scouting for a location for her to open up her own music school. She hadn't met her yet—they were too afraid she'd slip up and tell her mother, but Meiling was hoping she could teach his older daughter, Ariel, to play. Maybe they could share a love of music.

Adam didn't know what he would do next, once he sold the business, but he said he didn't care, as long as they were together. Probably work for another charter boat operation until he could get enough money to get a boat again. She told him he didn't need to sell his business and maybe resent her later, but he insisted and said he could never resent her for anything.

He wanted to make sure his kids didn't hurt for anything. He planned on giving his wife most of the money, and with a chunk of cash, she could buy a small house or go back to school, whatever was best for the kids in the long run. He didn't love his wife anymore—they had nothing in common but their daughters—but whatever was good for her would be good for the kids. He had just bought her a newer model car, too, so she'd have reliable transportation.

Meiling sighed and looked in the bathroom mirror, touching the small, pearl earrings she always wore. Adam was a good man and she knew his wife had cheated on him several times before, but somehow that didn't make her feel any better. She just wished the whole situation wasn't so complicated. If only they had met years ago. Maybe they could still have children of their own. The thought cheered her.

Splashing her face with cold water and patting it dry, she adjusted her cross-body bag and pinched her cheeks. If she left now, she'd get to the Hosteler's home right on time. It was a beautiful day, but she went back to her room and grabbed a knit hat to stuff inside her jacket pocket, just in case. You never knew at the coast.

It was only half a mile to Little Whale Cove and she wanted to walk. There was a path that ran between the forest and the highway. She'd be there in twenty minutes.

At 11:40 a.m., she rang the bell.

She was surprised when a woman she didn't know answered the door. Tan and trim, with a sprinkling of freckles across her nose, wavy, auburn hair curled around the tall woman's shoulders. She looked athletic and had a direct gaze and a warm, friendly smile.

"Hi, I'm Logan. Mrs. Hosteler asked me to get the door. She's got her hands full in the kitchen. She's made enough food for an army, but it all looks great. Hope you're hungry!"

Lunch was crab salad, french onion soup, and a New Zealand sauvignon blanc. Meiling didn't drink often, but the wine was cool and refreshing. Dessert was leftover goodies from the concert, including a cherry cheesecake and giant, oatmeal cookies.

Meiling's apology for missing her performance was accepted and after singing the young violinist's praises, Vivi told Logan how much she wished she could have heard her play last night. Then Vivi offered her own apology.

"Adam was supposed to join us for lunch, but he must have been delayed. Those tourists always want one thing more and he just can't say no. He promised me he'd have a two-hour break between his morning fishing trip and his first whale watching excursion today, but maybe someone twisted his arm and he fit in another one."

Meiling said nothing, her face expressionless, hands in her lap. Adam wouldn't have cancelled this lunch just to fit in one more trip, would he? He knew she was leaving the next week. Maybe he changed his mind. She couldn't call from here and there wasn't good cell reception on the way back. She'd have to try to reach him when she got home.

They adjourned to the living room, and Vivi was just getting out her travel albums from last year's trip to Belgrade when the doorbell rang again. This time, Vivi answered the door. Two men in suits stood on her porch, just outside. One man, in his late fifties, paunchy and pale, with a full head of wavy, coal black hair, stood on the top step, the younger one looked down at his shoes.

"Mrs. Hosteler?" the first man said.

"Yes . . . ?"

"My name is Detective Monson and this is Detective Grant. We're with the Lincoln County Sheriff's Department. May we come in?"

"What's this about?" Vivi said, hesitating.

Meiling watched with interest from the living room, where she and Logan just settled in on the couch, photo albums in their laps, refilled wine glasses in hand.

"If we could just speak with you for a moment inside," Monson said.

Vivi opened the door so they could come in, but stopped there, and remained standing in the hallway.

"Are you sure you wouldn't like to go into the living room . . . maybe sit down, first?" the detective said.

"No, this is fine. What can I do for you?" Vivi asked, somewhat impatiently.

"Is your husband at home, ma'am?"

'No, he knew I was having guests for lunch and went to the hardware store to pick up some paint. We're redoing the deck . . . what's this about? Is Stan okay? Has there been an accident?" she said, alarm creeping into her voice.

Detective Monson took a breath and said, "No, as far as we know your husband is fine. I am so sorry, but we regret to inform you that your son, Adam Hosteler, was found dead aboard his boat early this morning."

Detective Monson barely caught Adam's mother before she crumpled heavily onto the slate entryway floor. He hated making these calls.

At the same time, the detectives heard a young woman cry out from the living room and a glass shatter.

23

Logan watched as both Vivi and Meiling collapsed at the same time. The detectives were taking care of Vivi, who had fallen to the floor in the entryway, so Logan helped Meiling. Something was definitely out of the ordinary in the young woman's reaction. Had she known Adam? Logan hadn't gotten that impression when they were talking at lunch.

Her face pale, it looked like Meiling was going into shock, so acting on barely-remembered first aid training, Logan lifted her legs onto the couch and put several pillows under her feet, instructing her to stay put. The young woman nodded mutely.

Stepping over several broken wine glass shards, Logan dashed to the kitchen, found a couple of dish towels and ran them under cold water in the sink. Wringing them out quickly, she handed one to Monson, who was just coming into the kitchen, and brought the other one back to lay on Meiling's forehead. She went back for two glasses of water. Monson had Adam's mother seated on a chair in the foyer and was talking to her in low, soothing tones.

Logan sat on the edge of the couch beside Meiling, holding the water to her lips, encouraging her to drink a few sips at least. When the color started returning to her pale cheeks, Logan asked, "You okay?"

"Fine," Meiling said, then whispered, "Fine . . . I need to go back. I cannot be here."

"Just wait," Logan said, "Stay here for a minute until you can sit up without feeling dizzy. I'm going to get my jacket. You're in no condition to walk home. I'm taking you home."

While Logan grabbed her jacket, Meiling recovered enough to sit up and take a few more sips of water while Logan picked up the broken glass pieces and mopped up most of the spilled wine. No sense anyone getting cut in addition to everything else.

Just then, Stan Hosteler came in the front door with a puzzled expression on his face, looking at the two unidentified men standing in his house, "Hello?"

Then he saw his wife. She was sobbing now, face in her hands.

"Vivi!" he cried, running over and lifting her out of the chair into his arms. He asked his wife what happened, but as she was unable to respond, the detectives told him.

Not wanting to intrude on such a horrible, private moment, Logan caught the attention of the second detective, Grant, who got their contact information and helped them quietly exit past the grieving parents. He said they'd contact her tomorrow. Logan mumbled her condolences and promised to check in later. She had no idea if Vivi and Stan heard her or not. She couldn't imagine hearing such awful news.

Meiling made it to the car, but then began quietly crying again.

"I am so sorry," she apologized, crumpling into the seat.

Out of her depth, Logan decided to tread carefully, but try to figure out what was going on. She wanted to run next door and tell Amy where she was going, but didn't think she should leave her passenger alone.

"That's okay, Meiling," she said, "Why don't you give me the address where you're staying."

She did, and Logan reached for her phone to GPS it, but realized she must have left it at home. Luckily, it wasn't far and Meiling was able to give her directions. They remained silent while Logan drove through Little Whale Cove deciding whether she should butt in. Well, really, she'd already made up her mind to butt in, it was just a matter of how and when.

Wanting to know everything—immediately—was a character flaw of Logan's. She knew this, but couldn't seem to stop herself. She finally just decided to come right out with it.

"Did you know Adam?" she asked, turning north onto Highway 101. Fresh tears.

Okay, I guess that's a yes.

Meiling's voice barely above a whisper, Logan had to strain to hear her.

"Yes, we were . . . we were going to be together," she said, "His parents did not know yet. He was going to tell them today."

With this, she dissolved into tears again.

"I am so sorry, Meiling," Logan said.

Adam was married with a family. Logan felt bad for this young woman, obviously in shock and grieving, but wasn't sure how to feel about this news. She knew the world wasn't black and white, but still, Logan had a hard time justifying or accepting disloyalty of any kind.

Meiling got out of the car, thanked her for the ride, and was met at the door by her brother, Jian, who helped her inside.

That was weird. He didn't even ask why his sister was upset. It almost looked like he'd been waiting for her.

Still stunned from the events of the last couple of hours, Logan drove back to the house. Ben was prepping vegetables in the kitchen and Amy and Liam just took Ian out in the stroller to get him to take a nap.

Logan sat at the table and filled him in. He said the detectives just left. They'd come by and said they would get in touch with her tomorrow to take her statement.

"Do you think I should tell them about Meiling and Adam?" she asked, after telling him what Meiling had said.

"Not unless you think it has anything to do with why he died," Ben said, "Did they say he was killed or did he have a heart attack or something?"

"I couldn't hear everything, they were in the hall. They just said he died when they first came in," she said, "they didn't say what from."

"It's up to you," Ben said. "But I'm sure the parents have enough to deal with right now—and the wife and kids—without adding that to the mix."

"Yeah," Logan said, "Do you think she knows—the wife?"

"If she does," Ben said, adding the potatoes to the soup he was making for dinner down on the counter, "and it turns out he was killed, it's bad news for her. That would give her a classic motive."

The rest of the evening was quiet. Around five, Logan took a care package with some of Ben's soup, a salad, and some fresh rolls over to the Hosteler's. Stan answered the door and accepted the gift numbly, then retreated into the house. Logan felt so bad for them.

There wasn't much more she could do, so she came back to focus on her own family. It was a quiet night, everyone lost in their own thoughts. Ian, for once, cooperated with coos and loves, helping soothe Logan's jangled nerves, then went down for bed without a hitch around seven thirty.

SAFE HARBOR

Logan hoped sleep would come to the devastated parents next door, relieving them of their grief for a few hours. As for her, she lay awake wrestling with how much to tell the police tomorrow when they called.

24

The available members of the Lincoln County Major Crimes Team began assembling in the common room of the Depoe Bay Coast Guard station as soon as they got the callout Tuesday morning. Until they knew what they were dealing with, the ping pong table would have to suffice as a conference table. If they didn't find the guy right away, they would move to the Fire Department. They had a larger upstairs room that could accommodate them if they needed it.

Formed in just the last few years, the Major Crimes Team consisted of representatives from the Sheriff's Office, Oregon State Police (OSP), Newport PD, Lincoln City PD, Toledo PD, and an investigator from the DA's office.

Unless they had an active case, which fortunately only happened a few times a year, the team only met on the last Thursday of the month at the Lincoln County Sheriff's office, just to keep in touch.

This was different. They had an active homicide case. Everyone's blood pressure rose a few degrees, and the tension was tangible. The clock was ticking. They had five days. Five days of intensive effort from all Major Crime Team members to figure this out and find the killer, or the case would be transferred back to the agency in charge geographically. In this case, because the homicide occurred in Depoe Bay, the Sheriff's department would take lead.

It would fall back in the Sheriff department's lap, but without the manpower and access to resources of the Major Crimes Team. Knowing this, everyone was going full bore. Their families understood. Those five allotted days often ran eighteen to twenty hours long. As everyone knew from watching CSI or Bosch, the chances of murder cases being solved dropped dramatically if the killer wasn't identified and arrested in the first twenty-four to forty-eight hours. Everyone was focused.

Of the twelve members, ten were able to make it in today. Johnson from Toledo was on vacation and Abigail Trent, the Detective from Lincoln City, had liver cancer. Stage 3. Her husband drove her to Portland once a week for some kind of treatment for that. One of the disadvantages of living on the coast, away from specialists. Anything major you had to go to Salem, Corvallis, or Portland. Trent was sharp. She'd be missed. Johnson was an arrogant asshole. Nobody would miss him. He'd been a decent cop, but he was counting the days to retirement. And all of those days, he worked as little as possible.

Oregon State Police's Detective Clancy brought in a box of pastries donated by Gracie's Sea Hag restaurant when they heard what was going on, tossed it in the middle of the ping pong table, flipped open the lid and took out a bear claw. Detective Monson of the Sheriff's department grabbed a maple bar, took a bite, then placed it on a napkin for later. They'd all been running on coffee, so solid food was appreciated. Someone already had more coffee going and a white board set up.

Unlike in movies and popular TV shows, no murder book had been created yet. That would be assembled as reports came in from autopsies, interviews, and lab results.

Brushing his hands on his pants, Monson started the briefing.

"This morning, at 5:35 a.m., Western Communications Center received a call from an Eric Udall, a twenty-seven-year-old residing in Depoe Bay, reporting his discovery of a dead body on the deck of the *Mary Ann* when he arrived for work. Mr. Udall has been employed by the deceased, forty-five-year-old Adam Hosteler, also a resident of Depoe Bay, as a deckhand for the last two summer seasons.

"Mr. Udall called 911 from his cell phone, from the Coast Guard station. He said he immediately went to the station upon discovering the body. The guy on duty, a Seaman Apprentice Sean Pettigrew, then called someone to cover his desk and went to secure the scene until the Sheriff's office arrived and cordoned off the area. We took a preliminary statement from him, but he pulled a double, so if you want more details, you'll have to play Prince Charming and kiss him out of his beauty sleep. He's catching some ZZZs in the back room.

"Family's been notified and Newport's got a couple of officers canvassing anyone who may have stayed late or come in early to work and the neighborhood for witnesses.

"ME's preliminary report is death by a blunt force object, the head wound matches what we assume is the murder weapon, the bloody fishing gaff laying next to the body. We'll know more when the lab work comes back if there's any more to it, but it looks pretty straightforward. Any questions?"

"Time of death?"

"Again, the ME—most of you know Cyndi Birdwell—could only give a range. She'll give us a better idea when she finishes up, but right now she says somewhere between ten o'clock last night and two this morning."

Ron Caldwell, the investigator from the DA's office jumped in, "What was he doing down there? I don't think they allow liveaboards in the harbor."

"Permission or not, from what we could see from the deck into the cabin, he's been staying there a while—a few days, weeks, maybe. Couldn't be for long. It's a small boat. Gary's working on the search warrant."

Gary Smythe, a patrol officer from Lincoln City, was their go-to guy for search warrants. Everybody on the team had him on speed dial. Man had a golden pen.

"Anyone talk to the wife yet? Trouble at home? Gaff's not that heavy, a woman could have done it."

"Wife's been notified. We're heading down there to interview her again, but yeah, since he was almost certainly staying down on his boat, could be some kind of trouble at home. Grand Jury meets again Thursday, so Ron'll work his magic and get us our subpoenas for bank and phone records by tomorrow noon."

"Can't you just ask the wife?" asked one of the newer members of the team.

"Yeah, and we will," Monson replied, "we'll do both. Don't want to give the defense any ammunition down the road in case she decides to say she never gave her permission."

The detective nodded.

As soon as everyone had their assignments, the team dispersed into the field or onto their computers. They had a hell of a lot of work to do and precious little time to do it.

25

Detective Monson rolled his chair over to one of the folding tables set along the north wall of the large, upstairs room of the Depoe Bay Fire Department where thirty-eight-year-old Newport Police Department Detective, Jim Grant, was queuing up a video on his computer. Grant's professionally styled, sandy brown hair, crisp suit, and flat abs contrasted with Monson's pasty skin and lumpier edges. No one understood why, but the two men got along well.

"I say it's the wife," Monson said.

"Well, since there's no butler," said Grant.

His girlfriend had been binge-watching Agatha Christie murder mysteries and he'd been sucked into watching them with her. They weren't bad. He wished Hercule Poirot was on their team. He'd close the case in no time. They, on the other hand, were mere mortals and would have to slog through the investigation the hard way.

"Okay, let's say it's the wife. What's her motive?" Grant asked.

"Could be anything, money . . . other woman . . ." Monson said.

". . . couldn't stand his snoring . . ." Grant chimed in.

Monson snorted. His wife made him use a CPAP machine. He hated it, but it probably saved their marriage. She snored, too, but wouldn't admit it.

"So, what have we got?" he said, scooting his chair closer to the table.

"CCTV is hit and miss," Grant said.

He pulled up an image of the harbor in Google Maps and tapped on the screen.

"The fuel dock at the south end has good video, but nothing on it for Monday night or early Tuesday. Same with the buildings up top."

He pointed to a small, rectangular building on the far side of the parking lot, facing the harbor: Dockside Charters.

"Dockside has good coverage around their building, but it's patchy on the docks themselves. Other than that, everyone's kind of responsible for their own thing. They don't usually have trouble down there. Like I said, not a lot of theft. Not much left on board the boats at night to steal."

"No footage of the guy's boat, I suppose, the *Mary Ann*, or any of them on that dock, Dock 2. That would be too much to hope for."

Grant hit play on the video and fast-forwarded until he got to the place he wanted.

"They've got coverage at the south end of the dock, three down from our vic's boat. Nothing on that dock, Dock 2, then coverage picks up again near the Coast Guard station. That's where this footage is from. This stretch links the little docks together," he said, tracing a path with his finger along the screen, parallel to the parking lot.

"Only one way in or out for someone on foot, unless they swim, or jump from boat to boat," said Monson.

"Or fly," Grant said. His daughter read vampire books and they always managed to fly away and materialize someplace else at will. He looked at the time stamp on the recording—1:42 a.m.

"What about here, just before the station?" Grant said. "If they went through the parking lot, someone could go straight up between the houses there."

"Yes," Monson said. "That's a possibility, but if they came in a car, makes more sense they'd take the direct route—they'd want to jump in their car and take off."

"Time fits in the window the ME gave us for time of death. We get her report yet?" said Grant.

"Won't get the full report for another day or two, but yes, it fits the ten-to-two time frame," Monson said. "Can you get it brighter?" he asked. "Where is this?"

"Dock 1. In front of the Coast Guard station," Grant said.

Only part of the harbor was illuminated by security lights. This area was fairly well lit, but the person they were looking at crossed the dock at the edge of the frame, partially in shadow, exiting to the right toward the parking lot and town, with what looked like a bedroll or sleeping bag tucked under one arm. They weren't running, but crouching down, looking like they were trying to step quietly. They may even have been barefoot. It was hard to tell.

"I've watched this a dozen times, looks female, or a small male, maybe—think it's our killer?" Grant asked.

"No. I don't get that from this. They're leaving in a hurry, but they're not running. Body language looks scared to me. Looks like they're trying to get away, but hide from someone at the same time. If they'd killed the guy, who would they be hiding from?"

"Maybe they saw something, depending on where they were. What about the Coast Guard? They see this chick? Don't they visually monitor that area out of the station window? Where's his interview? If he's supposed to be watching this area, how come he didn't say anything?"

"Good question," Monson said. "We need to get back down there tomorrow and talk to him again, jog his memory. And we need to talk again with shop owners, workers—anyone who may be able to identify her or saw her that night, if it's a her. She has to live somewhere nearby.

"Oh, and pull up all video from nine or ten on—our killer may have come for a visit and stayed a while before offing our victim."

26

Monson scratched his chin and felt a rough patch. Must have missed a spot. No surprise. He'd finally gone home last night around 2:00 a.m., more for a change of clothes than actual sleep. He must have caught a few hours, though. Woke up around six o'clock, forced himself into the shower, then shaved in the car on the way over this morning.

He'd sent out a group text last night before he left, telling everyone to be here by eight. Everybody except Ron. He looked at his watch. The investigator for the DA's office was already on the road to Portland for the autopsy. Cyndi Birdwell ran a tight ship, but tended to be more open with Ron than other observers. He would bring back what information could be gleaned by paying attention as she recorded her results into the mic as she went through the exam. He took notes, but also had an excellent memory.

Clancy brought donuts again, this time from Pirate Coffee. By unspoken rule, local restaurants and stores stepped up, supplying cops and firemen with what they needed to do their jobs when disaster struck. Everybody out here pitched in. It was the way of small communities. They knew it might be them that needed help in the next emergency.

Monson waited as people filtered in and got settled, then summarized what they knew so far. They didn't know how it all fit yet, but the white board was filling up.

Monson tapped on a photo of Adam Hosteler, standing proudly on board his charter boat, the *Mary Ann,* arm around his wife, three little daughters seated at his feet, their legs dangling over the edge. The photo was several years old by the age of the kids. Everybody was smiling. Happy days. The wife had supplied the photo.

"Okay. We've got our victim, Adam Hosteler, charter boat captain, age forty-five, estimated TOD sometime between ten Monday night and 2:00 a.m. Tuesday morning. Preliminary cause of death, blunt force trauma to the head. Fishing gaff found here—he pointed to one of the crime scene photos—to the right of the body. Blood on the gaff is the same blood type as the victim, A+. Waiting for official test results, but it's his."

No one interrupted, so Monson went on, jabbing a finger back on the timeline.

"5:45 a.m. Western Communications Center receives a 911 call from victim's deckhand, twenty-five-year-old Eric Udall. Coast Guard helps secure scene until we arrive."

"Working backward, in the last forty-eight hours before the victim's death, he was business as usual, taking tourists out on his charter boat for half-day fishing trips in the mornings, and a few whale watchers in the afternoons. Johnson's got more detail on his exact whereabouts that day, but it doesn't look like Mr. Hosteler did anything out of the ordinary."

"What about his living on his boat? Anyone talk with the wife, yet?" Clancy asked.

"Yes, all indications point in that direction," Monson said. "Ron's doing some more digging. We'll know more once we get the records requests approved, but yeah, there's some dirt there. She was notified yesterday, but we're taking another run at the wife today now that we know she was there that night. Grant caught her on video exiting past the Coast Guard station at eleven fifteen. We'll get her story since it fits in the murder window."

They all knew what that meant. It meant the detectives found something on the boat, but couldn't use it until the warrant came through. They also knew that these were early days and Monson was an experienced investigator. He would make sure they meticulously followed every lead and wouldn't narrow the investigation too soon.

Monson turned back to the board.

"Which brings us to a person of interest we haven't been able to locate yet. Chris Larsen, thirty-six-year-old former employee who confronted our murder victim Monday morning at approximately 11:30 a.m. at his boat, when he returned to the docks from a chartered fishing trip. Plenty of witnesses—some customers and the deck hand, but two of his own customers were closest, a Logan McKenna and Ben Halvard. We're going out to talk with them today. Clancy, any luck on running this Chris guy down?"

Clancy looked at his own notes.

"Not yet. The last people to see him were the bartender and waitress at Pagoda Palace. Waitress said he was there with friends until closing Monday night, around one," Clancy said.

"That puts him there at the right time," Monson said. "She say what he was driving?"

"No, didn't go outside, he was gone when she locked up thirty minutes later," Clancy said.

"Okay," Monson said.

He didn't have to tell Clancy what to do next. He'd check to see if any vehicles were registered in Chris' name, current address, etc. They knew he wasn't working as of Monday afternoon, but he may have landed something since then or gone north to find work. For an employer not as picky as Adam about drug use. They'd track him down.

Monson then had Grant share the CCTV footage showing the unidentified person exiting the dock area early Tuesday morning. Everyone agreed it was probably a female. They distributed copies of the best screen shot they could get off the video.

"Ask around. Someone must know who she is. Doesn't look like the wife—too small, but we're not ruling it out. She could have come back."

The sheriff's department volunteers were coming up the stairs, gathering for their assignments, so Monson drew the short briefing to a close. Today was search day. They had a probable murder weapon, but in every murder case he'd ever worked, someone left something somewhere. In his experience, most people weren't seasoned criminals. And most seasoned criminals weren't all that intelligent.

In the meantime, after the briefing they'd keep plugging away, conducting interviews, reviewing the CCTV footage, and looking for witnesses until something broke.

1:30 P.M.

Monson heard someone clomping up the stairs. It was Ron, the investigator for the DA's office.

He looked at his watch, then called across the room, "Wow, that's got to be a record. How'd you get here from Portland that fast?"

Ron strode over and took a seat next to Monson's temporary desk. "Lucked out and got the first slot. Autopsy was over by eleven. Left right after," he said, pulling over a chair and folding himself into it. Ron was six-four. Most furniture was not made with him in mind.

Monson pushed a coffee over he just made for himself, two sugars, heavy cream. Ron gratefully accepted, took a deep slurp, then wiped his mustache off and waited. Grant arrived with a fresh cup for Monson, black, which Monson proceeded to bring up to his standards. Grant's Starbuck's thermos was filled with decaf. He didn't do caffeine after lunch. Not that they'd had lunch yet.

Ron didn't make them wait. He pulled out his notes.

"Until sometime between one and two o'clock Tuesday morning, August 14, 2019, Adam Hosteler was a forty-five-year-old male in good health. Cause of death was good old fashioned blunt force trauma to the head. Murder weapon, the fishing gaff."

Ron looked up from his notes. "Any good prints?"

Monson shook his head, "Weapon was partially wiped. Chris, Adam, Adam's wife, and Eric Udall's fingerprints were on there of course, along with several we're tracking down now—probably tourists on board during fishing or whale watching trips. Prints won't help us much."

Ron flipped to the last page of the notes he took during the ME's autopsy. He'd saved the best for last.

"She did have one thing for you, though," he said, smiling. "The victim was whacked on the head more than once. A non-fatal wound, delivered by the same weapon, before the one that did him in."

This got their attention. Monson raised his eyebrows and waited for Ron to explain.

"How do they know the non-fatal wound happened first?" Grant asked.

"Well, that one had Neosporin on it," Caldwell said. "Don't think our killer would whack him gently, then wait for him to go fix his owie first, before finishing him off."

27

Detective Monson from the Sheriff's office called earlier and said he would be stopping by to talk with Logan and Ben, since they both witnessed Adam being confronted by his former employee at the *Mary Ann* on Monday. Other people were nearby, but she and Ben were closest and had heard and seen the whole thing. Just routine, the detective said, covering all the bases, gathering information, all normal parts of the investigation.

Amy and Liam were leaving to take Ian to Lincoln City for some kite flying. Lincoln City had miles of open, sandy beach and a great kite shop in town. Logan had just finished strapping her grandson into his car seat and kissing him on the forehead when the detectives arrived. Mom and Dad were already in the car. Making sure Amy hadn't left her coffee on the top of the car, which she often did, Logan tugged Ian's seat belt again, shut the door and tapped the side door as a go signal. Amy waved, and they were on their way.

Not wanting to block in the SUV, the detectives had parallel parked on the street. After waiting for the car to exit the driveway, they followed Logan back into the house where Ben was waiting with iced tea, water, and coffee. They opted for coffee.

Detective Monson introduced himself to Logan, then did it all over again for Ben. They settled in the living room. There was plenty of room. The whole police department could have fit on the humongous sectional.

Detective Grant sank back into the low cushions, but Monson, the older detective, remained on the edge, leaning forward a bit to keep his balance, pencil poised, notebook on one knee.

Ben handed them each a mug of hot coffee, placing cream and sugar within reach. They thanked him. Grant doctored his cup with lots of cream, no sugar. Detective Monson drank his black. They resumed their positions.

"Nice," said Grant, nodding toward the sweeping view of the ocean out the large picture window.

"Yes," Logan agreed. She wished they'd get on with it. She knew they had to do their job and talk to everyone, but neither she nor Ben knew these people well and the argument they witnessed may or may not have had anything to do with the murder. She hated the idea of giving the police ammunition against a guy who was already down on his luck, even if he was a jerk. Being a jerk didn't make you a murderer.

Monson took the lead, "We're just filling in the timeline of events leading up to the death of the owner of the *Mary Ann*, Mr. Adam Hostler. Mrs. McKenna, when . . .

"Oh, you can just call me Logan, Logan McKenna. My husband passed away several years ago," she clarified.

Monson looked at Ben, then continued, "All right, Logan. Let's start at the beginning—when you first met the deceased, Adam Hosteler."

For the next half hour, she and Ben answered questions, giving the times as exactly as they could remember them. Logan answered truthfully, but did not volunteer or embellish any negative information about Adam's former employee, Chris. The retelling made her wonder if Chris had any previous incidents of violence. Anyone could lose their temper once, but if there was a pattern, then she could see why the police were interested.

She asked Monson this question, but he ignored her request.

Google it is, then.

Logan was itching for them to leave so she could get on her computer. Monson asked how long they'd be staying in town and handed them his card in case they thought of any additional information.

"Ben and the kids are scheduled to fly back on the 19th, Sunday," Logan said.

"Yes," Ben said, "We may be driving to Portland Saturday night, since our flight leaves early Sunday morning."

Logan explained she'd be staying for another few days to a week. She promised Huey and Rita she'd fit in a couple days work at the New School before flying back. Saved grant money doing it that way instead of turning around right away to come up in September as she usually did.

Just after the police left, they heard a knock on the door. Ben was putting the coffee things away, so Logan answered. It was Vivi, looking nervous and upset. Logan was surprised to see her there.

"I didn't want to interrupt while the police were here," Vivi said, wringing her hands.

"Not at all," said Logan, stepping aside for her to come in.

"I just wanted . . . is this a good time?" Vivi asked, hovering near the entrance, seeing Ben in the kitchen.

"Yes, of course," Logan said. "You can come by anytime, Vivi. What can I do for you?"

Ben excused himself and went upstairs. Logan went to get some iced tea for Vivi. She followed her into the dining room, so they just sat down at the table in there.

"How are you and Stan doing?"

"We're okay, dealing with things—no one tells you how much has to be done when you feel least up to it—I feel like I'm sleepwalking through it. Adam was so . . . I still can't believe it, you know," she said. "Nothing seems normal or right . . ."

Vivi teared up, but got control of herself and continued, "The service will be Saturday after next. The funeral home said they'd be able to get him back by then—they do the exams . . . the autopsy . . . up in Portland—they said they'd have him back in time for this Saturday, but I don't think I can be ready by then, and we have relatives coming from out of town. They'll let us know. You are welcome to come, of course, although I know you only met Adam the one time."

"Thank you," Logan said. "We'll be gone before then, but it's very kind of you to invite us."

She asked again if there was anything she could do.

Vivi pushed her shoulders back and sat up straighter, "I'm fine. My book club friends are helping me with the arrangements. I thought I could at least take that burden off of Debra, Adam's wife. She has her hands full with the girls. It's Debra I've come about, actually."

28

Logan waited to hear more.

"Debra is very upset. When the police came back to talk with her after the notification yesterday, she said they weren't very nice at all. It sounded like they think she had something to do with Adam's death," Vivi said.

Logan wondered what this had to do with her. Vivi's next sentence answered that question.

"Rita told us about how you helped that woman a couple of years ago, and other friends before that, one in California and one up here in Portland," Vivi said. "I want you to help Debra. I haven't always been my daughter-in-law's biggest fan, but she is the mother of my grandchildren, and even though she's had her problems, she has been a very good mother to them."

"Well, yes, I've been involved—completely by accident—with a couple of murder investigations, but I'm not qualified to handle something like this. Your daughter-in-law needs a good attorney, not me," Logan said.

"But Rita said you have a brother in law enforcement, so you know how things work with the police."

"Rick's the police officer, not me," Logan said. "I have absolutely no police or legal training."

Vivi pushed on, "Rita said you are smart, very capable, and more important to me, very loyal to your friends. Whatever you don't know, she says you'll find out."

Smiling, she added, "She said you're actually very nosy—but in a good way."

Logan had to admit, sticking her nose where it didn't belong did seem to be a genetic trait she'd never been able to shake. They'd be here another week-and-a-half. If it would help ease Vivi's mind, the least she could do was talk with her daughter-in-law and maybe convince her to obtain good legal counsel if she needed it.

"Did the police come right out and tell her they suspect her?" Logan asked.

"No, she just got that impression from the way they talked to her, the questions they asked."

"Okay," Logan said, "I can talk with her, see why she thinks the police are interested. Maybe she can clear things up easily by proving she wasn't anywhere near his boat that night. Has she done that?"

"I don't know," Vivi said. "She was just so upset when she called yesterday after they left."

Logan handed Vivi a pad of paper she'd seen in the junk drawer and a pencil for her to write down her daughter-in-law's address and phone number. She said she'd let her know as soon as they connected. The relief sheeting off Vivi's body was palpable.

"Thank you, Logan," she said. "I can't tell you how much I appreciate this. I know you don't know us, and you're supposed to be on vacation. Hopefully you'll be able to help her clear things up with the police and they can get back to finding out who really did this."

◊ ◊ ◊ ◊ ◊

SAFE HARBOR

A little later, Logan reached Debra on the phone. Vivi's daughter-in-law didn't seem thrilled with the prospect of a visitor, but said to come over in the morning, after the kids left for school. It seemed soon for them to be back in school—their father had only died two days ago—but Logan wasn't their mother, and she could only assume theirs knew what was best for them. Given the topic of their upcoming conversation, it was probably best. No sense upsetting them with talk of their father's death or the police suspecting their mother.

Since she couldn't go see Debra until tomorrow, and the kids wanted to just hang out at the cove again, Logan and Ben decided to spend the rest of the afternoon exploring Depoe Bay.

The town only being a few blocks long, it didn't take them long to do the walking tour. Starting with the shops on the east side of Highway 101, they picked up a cute t-shirt for Ian that said, "Having a Whale of a Time", and a glass float for Bonnie. The now familiar aroma of caramel corn pulled them into Ainslee's and they picked up a couple more bags for TV snacks later tonight.

Liam was hard to buy for. Nothing in the shops screamed Scottish botanist—she didn't even know if he wanted a souvenir—but she'd keep looking. Maybe something from the brass store they'd seen on the corner. The lease on Amy and Liam's rental home was up soon and they were house hunting, although with the prices in Southern California, they weren't likely to find anything they could afford. Liam's parents had offered to buy them a home, but wisely, Logan thought, Liam had declined. They'd manage on their own.

One shop had treasure chests, swirled, hand blown glass lamps, and a bunch of carved wooden bears in various sizes scattered throughout the store. One, about three feet tall, was similar to the one standing guard outside the home they were staying in. They must have bought it here.

After putting their packages in the car, Ben got them a couple of coffees to go. Wrapping their hands around the tall cups to keep warm, when the walk sign flashed, they made their way across the street to do a little whale watching.

It was overcast, but no one seemed to mind. The sole bench was taken, but they sat on the sea wall for a while, enjoying the spectacular view of the bay, including a bald eagle that flew past with a large fish in his or her talons. Logan wondered if male and female eagles had the same markings.

Next, they wandered through a white, hexagonal building on the south end of town, just at the start of the bridge, which turned out to be a whale watching center with quite a bit of information about the types of whales that came by and when, great viewing areas protected from the wind, and a little history of the town thrown in by the docent manning the station.

Outside, an excited bird watcher waved her companion over to the railing at the base of the whale center, right next to the narrow opening to the harbor.

She pointed down into the water, "Look! They're right there . . . see? Pigeon guillemots! They are so cool!"

He didn't look as thrilled about her discovery as she was, but obligingly peered over the edge. Logan came up beside him and looked down to see what a guillemot was. A small group of birds with bright, red legs were swimming energetically in a circle underwater, diving for fish.

Just then, the sun came out in full force from behind a bank of clouds, warming her face and painting the ocean in deep greens and brilliant blues, with bright white froth topping the incoming waves. These moments of pure, wild beauty still took Logan's breath away.

She smiled up into Ben's face and gave him a fierce hug. She was so glad they came.

29

Deciding to give Ben the night off from cooking, Liam went down to the Mexican place and picked up easy-to-eat-with-your-fingers burritos, tacos, guacamole, and salsa and chips. Ben couldn't resist getting in the kitchen and made everyone margaritas good enough to rival the ones at Juan's back home. They took everything out on the deck and talked and ate until it was dark. This was Logan's idea of a good time. She loved being with her family.

But when they went to bed, she couldn't get to sleep. She'd been itching to get on her computer ever since the detectives left. As soon as she heard Ben's soft snores, she tiptoed down the stairs. Taking her laptop onto the deck, she popped it open and checked her email. She'd emailed Huey last night. She wanted to know more about Adam's former employee, Chris. If she was going to help Debbie, she needed to see who else may have killed her husband. If Chris had a history of violence, it might also help keep Meiling's relationship a secret. There seemed no point in anyone finding out about that now that Adam was gone.

Last year, Huey Nguyen, the tech guru at the New School who worked with her in Fractals, helped her unlock some hidden files on a flash drive, which lead to the capture of a killer. Huey's methods were sometimes less than legal, but he could get into anything except maybe Homeland Security, so Huey was the first person Logan thought of to help her this time.

She needed to get into whatever database contained arrest records to see if Chris Larsen had a criminal record. She knew there were sites like that online you could pay for, but she was cheap and didn't want to waste time figuring out how to navigate them. Besides, she wasn't sure they would work anyway. Huey was faster.

If Chris had a criminal past, maybe she wouldn't feel so guilty about withholding information about Adam and Meiling's involvement from the police or deflecting the police's attention from Debbie. But the real reason Logan wanted to know was simply that she wanted to know. She hadn't asked to get involved, but now that she was, she wanted to get to the truth, whatever that truth turned out to be.

When the Mail window opened, Logan smiled. The second email was from Huey. She quickly scanned over the information he'd sent. Paydirt!

Huey had found two items of interest. One was recent, a drunk driving incident last month. DUI on his record, big fine, released after a night in jail.

The other entry was far more interesting. Huey, whose curiosity had been peaked by Logan's request, had done some digging into not just the regular police database, but sealed records, too. Juvenile records. This is where he struck gold.

Yowza . . . !

SAFE HARBOR

At the age of sixteen, Chris Larson almost killed a man, Karl Richards, his mother's live-in boyfriend at the time. According to the intake report, Richards had put his mother in the hospital more than once. Chris claimed Karl started drinking the minute he got home that night and was gearing up to go after his mother again. The seventeen-year-old knew the signs, so he made a pre-emptive strike and beat the boyfriend bad enough to keep him from ever coming around again.

The police may have looked the other way, given the family history, but unbelievably, the mom came to Richards' defense. Said he never hit her. Since Chris didn't have a mark on him, he couldn't claim self-defense. The judge didn't have much choice. The boy was in juvie for a year until he turned eighteen. Logan scanned the rest of the record. No incidents that she could see while he was locked up in the youth facility. Not much in the notes after that.

Interesting.

This information may not clear Vivi's daughter-in-law, but it definitely showed that someone else had not only ample motive, but a history of violence. The only catch was how to alert the police to this bit of Chris' personal history, without having to explain how she got it.

Logan's back told her she'd been sitting too long, so she logged out of the sites and went into the kitchen for some SleepyTime tea. She added a dollop of honey and took the mug back to the living room, grabbing her laptop from the dining room table on the way. Steam swirled up, warming her cheeks as she took a sip of the fragrant tea. Setting down the mug on the end table, she flipped open her laptop and curled up on the couch. Might as well catch up on emails while she waited for the tea to take effect.

Scrolling through her Inbox, she deleted all the ones from her mother without reading them. Then she saw one from Rick.

Hey Sis,

Tried calling, but you're not answering your phone. When were you going to tell me about mom?

Rick

Damn.

When their mother couldn't get through to Logan, she must have decided to contact Rick. Damn that woman! First she leaves them high and dry, then thirteen years later, waltzes back in and won't leave them alone! She'd disrupted Logan's life, talked her into giving her a chance to tell her side of the story, and when Logan finally agreed to see her, didn't show up at the restaurant. Logan felt she had every right to keep her from disrupting Rick's life and hurting her little brother all over again.

Frustrated and fuming, Logan hit Reply.

Rick,

Sorry I missed your call(s). I think I lost my phone. I'm sure it will turn up around here somewhere, but in the meantime, if you need me, call Ben or Amy and I'll call you back on theirs.

Logan's fingers hesitated over the keyboard. She took a deep breath, rolled her shoulders, thinking about what she could possibly say. She and Rick had always been close. She didn't want their mother coming between them now.

I'd borrow a phone and call you now, but I just got your email. I could use Ben's phone, but it's late and I can't call without waking people up. I can't explain any of this in a phone call or an email, anyway. Can we talk about this when I get home?

SAFE HARBOR

I don't want you to worry about this. Please wait until I get home. She just showed up, Rick, out of the blue. She's been gone for years, she can wait a few more days, okay?

Love you,

Logan

Powering down her laptop, Logan laid it on the coffee table. Nestling back into the couch cushions, she stopped to enjoy the stillness. With the lights out and her computer shut, she looked out from the darkened living room to the ocean. The calm, glassy surface rippled gently under an ivory moon.

Rick's email shouldn't have come as a surprise. Logan knew she would have had to deal with her mother sooner or later. She had just been hoping for later.

30

No matter how he sat, Pettigrew couldn't get comfortable.

He'd never been questioned by the police before. He'd never even gotten a traffic ticket. And now here he was, sitting across from two policemen. Detectives. *Homicide* detectives. They introduced themselves as Monson and Grant. They'd parked him at this table and told him they'd be right back.

This wasn't the police station, it was just a big room over the Fire Station two blocks away, but it looked pretty damn official. There were cops coming in and out all the time, a white board Monson turned around so he couldn't see what was on it. He didn't recognize all the different uniforms the cops wore, but whatever agencies or cities they were with, none of them smiled at him.

He had a pretty good idea why he was here. He'd just have to tell them and get it over with. He hoped it wouldn't get him trouble with his commander. He wanted to make the Coast

Guard his career. No sense starting with a big, black mark on his record.

Finally, the two detectives came over and sat down across from him. Monson, a large, rumpled man with dark hair and brooding eyes, spoke first. He must be the one in charge. Grant, younger by at least a decade, put his laptop on the table, opened it and started looking for something on it.

"Seaman Pettigrew," Monson said.

"It's Seaman Apprentice, sir, I'm not up for Seaman for another six months," Pettigrew said.

"That title is a little unwieldy for us landlubbers," Monson said. "How about if we just call you Sean? That's your first name, right?"

"Yes, sir. That would be fine, sir," Pettigrew said.

He needed to pee. He crossed his legs and hoped this wouldn't take long.

After going through the preliminaries, Detective Grant swung his laptop around so Sean could see the screen.

"We need to clear up a discrepancy in your statement, Sean. When we spoke to you yesterday, you said you didn't see anyone going past your station window during your shift," Monson said.

Yep, this was it. They knew. Sean remained silent.

Grant tapped on the play button of the video he had up on the screen.

"This is from your CCTV footage," Monson said. "We need you to identify this individual, Sean."

"I don't know, it's kind of hard to see her," Sean said.

"Then it is a female," Monson said.

"I didn't say that, I . . ."

"Look, let's not waste time, here, Sean. We went back a week or two and saw her again."

Grant pulled up another video, dated August 7.

"Who is she? The fact that you didn't tell us about a person you saw on the docks the night of the murder doesn't look good for you, Sean," Monson said. "You do realize this is a murder investigation. Withholding information like this is serious, Sean."

Sean folded his hands in front of him on the table and looked from one man to another. Grant looked friendlier, so he focused on him.

"I didn't say anything because she's not involved. She's a nice person!" Sean said.

"So you do know her," Monson said.

"No, I mean I don't *know* her, know her. I asked around and know who she is, but . . . we've never actually met," he said.

Grant looked surprised, "So you've never even talked with this girl?"

"No," Sean mumbled.

Monson was not concerned with Sean's love life or lack thereof. His expression remained unchanged and he got the interview back on track.

"What's her name?" he asked.

"Karen. I don't know her last name, but she works up at the Horn some nights. Waits tables," he said miserably.

Monson then had him go into great detail about every time he had seen her and what he had observed her doing.

"She never bothers anything and always leaves everything nice. She just sleeps on boats a few hours a night and is gone before the deckhands start coming in. She's a student down at the college in Newport. Just having trouble at home. That's why she's camping out down here sometimes. And it's not every night . . ."

Monson was already getting up out of his seat. He placed

his business card on the table in front of Sean and tapped it.

"If you think of anything else, Sean, you call me. We'll drop you off on the way."

On the way where, he didn't say and Sean didn't ask.

Neither detective had mentioned talking with his Commander or any further contact, so he could only hope this was it. He'd know when he got back if he was in trouble. He really wanted to stay in the Coast Guard.

Of course, once they found Karen and told her he'd ratted her out, it would ruin any chance he had with her. She'd hate him. He had just been waiting until he figured out how to approach her, and now it was too late.

On the way out, he didn't dare ask to stop and use the bath-room. Hoping he wouldn't disgrace himself and pee in the patrol car, Seaman Assistant Pettigrew did as instructed and followed the detectives out. Monson trotted down the stairs briskly.

He moved pretty fast for an old guy.

31

Tim Hayes, an easy-going gentleman, waited for his search buddy, Bill, who was working his way up the opposite side of Seal Street. Bill took a little longer than he did to get to the top.

Pushing seventy, Tim didn't look a day over sixty thanks to good, German genes on his mother's side, weekly pickle ball tournaments and kayaking as often as he could get his boat in the water. He and Bill were part of the retired volunteer force affectionately referred to as The Posse, called out by the Lincoln County Major Crimes Team when they needed extra manpower to get the job done.

They'd been at it several hours already. As soon as they finished this grid, they'd break for a late lunch, then move on to the next. They didn't know what they were looking for exactly, just anything that looked out of the ordinary or might be connected in some way to Tuesday's homicide in the harbor. Or maybe Monday's. The exact time of death was still unknown. At least to them. They weren't official law enforcement, so weren't privy to all the reports.

The one thing they weren't looking for was the murder weapon. They already had that, but there was always something. They'd know it when they saw it.

While he waited, Tim placed his foot against a large hunk of driftwood delineating the end of a small parking area behind a shop that sold brass portholes made into mirrors, ship's bells, and other nautical-themed items. Lifting the weight of his body up out of his hip socket, so as not to strain his lower back, he bent forward, reaching for his toes and started his stretches. Keeping limber helped prevent injuries.

At the end of his stretch, a bright bit of color in the blackberry bushes on the other end of the lot next to the dumpsters caught his eye. The large, metal containers had been pushed back a couple of feet during this morning's trash pickup, exposing that section of brush.

Sure it was nothing, and knowing this parking lot was part of the search grid they'd be working after lunch, Tim almost decided to wait, but couldn't resist going over to take a look. One look is all it took.

"Well, I'll be damned!" Tim said.

5:00 P.M.

LINCOLN COUNTY MAJOR CRIMES TEAM

INCIDENT COMMAND CENTER, DEPOE BAY

"What'd they find?"

Monson signaled to the Sheriff's Deputy who'd ask the question to wait until everyone was assembled and found a seat, then began the briefing.

"As most of you know by now, earlier today, we caught a break. Two members of the search team, Tim Hayes and Bill Goddard, discovered probable pieces of physical evidence in Grid Two, back of Poseidon's."

Here, Monson gestured to the white board behind him, where he had taped some pictures.

"The items were found three feet into some blackberry bushes. They almost missed it, but for the color. The dumpsters would have kept it hidden, but trash pickup was today and they had a new guy. Dumpsters got put back a few feet off their normal spot."

He showed several more shots of the items from different angles, *in situ*, then pointed to the next photo, a sweater, removed from its discovery location and spread out on a flat surface. A small, thin, silk sweater, one sleeve splotched with dark stains.

"Woman's sweater. OSP techs are working on the blood now. Sample sent up to Portland for DNA testing. They put a rush on it, but as you know, that may take a while. They were able to type it before sending it out—A+, second most common blood type. Doesn't narrow it down much, but it's our victim's type as well. It's a start."

Everyone was paying attention. It didn't always happen, but any break in a case was cause for hope.

Monson continued. Rolling the white board over so everyone could see it better, he said, "Underneath the sweater—actually wrapped in it—was our second item. A phone."

A low rumble ran through the group. Phones were good. People lived on their phones. Phones were a treasure trove of information and most people weren't too careful about covering their tracks. This could be the break they needed. If things went their way, they might all be home for the weekend.

Monson ignored the hope.

"Samsung, cracked lens, 2015. Ron's already on it. Grand Jury meets tomorrow. He'll have records for us hopefully after lunch."

The team knew better than to ask if he knew whose phone it was. Technically, they were supposed to wait for the warrant, but he probably already knew. He just couldn't say. They'd had leaks to the press before and Monson didn't like releasing that kind of information until he was ready. None of their departments needed any more bad press. Law enforcement officers everywhere were increasingly mistrusted by the public and under intensive scrutiny. The Lincoln County Major Crimes Team was no exception.

Most of the team were running on fumes. Few had caught more than a few hours sleep in the last thirty hours, so Monson sent them to homes and dinner, knowing they'd ignore his orders to get some sleep. They'd all be back at it later tonight. Everyone wanted this guy caught. Even though he was still technically considered an outsider, Adam Hosteler had earned a good reputation among the locals and was well-liked and respected in the area.

Monson and Grant decided on dinner at the Horn. The night manager wasn't in, but the day manager got him on the phone. He gave them Karen's home address and verified she was working tonight. Monson didn't want to spook their only potential witness, so chose not to contact the mother. If her daughter was choosing to live rough instead of at home, he doubted the mother would know where Karen could be found, anyway.

They tried the college next. The registrar's office confirmed her enrollment but said she didn't have any classes today. For now, showing up at her work unannounced looked like their best chance for detaining her. She may or may not be involved in the murder, but she was there that night.

Even though he was in a hurry to solve this case, Monson was experienced enough to realize they couldn't shut down any avenues of investigation yet. They were looking at several people: Chris Larsen, the volatile former employee, seen in a physical confrontation with him the day before the murder, the guy's wife, Debra Hosteler, and a woman he planned to speak with next. No direct evidence yet linking the wife to the crime, but she hadn't been exactly forthcoming about the status of her marriage.

There was evidence of the guy living on his boat recently. And he was particularly interested in his phone. Because of recent leaks on a previous case, he hadn't shared this information with the team yet, but he thought he might have something. As soon as he was sure, he'd share.

The beginning of a case always felt like working on a jigsaw puzzle with a gazillion, tiny pieces from different puzzles all mixed together. Police work was trying each piece, one at a time, finding which ones fit, throwing the rest away, until hopefully the picture became clear.

When he went through the crime scene yesterday, he'd quickly scrolled through the victim's phone before bagging it. From the last message, it looked like Adam had someone on the side he was arranging to meet that night. Monson couldn't be sure, but if memory served, it matched the number on the cell phone they found this morning.

And guess whose phone that was?

The Logan McKenna woman. Her name kept turning up. Her driver's license picture was already on the board. She'd visited the area before, and showed up again this year, renting a home next to the victim's parents. She'd secured a place on Adam Hosteler's charter fishing boat the day before he turns up dead. She and her boyfriend seemed to be pointing the finger at Chris, the disgruntled employee. They were the only ones who heard him threaten Adam directly. And now the phone.

Yeah, Logan McKenna was connected somehow. There were just too many overlapping data points to be a coincidence. And Monson didn't believe in coincidences.

The search warrant would give them a deeper history and a much clearer picture of what was going on there. Until then, they had a lot of legwork to do. Before they talked with the wife again, or the McKenna woman, they needed to learn what the homeless girl, Karen Monahan, knew. Whatever she witnessed—if she saw or heard anything at all—would hopefully help them narrow down the field of potential suspects and save them some time.

In an ideal world, Karen would identify the killer tonight, they would arrest him or her, and they'd all go home, but he wasn't expecting that kind of luck.

32

Karen was terrified. Panic seized her, but she forced herself to calm down. As quietly as possible, she gathered her sleeping bag and backpack. She didn't know if whoever ran past her just now was still there. Did they keep on running, or double back? Were they watching her right now?

For a minute, she'd just stood there, frozen. She strained forward, but all she could hear was the lapping of the water on the side of the boat. Finally, she made up her mind. She had to see if the guy on his boat was okay. He might need help. Laying her gear down quietly on the deck of the *Miss Behavin'*, Karen crept back toward the *Mary Ann*.

She found him, lying on the deck, not moving, his head bashed in on one side. He looked dead, but she didn't want to leave him if she could help. Shoving down the panic, she forced herself to step on board, lean down and check his pulse. He was beyond help.

Helplessly, she looked around. The black night beyond the boat held nothing but terror.

Karen bolted down the dock, grabbing her gear on the way. As she approached the Coast Guard station, she forced herself to slow down so as not to alert anyone who may hear or see her from inside the station. Once she was safely away from the harbor and was confident no one was following her, she made her way up the hill and hiked up an old logging road, crawling into a still-forested area until she felt safely hidden behind some brush.

For the next few hours, until daylight, she lay awake, shaking. Only a strong need to go to the bathroom forced her to come out. Finished with her business, she stood perfectly still, looking and listening. No bears. No bad guys. Just some noisy crows.

Karen wasn't ready to come out of hiding yet. She needed time to think. Digging around in her backpack, she pulled out an apple, some beef jerky, and half a bottle of water. It would have to do. From the logging road she could make out all the police activity down at the docks. Part of her felt guilty for not going down there and telling them what she knew, but really, she didn't know much.

She didn't know who killed that man . . . she didn't want to get involved. In the light of day, some reason had returned. The man was dead—she couldn't help him.

After finals, she was out of here. Fall classes started in three weeks at her new home, the University of Oregon in Eugene. She had a scholarship. She had a work-study job lined up. She had to show up for work tomorrow—she needed money to get out of here, but she'd hide out here one more day.

SAFE HARBOR

Thirst drove Karen into town. Before it got crowded, she took a spit bath in the sink at the public restrooms near the shops and used the facilities. She had started her period. Great—as if she needed something else to deal with.

She didn't get there in time, so she had to throw out her underwear. After cleaning up the best she could, she pulled on the one other pair of panties she had and lined it the best she could with some scrunched up toilet paper. She'd go down to the Shell station later and use some of her dwindling cash for tampons and snacks. Finishing her morning toilette, she pulled a clean t-shirt on and brushed and braided her hair again.

She felt almost human. It was as if the events she had seen hadn't happened. They didn't seem real. Just a very bad dream.

She didn't have any classes today, so hitched a ride to Lincoln City and spent the day walking in and out of antique shops and the outlet mall, doing her blend-in-with the tourists thing. Anything to be as far away from Depoe Bay as possible until finals were over and she could get out of town.

She debated whether or not to go in to work tonight, but work was the one thing she could not skip. She needed the money.

A nice couple from Seattle gave her a ride back. She had them drop her off at the whale-watching center, then walked across the street to the Horn. Hanging her backpack up on a coat hook with her jacket, she tucked her wallet and ID into her waistband wallet. She didn't trust the dishwashers. Tying an apron around her waist, she waved at one of the cooks, nodded at the bartender, glad to see they had the good one on tonight. Barry was fast and accurate. Helped her tips. Grabbing an order pad and a pencil, she slapped a smile on her face and went to her first table.

5:23 P.M.

Happy Hour was revving up. For a Wednesday, it was pretty crowded. A spandex brigade took up three of her tables in the back of the bar. A bike club riding from Cannon Beach to Brookings, mostly guys, they would cross their halfway point tomorrow and were celebrating early. At least they were good tippers.

Table Four ordered another round and Table Six needed more napkins. In the zone now—she liked it when it was busy—Karen smoothly filled their requests and told the two men at Table Three she'd be right back to take their order.

"What can I get for you gentlemen?" Karen said.

Without asking the other guy what he wanted, the older man said, "What's good here? What do you like?" he asked.

"Fish and chips are good, but I like the cheeseburgers, myself," Karen said.

"Okay, you convinced me, we'll have a fish and chips and two cheeseburgers."

Must be hungry. But the big guy could probably put it away. It didn't look like he missed too many meals.

"Curly or regular fries?" she asked.

"Surprise us," he said, handing her back the menus, "and we'll take them to go."

"Can I get you a something to drink while you wait? We've got some good local beers on tap," Karen said.

"No thanks, we're good," the man said.

Before she could bring the to-go bags back to the table, the two men got up and met her as she came out from the kitchen. They didn't make a big deal of it, but each stood in the aisle, essentially blocking her way.

"Karen Monahan, we need you to come with us," he asked in a normal tone of voice. He'd gotten her last name from the manager.

She looked at the bartender, but he was avoiding eye contact with her, so she turned on her heel and went back into the kitchen. When she got there, she turned to face them, folding her arms.

"Cops?" she said.

"Detectives Monson and Grant," Monson said. "We're investigating the homicide that occurred aboard the *Mary Ann* down at the docks in Depoe Bay Harbor late Monday night or Tuesday morning. We'd like to ask you some questions about that."

33

Just the thought of what she saw that night made Karen feel sick.

"Am I in trouble?" she asked.

"No, ma'am, we're not pursuing any civil violations you may or may not have committed. We're not interested in that. You've been identified as being in the area at that time, and we need to ask you some questions about what you may have seen or heard between the hours of 5:00 p.m. Monday night and 2:00 a.m. Tuesday morning."

Not knowing what else to do, Karen handed them their food, which she was surprised to learn they'd already paid for, sighed and retrieved her jacket and backpack.

Monson indicated she should gather her personal items and exit the building walking in front of them. The temporary command center wasn't far, he said. When they got to the car, Grant, the younger of the two detectives, opened the door for her, smiled and said, "Thank you for cooperating, Miss King. For your assistance, we'll even let you choose your entree and side dish—would you like curly or regular?"

True to their word, the 'temporary command center', which was just a big room over the fire station, was only a few minutes away. The cops didn't ask anything about her sleeping on board other people's boats, but spent what felt like hours having her repeat what she had seen and heard over and over again.

She started with the first night she saw Adam arguing with his wife, Debbie, on the *Mary Ann* two weeks ago. They were most interested in this past Monday's fight—exactly when the wife arrived and left, what they argued about, and how she phrased her sentences at the end of their yelling match. She told them she only saw her there on the *Mary Ann*, she didn't know when she arrived or when—or even if—she left.

Then she got to those dark hours early Tuesday morning. Those frightening moments were seared into her memory. She told them everything, but didn't think she was much help.

"I'm not even sure if it was a man or a woman I saw running past the *Miss Behavin'*, from where I was—I was on the port side. But, if it was a man, he wasn't a very tall or big one."

Yes, she heard some voices. Voices woke her up, but she was too groggy with sleep to say for sure whether it was female or male. Then there was a clanking sound and a crack, followed by a kind of heavy thud.

She replayed the scene over and over for them, trying to find details that would help them identify the killer, but all she'd been able to positively say was that whoever it was wore blue jeans and black or dark gray Nikes. A flash of light illuminated the outside of his or her leg as they ran by and the white swoop on the Nike's stood out. And then they were gone. She only saw whoever it was for a couple of seconds.

As soon as she had checked on Adam—the police didn't seem to judge her for not calling them then—she had grabbed her bag and ran, slowing down at the end of the dock, trying to escape quietly, in case the killer was still there. That's the footage they saw of her on the Coast Guard CCTV video.

They didn't say how they found her from that. The image they showed her on the younger detective's computer was dark and grainy.

The two detectives were nice. Grant found her a Snickers bar and some hot chocolate after she polished off her cheeseburger and most of his fries. She wasn't brave enough to steal Monson's.

As the interview wound down, she started getting nervous, wondering where she was going to sleep. Would they just let her go, knowing she was just going to go camp out somewhere illegally when she left?

Detective Monson pre-empted that conversation by handing her a one-night voucher to the Travelodge in town, and four twenties. She started to protest, but Grant stopped her. Monson was already halfway down the stairs, expecting her to follow.

"Hey, if Monson's buying, let him! You probably missed out on at least that much in tips tonight," Grant said.

Karen didn't know it, but neither the hotel voucher nor the twenties came out of any official fund. Monson, being a dad, had stopped by Travelodge on the way to the Horn, and picked one up for her.

He'd done a little digging into Karen's home life. The school said she made good grades. She wasn't typical, that's for sure. He hoped the kid made it.

34

The Hosteler home was a modest, 1940s Cape Cod, a few streets east of Highway 101. With a sagging second story balcony, the white and gray boxy house probably hadn't been seriously renovated since the seventies, but it was recently painted, relatively moss free, and the yard neat and trim. Two overgrown pines dominated a pine needle-strewn patch of struggling lawn.

Debbie—only her mother-in-law called her Debra—said to come after she got the girls off to school. She'd be home. The younger girls were back in school, she thought that would be best for them. They really didn't understand what was going on, but the oldest, Ariel, eleven, was well aware of what happened and wasn't ready to go back yet.

Logan double-checked the address, pulled into the driveway and parked next to a fairly new model, blue Kia in the gravel driveway. Wondering for the nth time what in the heck she was going to say to Adam's widow and why she'd agreed to come, she walked up the steps.

Debbie must have heard her pull up, because she opened the front door before Logan got the chance to knock. Taller than she remembered, Logan had to look up to meet the woman's eyes, which were red-rimmed and vaguely unfocused. She was also about forty pounds heavier than Logan, though not fat. Baggy sweat pants, what looked like her husband's t-shirt, and dirty, white slippers completed the just-got-out-of- or never-went-to-bed look. Logan wondered if she drove her kids to school today or if they got themselves there this morning.

She followed the new widow down a dark hallway to a linoleum-floored kitchen and dining area. The house was deathly quiet and smelled stale. Logan longed to open a window, but understood the woman's need to create a solitary den in which to grieve. She'd felt the same way when Jack died. Amy was grown and away in Africa at that time, so she'd had the luxury of shutting out the world. This woman still had three young children at home, depending on her. Logan hoped she could help. If nothing else, she was a good listener.

They sat at a scratched but solid, Early American style dining table with six chairs. Five of them matched. Logan wondered what happened to the other one. Debbie motioned toward the counter, which was covered with what Logan assumed were neighborly offerings of cakes, cookies, rolls and liters of soda.

"There's more in the fridge, can I get you anything?" she said. "And there's coffee still in that pot over there."

Logan declined, saying she just had breakfast.

Debbie said nothing more, so Logan jumped in.

"Your mother-in-law told me you were concerned about some questions the police asked you yesterday," Logan began. "I'm not sure if I can do anything to help, but I may be able to suggest people you can talk to who can. Do you still want to talk with me?"

"Yes, thanks," Debbie said, fidgeting with a ceramic, turkey-shaped saltshaker, one of a set near the napkin holder in the middle of the table.

Just then, a young girl with long, Alice-in-Wonderland hair stood tentatively in the doorway, still in her pajamas. Looking at her mom, she waited.

"Ariel, honey, I have company for a few minutes. Why don't you go take your shower, now," she said. "You can use the shampoo in my bathroom."

"Okay." Ariel silently slid back into the hallway and within minutes, they heard the bathroom door shut and the shower water running.

Debbie turned back to Logan. "I don't know where to start."

"Anywhere, really. What was it about the questions the police asked that made you feel concerned?" Logan said.

Debbie took a drink from her coffee mug. Logan noticed she was a leftie, like Amy.

"Well, the first time they came, Tuesday, when they made the official notification, they were nice. They didn't ask a bunch of questions then. But when they came back, they just started asking all kinds of things. They started with did Adam have any enemies, had he been sick, things like that. Then they got into it, asking me did we have money problems, why was Adam spending nights on the boat, how was our marriage . . . I'd just lost my husband!"

"What did you say?" Logan asked.

"Everyone has money problems. We get by, though. Adam has always been a good provider. And our marriage is fine. Adam was a wonderful husband and father," Debbie said, her mouth firmly set. "I know they didn't believe me. They kept badgering me. Wanted to know where I was Monday night. I know they'll be back. I just don't know what to do!" she said, her voice rising. "They even asked if they could see our bank and phone records."

An alarm bell went off in Logan's mind.

"What did you say?" she asked.

"I told them yes. I didn't want to look like I have anything to hide," Debbie said. "Should I have said no?"

She wanted to shout, *'Yes, you idiot—don't you know not to volunteer information?'* but she couldn't bring herself to say that. It was only a matter of time before the police got warrants for all that anyway. She would have only put off the inevitable.

Logan felt bad for Debbie, but on the other hand, she knew the woman was lying.

According to Meiling, Debbie knew her husband was planning on leaving her. If her husband was having an affair, if he and Debbie had exchanged angry texts or if he'd contacted a divorce attorney—it would all be in the phone records, as would evidence of his affair with Meiling, unless they were careful, which people generally weren't when caught up in the infatuation stage.

Every natural instinct Logan possessed pushed for her to get involved, to help this woman; but what if she was guilty? Adam seemed like a nice guy when they met him, but maybe he was abusive in addition to being a cheater. She'd learned a little from her neighbor last year about how charming abusive spouses could be to those outside the home. Maybe it was self-defense, maybe he deserved to be whacked. Maybe she'd done it in a fit of rage and frustration. Normal people snap.

Or maybe Debbie was a stone cold killer.

35

Logan pulled herself back from that line of thought. She promised Vivi she'd help, and she was a woman of her word.

"What did you tell them when they asked where you were? Were you home?" asked Logan.

"Yes, I was home helping Ariel with her science project. Earlier, I was at his parents' house. With Adam. He brought over some crab he had extra. I went home to the girls."

"Then he went home with you?" Logan said.

"Well, no," Debbie hesitated, "Adam had some work to do on the boat, then he was going to come home. That was the last time I saw him."

Logan didn't challenge this version of events, even though, from what Meiling said, she doubted the man was planning on going home to his wife that night. Debbie seemed hell bent on presenting an image of a happily married man.

"Did anybody see you after that, a neighbor maybe? If you have a land line and talked with anyone, they might even be able to verify that you were home that way."

"I don't think so," Debbie looked at the table and rubbed her thumb up and down her coffee mug handle. "It was just the two of us. The other girls went to bed around eight-thirty."

"So, you were home all night, but only your daughter saw you after 8:30 p.m.? What time did you guys wrap up the project? When did Ariel go to bed?"

Debbie looked nervous, "Ariel's project was due the next day and the black marker she'd been using ran out of ink. It was late. I told her to go to bed and drove to Freddy's to pick one up. She could finish lettering what she needed to do on the poster board in the morning."

"What time was that?"

"Around ten maybe? I don't remember."

"Did you pay with a card?" Logan asked.

"No, I had a five in my wallet," Debbie said.

"Did you keep the receipt?"

"No, I don't think so. I'll check, but I don't think so, and the trash has already been picked up," Debbie said.

"Try and remember what time you went," Logan asked, knowing the store could probably find the transaction. Everything was computerized now. But that wouldn't help her much, since it was cash. But they might have security cameras that could verify.

"It was about ten-thirty Mom," a voice from the doorway said. "You said Freddy's would be open 'til eleven."

Ariel must have heard them talking. Logan wondered how much she'd heard of their conversation. Not something an eleven-year old child should have to hear or worry about. Straight ash-blonde hair hung to the girl's thin shoulders. Gray-blue eyes stared defiantly at her.

Ariel thrust her chin out and said, "My mom was here helping me with my science project. It's on wild mushrooms. All last year, I kept track of which ones grew where and when they came out. There are some here, but there are a lot more different kinds in the forest where Grandma lives. Chanterelles—you can eat those—and other kinds, like the Jack o'Lanterns. They look just like the edible ones, but they're really poisonous. I was drawing diagrams about how you can tell the difference when one of the markers ran out of ink. Mom went to get some more.

"The car made that screeching sound when she backed out. Dad said it needed new brakes . . . he was going to fix them this weekend," Ariel said, tearing up, but not giving in to crying.

Her mother reached out, enveloping her daughter in her arms.

"That's right hon, Daddy was always good about keeping the cars running, wasn't he?"

While Debbie comforted her daughter, getting her a glass of water, Logan thought about the timeline.

If what Ariel said was accurate, that meant she knew when her mom left, but not when she got back. This wasn't good news. She would ask Debbie if anyone at Fred Meyer's—or Freddy's as her daughter called it—remembered her being there, but right now, other than her very loyal daughter's corroboration, and possibly a sales cashier or someone else, Adam's wife had absolutely no alibi from after she left Vivi and Stan's earlier that evening.

She could have been anywhere and done anything, even kill her husband, during those long, dark hours. Debbie was obviously lying about the status of her marriage and her knowledge about her husband's affair with Meiling, but did that make her guilty of murder?

Advising Debbie to obtain the services of a competent attorney before talking to the police again was about all Logan felt qualified to do to help the woman. She left mother and daughter packing up her science project to take to school. She over-heard the teacher in charge of the Science Fair when Debbie put her on speaker. She said that under the circumstances, of course she'd accept Ariel's project if they could get it in and set up before four o'clock. The annual event began at five in the cafeteria.

As she turned south on Highway 101, Logan remembered something Vivi's daughter-in-law said that didn't make sense. When Debbie woke up Tuesday morning and her husband wasn't there, wouldn't she have been worried? Of course she would. Any wife would.

But she hadn't said anything about trying to contact him. Had she tried to call him? And if she did, when he didn't answer, why didn't she drive down to the boat to make sure he was okay? Of course, maybe they were separated and Adam was sleeping on his boat. That would explain it. But if they had patched things up and she was telling the truth, then she should have been on the phone, calling hospitals and highway patrol. She would have gone down to the boat when she woke up and he wasn't there.

Unless she already knew he was dead.

By the time she got back to Little Whale Cove, Logan was completely drained. The more she thought about various scenarios, the more unlikely any of them seemed. And keeping secrets was exhausting. She didn't feel it was her place to tell any of the Hostelers about Adam and Meiling, but she knew it wouldn't be long before the police discovered the affair. When they did, Debbie would become a suspect, maybe their prime suspect. Or Meiling for that matter.

Yes, the police already knew about Chris, the guy Adam fired for drug use, but Debbie was the rejected wife, and a lying one as well. The police didn't take kindly to being lied to, and a jealous wife probably trumped a disgruntled employee any day.

Unlike Chris, Debbie had a lot more to lose than a job.

36

Debbie watched from the living room window as Logan got in her car and drove away.

"What did that lady want, Mom?" Ariel asked from the hallway, wrapped in a robe, hair dripping from the shower.

"Oh, nothing, honey," Debbie said. "She's just a friend of Grandma's. Do you need any help with your hair?"

"Can I use your blow dryer?" Ariel asked.

"Sure. It's in the second drawer," Debbie answered, distracted. "You know where it is."

Debbie listened until her daughter padded back down the hall and she could hear the whine of the blow dryer start up, and then returned to the kitchen and slumped down in her chair. She closed her eyes, took a ragged breath, and then, bending forward, let her head drop into her hands—as if holding it up had cost her her last ounce of energy. She allowed herself to release the jumble of fear and grief she'd been keeping tightly locked inside.

What was she going to do? They were going to find out! The police were only stupid in movies. She'd been there that night. It was all so awful, she'd been too upset to try to cover her tracks. Her fingerprints must be on the fishing gaff and god knows what other evidence she left behind.

Why had she lied? Why had she gone down to the boat Monday night? Why? It wasn't going to change anything. She knew that! Adam was leaving her.

She had thought there was a chance. She had to try. She had to go and see if she could talk some reason into him—look into his eyes, help him see the woman he'd fallen in love with, lived with, had children with. Why couldn't he see her anymore? It was as if she'd become invisible to him.

It was that Chinese bitch. She stole him! Blinded him! It was like he never loved her or the girls. Everything erased—just like that! What did Meiling have, besides youth and musical talent, that she didn't have?

Adam used to love her just as she was. He said he didn't care about all that. About education and polish. He'd had that with his first wife—the one in New York. He'd had that life and look how that turned out. He said what mattered to him was her solid soul, her desire to have a family. Her work ethic.

She remembered when they first got together. Even though he'd been coming to the coast for years, he and his family were still considered outsiders. They had money and east coast habits. He'd been to Europe three times. They only dated a short time before he proposed.

She was worried his family wouldn't accept her, but they did. Though she knew his mother still looked down her nose at her, tolerating her only because she bore her grandchildren and was married to her son. That was okay. She didn't like Vivi, either. Adam's mom never had to work, just did volunteer stuff—always the president of this or that club. They had nothing in common.

Debbie dragged her mind back to Monday night. She hadn't planned on going to the boat. She really was trying to play hard-to-get, leave Adam to himself for a while until he realized what he was missing, until he missed her—missed his family. It wasn't too late.

It started out okay. She hadn't made a fuss earlier that night at his parents' house, after the concert, when he said he was staying on the boat again. It took everything she had, but she'd straightened her back and acted like she didn't care.

She came home to help Ariel. Ariel had a Science project and they were working on that together—doing the tri-fold presentation board her teacher required. The marker Ariel was using ran out of ink and she got upset. Debbie had found another marker, but it was blue, not black. Using another color would look bad, her daughter informed her. It had to match! Unlike her mother, Ariel was an A student and wanted everything to be perfect.

To avoid her daughter having a meltdown because of ink color, Debbie agreed to go to Freddy's and get a new one before they closed. She told Ariel to go to bed and when she woke up, she'd have a new marker full of bright, fresh, *black* ink. She could finish the lettering on the board in the morning.

The Kia started right up and hardly anyone was on the road. The parking lot was empty. Debbie went in, got the marker, and a Snickers for the road. She deserved it.

Sitting in her car, chewing the last of the candy bar, an unfamiliar rage welled up. She balled up the wrapper, threw her car into gear, and headed for Depoe Bay harbor. It was only twenty minutes away. She'd get back in plenty of time to check on the girls.

Adam had to listen to reason. He just *had* to!

37

Ben had been patient, but he wasn't a saint. He hadn't complained, but Logan knew he'd rearranged his whole work schedule for this vacation, and so far, he'd been doing most of the work, keeping everyone fed and watered. The whole point of this trip was to spend time together as a couple and as a family, to relax and have fun.

Of course, it wasn't her fault the captain of the charter boat they'd gone out on had been murdered. None of them could have predicted being dragged into a homicide investigation, but still. She'd done her neighborly duty and talked with Vivi's daughter. She'd been a good citizen and answered the police's questions yesterday. She'd kept from getting further entangled by not revealing Meiling and Adam's affair to anyone.

Today was Ben's turn. She was going to make it up to him. She'd called ahead for reservations at Tidal Raves, a local restaurant overlooking a corner of Depoe Bay called Smuggler's Cove. Amy and Liam told them they'd read up on it and during Prohibition coves up and down the central Oregon coast actively participated in the dangerous but lucrative business of rum-running. After lunch they planned on a leisurely walk around town and an afternoon 'nap' if time allowed before the kids got back from Lincoln City.

4:30 P.M.

Watered, fed and 'napped', Logan did a full cat stretch and popped out of bed, gathering up her clothes. She loved afternoon naps. Ben was already downstairs starting dinner, so she dressed quickly and went to join him.

"You sure you don't mind if I run over and give her an update?" Logan asked.

Vivi hadn't been home this morning when she stopped by to let her know she'd talked with Debbie, or Debra, as she called her.

"Of course not, no rush—take as much time as you need," he said, his head in the refrigerator, his attention already diverted.

"Okay, be right back," she said, slipping on her flip flops, letting herself out the front door.

Vivi answered and took Logan out to the back deck, where Stan was fiddling with a latch on a gate. Must have been the project he'd been working on before they got the news. She was glad he had something to do. Bent over the railing, he reminded her briefly of her dad and how he had coped after his wife had left. He'd gone around the house looking for things to repair and when he ran out of those, started in on things that didn't even need to be fixed. Some men grieve best with a hammer in their hands.

Logan did her best to summarize her visit with their daughter-in-law and re-emphasized her recommendation to have Debra obtain the services of a good, criminal attorney. She might not need it, but it wouldn't hurt.

Vivi half-heartedly invited Logan to stay for dinner, but she made her excuses—Ben was already working on it and she needed to get home. If Vivi and Stan were going to help their daughter-in-law, they would need to make some phone calls, and Logan well knew how many details they probably still had to handle just from their son's death alone, even if he hadn't been murdered.

In truth, she had another reason for wanting to get out of there. Logan didn't feel strong enough to be in this house of pain. It was too close a reminder of the years after her mom left and the year she lost to grief after Jack died.

Vivi didn't mention Adam's involvement with Meiling, so Logan could only assume she didn't know about it yet. She wondered what she'd do when she found out. Meiling and Jian were still in town, doing workshops at the schools until Friday, so if they decided to, they could talk. Logan hoped she wasn't around when that particular bomb dropped.

38

Taking a shortcut across the yard through the bark chip, she aimed the remote at the car and locked it for the night, then let herself in the front door. Ben was already out on the deck, beer in hand, looking at the ocean. Just the sight of his strong, solid back sent a wave of warmth through Logan's body. She was so glad to be home. Another glass of wine and a snack tray waited on a low table between two sturdy, teak chairs, similar to hers back home.

Tossing her jacket and purse on the couch, she walked out to join him, slipping her arms around his chest and pressing her body against his. Ben was her rock. Her rock in swirling waters. When the rest of the world got crazy, she could count on him.

He squeezed back, then turned around and greeted her properly before they sat down in the chairs. Logan kicked off her shoes and put her feet up on the railing.

"Where are the kids?" Logan asked.

"Down at the clubhouse," Ben said. "They came back, but then decided to take Ian to the pool. They got their suits and some towels and walked down. They'll be back for dinner. I told them we'd push it back an hour. That okay with you?"

"Absolutely," Logan nodded, taking an appreciative sip of her wine, looking at the label. She didn't recognize it, but it was good.

"Mmm . . . thanks."

"How'd it go?" he asked.

She took a longer drink of her wine and brought him up to date. He already knew about Meiling and Adam and agreed with her it wasn't their place to tell either Adam's parents or his wife. No sense adding to their burden.

"Sounds like you gave her some good advice," Ben said. "I don't like attorneys either", (his ex-fiancé was an unscrupulous one), "but you need someone who understands that world."

He popped a couple of Greek olives into his mouth.

"Do you think she could have done it?" he asked.

"If she found out about Meiling," Logan said, "maybe."

Before Logan could answer, something beeped in the kitchen and Ben went to check on dinner.

"Do you want any help?" Logan called.

"No, I'm good. Why don't you just enjoy the sunset? Relax. I'll let you know if I need anything." Ben said.

At this latitude, the sun wouldn't set for hours yet, but she wasn't going to get technical. Taking Ben up on his offer, she closed her eyes and listened to the seagulls and the waves crashing on the rocks below.

"Put your seat back—the chair's got an adjustment on the side," Ben directed from the kitchen.

Logan found the knob, lifted it and pushed against the seat back at the same time until it lowered half way down, then dropped the lever back into place, jiggling it to make sure it was secure. Feet up and seat back, all pressure was off her lower back. Zero gravity.

Perfect.

"Got it! Thanks!"

She opened her eyes, leaving them slightly unfocused, and took in the view. Clouds hung, suspended, then slowly floated past, morphing into polar bears, ferris wheels, and old gypsies.

Ahhhhh . . . .

The sun was low in the sky, but still well above the horizon when Ben shook her shoulder. She must have dozed off for a minute.

"You've got company," he said, nodding toward the living room, where Detectives Monson and Clark stood by the door.

"What the . . . ?" she muttered.

The kids must have come home while she was asleep, because Amy was setting the table and Liam was trying to get Ian to eat pureed carrots.

Enticing aromas emanated from the kitchen, making Logan's mouth water. Ben's enchilada casserole. She'd drifted off before she had a chance to eat anything, and all she'd had was a glass of wine. She felt a little lightheaded. She wondered what the police wanted. From the looks on their faces, it was something serious. Might as well find out. The sooner they left, the sooner she could eat. She walked over.

"Detectives," Logan said, stopping several feet away. "What can we do for you?"

Detective Monson didn't waste any time.

"We'd like to ask you to come down to the sheriff's office with us, Ms. McKenna. In light of some new evidence in the case, we need to ask you some more questions."

"New evidence? What does that have to do with me?" Logan said.

"It would be much easier if we could talk with you in private," Monson said.

"What's this all about?" Logan asked, fully awake now.

She was tired and hungry and getting more than irritated at being dragged into all this. She knew she sounded snippy but couldn't help herself. She crossed her arms.

"Look, I am very sorry for what happened to that poor man, but other than going on a fishing trip on his boat and seeing him briefly at his parent's house that night, there just isn't anything else I can tell you. Can you just ask me whatever it is you want to ask me here? I'll be happy to help in any way I can."

Detective Monson asked, "Are you refusing to cooperate, Ms. McKenna?"

"No," Logan said, "Of course not. That's not what I said . . ."

Amy slammed the silverware she'd been holding onto the table and started toward the stand-off at the front door.

Glaring at Detective Monson, she said, "Look, if my mother says she didn't know this guy, she didn't know him!"

Ben motioned Liam to stay back with the baby and came forward to join Amy at the O.K. Corral.

Monson kept his eyes on Logan. He wasn't going anywhere without her. It was obviously her call.

Logan let out an exasperated sigh, but agreed to go with them voluntarily.

"Do you want me to call Uncle Rick?" Amy asked her mom. Then, turning back to the detectives, she added, "My uncle's a cop!"

Logan put her hand on Amy's arm to reassure her. This was ridiculous, but the faster she went down to clear it up, the faster she could get home. She pulled on her shoes and a jacket, grabbed a couple of warm, corn tortillas on the way out the door, and told everyone not to worry, she'd be right back.

39

Logan folded her hands in her lap, trying to remain patient. It had been over thirty minutes since they parked her in this tiny, cement room and asked her to wait. It was just like on TV. Gray cement, metal table, wobbly, plastic bucket chairs—one for her, two opposite, and a large rectangle of glass she assumed must be a two-way mirror. Other than what they'd said about having some new evidence, she still didn't know why she was here.

Finally, Detectives Monson and Grant came into the room, carrying one of those multi-use grocery bags. Placing the bag, unopened, on the table, he pulled out one of the two plastic chairs on the other side and took a seat opposite her. Next, he took out his phone and made some selections on the screen. Laying the phone flat on the table between the two of them, he began.

"Let the record show that the date is Thursday, August 16, 2019 and the time is 5:22 p.m. Detective Monson, Lincoln Sheriff's Department, Detective Grant, Newport PD and Ms. Logan McKenna of Jasper, California. Present."

Logan spoke up, "I'd like it to be noted that I came down here and am speaking with you voluntarily."

"Noted," Monson said, then settled into his chair and looked directly into Logan's eyes. He had all day.

"How well did you know the deceased, Adam Hosteler?" he asked.

"I didn't," Logan said. "Other than meeting him when we went on one of his half-day fishing trips, and then seeing him at his parents' house where we had attended a concert, I'd never seen the man before."

"You've had absolutely no contact with him either before or after those two instances?" Monson asked.

"I just said that," Logan said.

If they were fishing, they weren't very good at it. She just had to stick to the truth. This shouldn't take long. She gazed directly back at him, confident now.

"You're lying, Ms. McKenna," Monson said.

"Excuse me?" she said, "What makes you think I'm lying?"

Detective Monson took an Android phone out of the bag and placed it in the center of the table, directly in front of her. The screen was black except for the time of day.

"How do you explain this?"

Stunned, Logan stared. The protective case was an easily-recognizable, gun-metal gray she picked up at the Otter Festival last year. She reached for it.

"That's my phone! Where'd you find it, I've been looking for it?"

Monson ignored her question and moved the phone out of reach.

"Are you identifying this phone as your property?" he asked.

"Yes, as far as I can tell. If you give it to me I can tell you for sure," she said.

"That won't be necessary. You say you lost this phone. When did you lose it? Did you call your insurance company or go to the Verizon store in Newport to purchase a replacement? Do you have any proof that you reported it lost or stolen?"

"I'm not sure when I lost it. It could have been stolen, I guess. And I didn't report it to my insurance company because I wasn't sure it *was* lost. Being on vacation I assumed I'd just misplaced it and it would turn up in a day or so. Then all this happened."

She looked up defiantly, "It hasn't been my first priority."

Next, Monson slid the phone aside and lifted a thin, pink sweater out of the grocery bag. It was encased in a large, plastic baggie. Logan's eye was drawn to two dark, maroon-brown stains, one on the sleeve, the other along the bottom hem, as if it had been dragged in hoisin sauce.

"Is this your sweater?"

"No," Logan said.

That stain had to be blood.

Leaving the items on the table in front of her, Monson asked, "Please look again. Is this your sweater?"

"No, it's not," Logan said, trying to look at it more closely without appearing to. She didn't want to say anything yet, but she was pretty sure she knew who it did belong to. She'd check when she got home. If they let her go home. She needed time to think.

Monson continued, "Ms. McKenna, we know this is your phone. How do you explain the fact that you used it to text the deceased the night he was killed, asking him to meet you on his boat?"

"I can't, because I never did that. Whoever found or stole my phone must have sent that text," Logan said.

Monson's voice increased slightly in volume.

"Let me get this straight. You're asking us to believe that you just *happened* to rent a house next to the parents of the deceased, just *happened* to charter his boat for a fishing trip on Monday, lost your phone somewhere during that time—which you didn't bother to report stolen—then some random person just *happens* to find your lost phone, uses it to arrange a meeting with Adam Hosteler Monday night, and that very night Adam Hosteler gets killed?"

Silence filled the intervening space.

"Oh, and I forgot," he added, "Your phone just *happens* to be found wrapped in a woman's bloody sweater and thrown into the bushes not far from the victim's boat, where he was found murdered."

He held his finger up to add one more point, "And the blood type's A positive, which just *happens* to match the victim's."

Monson let the silence stretch and linger, then placed his forearms on the edge of the table and leaned forward.

"I'm just trying to get at the truth here. If you have an explanation for any of this, I'm willing to listen."

Monson waited for several beats, then asked, "Anything you want to tell me before the DNA results get back?"

"No, I can't explain any of this, but I did lose my phone. Someone else must have used it. I didn't know him and never had any communication with Adam Hosteler other than as a charter boat customer on one of his fishing trips."

Monson let out an exasperated sigh.

"You were at his parents' house when they were notified of their son's death. You chartered his boat, your phone was used to contact him and set up a meeting. We've subpoenaed the records. It all checks out. You and Adam Hosteler texted the night he died. The last time he had phone contact of any kind with anyone was the text from your phone.

"You obviously knew the victim better than you're letting on. The sooner you tell me, the better it's going to be for you. I can work with you now, but I have a lot less leeway once the DNA results come back."

"Look, if I was guilty of anything, I'd be asking for an attorney right now. I'm not. I have nothing to hide," Logan said.

"Well then, get comfortable, Ms. McKenna. We're going to be here a while."

40

Logan reached for her phone. Then she remembered.

Damn.

The police still had it. She'd have to find a Verizon store and buy a replacement. Who knew how long they'd hold onto it. They hadn't actually arrested her last night, just kept her in that awful interrogation room for hours, then told her not to leave town in case they had more questions. She had a feeling the lead detective, Monson, was holding back something, but if he was, he must be waiting for more ammunition before hitting her with it.

If they had arrested her, she wouldn't have had far to go, the stuffy interrogation room was conveniently located in the same building as the Lincoln County Jail. She'd seen the sign on the way in.

They were going to fingerprint her until she told them they were on file with the school district in California. At least she was saved that humiliation.

She looked at the clock radio next to the bed. 6:20 a.m.

Ben was already up, probably making breakfast.

Logan rolled onto her back, folded her arms on her chest and looked up at the ceiling. She felt heavy, stiff, and not remotely rested, but too awake now to go back to sleep. Bacon smells wafted up the stairs. Throwing on a navy-blue, front-zip hoodie she'd picked up at the Sea Otter Center in Jasper where Amy worked over her camisole and cotton PJ bottoms, she padded downstairs and gratefully accepted a steaming mug of coffee from Ben.

"You could have slept in, you know," he said.

Amy came around the counter, where she'd been making some scrambled eggs for Ian, giving her mom a fierce hug. Liam waved, then turned his attention back to Ian, bouncing him on his hip, distracting him until Amy got his breakfast ready.

"I know, but I'm awake, so might as well get up," she said, hugging her daughter back.

The kids fell asleep on the couch waiting up for her last night. Only Ben was still awake when Detective Monson brought her back. She was wired and could have stayed up all night, but after summarizing the night's events, Ben insisted she get some sleep and they could talk in the morning. As usual, he was right. She was out like a light the minute her head hit the pillow.

"So," Ben said, taking a sip of his own coffee.

Logan waited until Ian was in his chair, then filled them all in. It didn't take long. There wasn't much to tell, because the police essentially spent those hours asking the same few questions over and over.

"Do you think they finally believed you?" Liam asked, "Is that why they let you go?"

"I don't think they believe anyone, but they had no reason to hold me. I didn't make any calls or text Adam that night. I can't prove it wasn't me, but they can't prove it was, either."

"Did they find your fingerprints?" Ben asked.

"No, they said the phone was wiped clean," Logan said, "and they didn't mention the sweater, so I guess there was nothing on the buttons or anywhere."

"Well, that should be proof, right?" Amy said. "If it was your phone, you'd have no reason to wipe your prints off it. Someone else must have used it."

"That's what I pointed out, and they must know that, but I think my phone is the only lead they have, and they just wanted me to be involved somehow."

"Well, you're not," Ben said. "I'm just glad you're home."

Grabbing some potholders, he removed a foil-lined cookie sheet, sizzling with a dozen strips of thick pepper bacon, out of the oven and turned it off.

"Otherwise, I'd have to eat all this by myself," he said, grinning.

"Fat chance, big guy!" Amy broke off the end of one of the pieces with the tips of her fingers and popped it into her mouth.

Ben transferred the rest onto paper towels, blotted the excess grease, and arranged them on a platter of scrambled eggs and hash browns he had warming on the stove. Pastries, berries, and fresh squeezed orange juice were already on the table.

Amy took over the feeding of Ian and everyone dug in. For the rest of the morning, all thoughts of murder faded into the background. Amy put Ian down for his nap and she and Liam decided to walk into town. Logan looked online and found Verizon stores in Lincoln City and Newport.

She chose the one in Lincoln City. She'd promised Rose, one

of Thomas and Lisa's artist friends she met at the Otter Festival a few years ago, she would stop by for a visit. Rose wanted to show her how the remodel of her 1940s Cape Cod turned out. The last time Logan was here, she'd seen her weaving shop, Coastal Threads, and they'd had lunch in town, but she hadn't been to her home because parts of it were still torn up at the time. Solid and strong in both body and spirit, usually draped in greens and russet tones, Rose reminded Logan of a Redwood Forest Goddess. She didn't agree with her on everything but looked forward to seeing her again.

Ben said he'd stay and babysit.

What Logan failed to mention was that she planned on making a stop in Depoe Bay on the way. She'd sort of lied to the police last night. The pink sweater wasn't hers, but she recognized it. It was the same one she'd seen Meiling wearing in her photograph on the cover of the program for the evening concert she and Ben had attended at Vivi's house.

Logan didn't have the address, but she'd dropped Meiling off there when she took her home after the police came by to notify Vivi and Stan of Adam's death. She was pretty sure she could find the street again.

She could have gotten Meiling's number from Vivi, but decided not to call ahead. Logan had no idea what Meiling's reaction would be when she confronted her. She did know she and her brother were still in town. Vivi said they always gave workshops at the local schools the week following their concert. Today was the last one. They were flying out the next week to the next city on their tour.

Logan would just have to show up and hope she was there. It shouldn't take long. She only had one question.

How did Meiling's sweater get blood on it and why was it wrapped around Logan's phone and tossed into the bushes not far from where Adam was killed?

41

It took Logan a while to get through town. When inland temperatures hit triple digits, even more people flocked to the beach in droves. But once she turned right at Bay Street and got off Highway 101, traffic opened up.

Meiling and Jian's host home was the third house down on the left. A boxy, white-and-brown two-story, the garage was on the left, a small front porch was smack dab in the middle, with living area and bedrooms on the right. Several houses on the street had similar floor plans.

A steep driveway, already filled with a boat and an old truck that didn't look like they'd been moved in a very long time, led to a two-car garage, left no room for visitors, so Logan parked across the street.

She couldn't help but make comparisons to California. Since much of the town of Depoe Bay rose directly up from Highway 101, many of even the most modest homes had an ocean view. Logan had been browsing real estate sites with Ben and she guessed this one probably would list for as low as $350-400,000.

In Jasper, or anywhere else in Southern California, it wouldn't go for less than a million. When she bought her beach cottage fixer-upper a few years back, she was lucky to pick it up for a very reasonable price. With the improvements she'd made since then, and the increasingly hot real estate market, it had more than doubled in value. Not that it mattered. She had no intention of selling her home anytime soon. To Logan, it was a symbol of her new life, of resurrecting herself after Jack's death. Something she'd done all on her own.

Before crossing the street, Logan looked back over the roof and noticed a narrow, grassy footpath running between two houses, down to the harbor. Bright sunlight glinted off the colorful boats bobbing in the harbor. She spotted the *Mary Ann*, tied up to the end of the dock as it was the day she first stepped aboard. You'd never know a brutal murder had occurred there just days ago. The crime scene tape had been removed. From here, it didn't look like anything bad could ever happen there.

But something had, and somehow, Meiling was involved. How had she gotten Logan's phone? Why hadn't she used her own phone to contact Adam? That made her look like she was trying to hide something. Had she gone down to the boat that night? She was looking forward to spending the rest of her life with Adam. She planned on giving up her musical career for him.

Had he changed his mind? Said he was going back to his wife? Could Meiling have killed him?

Anything was possible, but Logan didn't believe it. Meiling's reaction to the news of Adam's death was genuine shock. She couldn't have faked that, could she?

The only way she was going to find out was to ask. Logan had no problem with direct confrontation. She needed answers. If Meiling didn't or couldn't give her a good explanation about the phone and the sweater, she'd call Detective Monson and let him take it from there.

Ben and the kids were leaving in two days and Logan wanted this straightened out so she could spend the rest of the little time they had together focusing on something else besides murder.

She locked the car and in several long strides was across the quiet street. Stepping onto the small porch, she knocked on the front door. She waited, but no one answered.

To her right, narrow Venetian blinds rattled in the slight breeze against a half-open sliding glass door, leading from the deck into what looked like one of the bedrooms. She could see some kind of nondescript, beige carpet, the corner of a bed, and a small nightstand against one wall. It was separate from the front porch—probably an add-on.

If no one was home, she wondered why they'd left the door not only unlocked, but wide open.

Just as she was about to give up, she heard footsteps and someone opened the door. It was Meiling, dressed in a pair of white capri pants, black leather flats, and a light blue blouse. She looked surprised to see Logan standing there.

"Hello," she said, opening the door all the way, stepping aside so Logan could enter, "Please, come in."

Logan did and followed her into the kitchen, where Meiling took a hot bowl of something that smelled delicious out of the microwave.

"I was just going to have some lunch, would you like some? There's more. It's just soup, it would just take me only a minute to warm it up for you."

"No, thanks, I had a big breakfast, but please, you go ahead," Logan said, sitting down at the kitchen table.

Meiling got her soup and joined her.

"Were you giving a workshop this morning?" Logan said.

"Yes, last one," she said.

"Where is everyone?"

A pair of chopsticks poised above her bowl, Meiling said, "The Andersons went to Bend to visit her sister, so it is just us here. I don't know where Jian is. He said he was sick this morning, but he must be feeling better, or maybe he went into town for some medicine."

She sounded puzzled, not worried.

Gracefully lifting some of the steaming noodles up to her mouth, Meiling somehow got them into her mouth without dribbling any soup on her chin. Logan was impressed. She could use chopsticks, but not so neatly.

Meiling finished, put her bowl in the sink, and returned to the table with a couple of glasses of water. Quiet. Waiting.

Seeing Meiling again in person made Logan not want to upset her by assaulting her with a bunch of questions right away.

"How are you doing?" she asked. "Have you seen or talked with Adam's parents yet?"

"No, I have not," Meiling said quietly.

"We are not going to be here for the service," she added, "We have to be in Baton Rouge soon for our next concert. We are leaving in a few days."

"Have you decided to tell them?" Logan asked. "Later, maybe?"

"I do not know," Meiling whispered. "It does not matter, now, does it?"

Logan didn't have an answer for that. She decided to jump in and ask the uncomfortable questions she came to ask.

"Meiling, I need to talk to you about a few things," she began.

Meiling looked up at her, distracted from her grief momentarily.

"The police talked with me," Logan said. "In fact, they talked with me twice. The first time, they came to the house and wanted to know about the argument Ben and I overheard from Adam's former employee."

Logan paused. "But last night they came by, and this time it was not a friendly conversation."

42

"Why?" Meiling asked.

"I lost my phone in town the other day, and the police found it."

"Oh, well, that's good, yes?" Meiling said, sounding relieved, but still confused. "What did they ask you about?"

"They said someone used my phone to text a message to Adam," Logan said.

"A message?" Meiling said, putting her glass of water down.

"Yes, it was sent the night he was killed, Meiling, and they said it was someone arranging a meeting. I know it wasn't me, and you said he and his wife weren't getting along. It sounds like it came from you."

Meiling just stared at her, so Logan looked her in the eye and asked, "Did you find my phone and use it to contact Adam that night?"

"Of course not! I have my own phone," Meiling said, picking it up from the table to show Logan.

Okay, on to Exhibit B . . .

"There was something else, Meiling," Logan said. "When

they found my phone, it was wrapped in your sweater and hidden behind a dumpster not far from here."

"My sweater?" Meiling asked.

"Yes, the pink one. I recognized it from your picture on the program at Vivi's house that night. The photo is black and white, but it's definitely the same one. It has pearl buttons and scalloped edges."

Meiling jumped up and ran upstairs. In a few minutes, she was back, looking alarmed.

"You're right. It's gone!" she said.

"And that's not all, Meiling," Logan said.

Time to hit her with the big news and see how she reacted.

"It looks like one sleeve and part of the bottom edge had been dragged through some blood—Adam's blood—at least that's what the police think. They said it was the same blood type. Can you explain how it got there?"

"I have no idea!" Meiling said, starting to cry.

Logan watched her closely, not sure whether to comfort her or push her to confess. She was either innocent in anything involving Adam's murder, or a very good liar.

Digging the heels of her hands into her eyes to stop the tears, Meiling lifted her head. Her words came out in quiet disbelief, mounting to jumbled panic.

"I don't understand. We were so happy, everything was wonderful. We were going to be together, and now one bad thing after another happens and none of it makes any sense!"

Logan hesitated only for a moment. She couldn't explain why, but she believed her. The only thing she appeared to be guilty of was getting involved with a married man. A man with enemies—at least one who hated him enough to kill him.

Meiling went to the sink and splashed her face with cold water, drying it off with a paper towel. Somewhat more in control of her emotions, she returned to the table and sank into her chair.

"Look, Meiling. I don't think you sent that message," Logan said.

Meiling looked relieved but doubtful.

"Right now, the police don't really know," Logan said. "But they think I did it."

"Did you tell them that was my sweater?" Meiling said. "I need to tell them."

"No, I'm not sure why I didn't tell them, but I wanted to talk with you first. I'm glad I did, because if you go tell them now, that will cause them to focus on you. They'll stop looking for whoever really did this."

Meiling nodded.

"My brother is a cop, so my guess is that someone, probably one of those detectives—either Monson or Grant—took a quick peek at Adam's phone, but don't have all the records yet. That's how they knew someone had texted him, and that number matched up with my phone when they found it. They'll get all the official phone records soon, though. Which means they'll find out about you two on their own at some point, Meiling, so we don't have much time to figure this out."

"Okay," Meiling said, sitting up straighter. "What can I do?"

"The first question we need to answer is who found or stole my phone, then used it to contact Adam, pretending to be you?" Logan said. "Try and think, Meiling. Can you think of anyone who would benefit from doing that?"

"The only person who knew about Adam and me was his wife. They fought about it. She did not even love him anymore, but she would not let him go. He was supposed to tell her it was over, once and for all, but when we talked before the concert Monday night, he said he had not yet. That is why I was too upset to perform.

"Then later, he called and told me it was all right, everything was okay and we would continue as planned. Whether his wife accepted it or not, he was planning on telling his parents about us at lunch on Tuesday."

Meiling dissolved into tears again for a few minutes, "I was so stupid."

When she regained her composure, Logan said, "Debbie could have gone down to the docks, had it out with Adam and things got out of control."

"I suppose so," Meiling said.

"But to set things up by pretending to be you would mean she was planning all this," Logan said. "Anyone could be emotional enough, but I talked with her yesterday, and I don't see her as a cold-blooded killer."

"Besides," Logan added as an afterthought, "How would she get my phone?"

Neither woman had a good answer for that. No one spoke for a few minutes.

Logan broke the silence. "The phone was either lost or stolen. Last time I remember using it was to confirm our reservations for the fishing trip Monday morning. I'd been to the store, I hung out in the charter office. I was at Vivi's house. Anyone could have stolen it. And if I lost it, anyone could have found it. That's a dead end for now."

She decided to move on to the sweater.

"How did someone get your sweater? And why did they take it? How did Adam's blood get on it—if it is Adam's blood—the police said something about sending a sample out for DNA analysis. I assume they'll know one way or the other about that soon, but they're pretty sure it's his."

43

Trotting up the stairs, Frank Walters, the FBI's representative on the team, was the last to come in. Monson nodded and waited until he was seated. He looked around the table as people settled in. Ron, Grant, Smythe, he respected these men. Other than the Statie, with whom he hadn't had the best working relationship, he'd miss all these guys. But, unless something broke today, the team would be disbanded tomorrow and he'd be left to solve this one on his own.

This was reasonable, he knew—the county couldn't afford to keep the Lincoln County Major Crimes Team focused on any case indefinitely—each of these officers had work waiting for them back in their home offices.

Everyone knew the deadline, so Monson didn't waste time bringing it up. Instead, he got right to it. Going around the room, he asked each member of the team to brief the rest of them on their progress. The official written reports, which were already piling up on his desk, would eventually be compiled into the murder book he would create back in his office. But here, sitting around the table, members of the team could share things they may not put in writing. Monson encouraged this.

First, Ron shared the official autopsy report, including the non-lethal blow Adam incurred prior to the mortal blow.

"So, the guy was attacked twice? Same person?"

"Don't know, but same weapon, according to Cyndi," Ron said, "the fishing gaff. The one we found next to the body."

He illuminated further for the OSP officer, who, being from Salem, wasn't familiar with the equipment found on fishing boats and he hadn't been at the scene when they first arrived. He'd seen the pictures but hadn't asked. Probably didn't want to admit his ignorance. He knew he was the outsider.

"A gaff is a strong metal pole with a hook on the end, used to bring in fish too large to reel in when they go out for the big ones. This one was a seven footer."

"Fingerprints?"

"Just the ones you'd expect—Adam, his crew, his wife," Monson said.

"How far apart?" Frank asked.

When Monson looked confused, he clarified, "Time wise, how far apart were the injuries inflicted?"

"An hour, maybe," Monson said, "That's Birdwell's best guess. Long enough for him to put some Neosporin on it and stop the bleeding."

"So, it could have been two different people," Grant said.

"Of interest is the location of each blow," Monson said. Getting up from his chair, he flipped the chart paper over for a fresh sheet. Grabbing a marker, he made a line drawing of a man's head, with arrows. "There's a more exact diagram in the report, but basically, one came across from the left, here, made contact with the side of his head near the temple. That one didn't kill him, although Birdwell said it probably knocked him out. The lethal blow came from the right. More of a direct hit."

"Angle?"

"Angle doesn't help us," Monson said, "Both hitters were about the same height. Roughly five eight, five nine."

"So, could have been a short man or a tall woman," Ron said.

"Or a midget standing on a stool . . ." the Statie chimed in, pointlessly.

Monson ignored him and had Grant summarize what they'd learned from their only almost-witness, the young woman sleeping rough on a nearby boat that night.

They went over the CCTV footage, the interviews and the Coast Guard guy's statement. They'd established a hot line to collect leads in case anyone they hadn't talked to already had seen or heard anything. Ron was still working on tracking down the disgruntled former employee, Chris Larsen, who'd threatened Adam the day before he was killed.

"So far, nobody's heard from him. His girlfriend said she hadn't seen him since she left for work Monday. When she got off work, her truck was gone. She got a ride home from one of the cooks. Said Chris never came home that night and hasn't been in contact."

"Did she try and call him?"

"Yeah, just goes to voicemail. The mailbox is full now," Ron said.

"They ever find her truck?"

"That's what's weird. The next day, she got a ride to work and there it was, in the parking lot, right where she left it the night before."

"Why would he borrow it and return it without taking her home?" Smyth asked. "They get in a fight? You think she's telling us everything?"

"Don't know," Ron said simply. "Working on it."

Without much else to report on that front, Monson wrapped it up.

They were waiting for the official DNA report to come back on the blood on the sweater, but that would only verify what they already knew. It wouldn't get them any closer to finding out who put it there. There was a partial print on one of the pearl buttons, but so far they hadn't been able to match it with anything. Frank was following up on that. The FBI had a deeper reach than what he had access to.

As for the phone, Monson shared what they'd learned from the McKenna woman, which wasn't much. Thursday Ron got the subpoenas, but they were still waiting for the official records to come through from the phone company. Luckily, Logan McKenna had given them permission to look through her phone—said she had nothing to hide, in fact, it would prove she didn't know this guy. Even after pouring through her texts from the last two years, it looked like the only time her phone had been used to text or call Adam Hosteler was the night he was killed. She could have had a burner, though. As far as Monson was concerned, she wasn't off the hook, yet.

Monson brought the briefing to a close, telling them he'd let them know tonight if they were reconvening or released back to their usual assignments. He might be able to get a one or two day extension, but unless something broke this weekend, Monday they were done.

SAFE HARBOR

After everyone left, Monson looked over the white board and tapped Logan's picture on the board. He'd interviewed a lot of suspects in his years on the job and the McKenna woman was holding something back. She knew something she wasn't telling them. He just had to find out what it was.

44

Logan was on a roll now, talking faster as one thought lead to another, "When was the last time you think you wore it?"

Meiling looked around the kitchen, as if the answer might be there, hanging on the wall, "Um . . . I don't know. I was going to wear it at the concert Monday night, so I must have had it with me at Vivi's. I was up in one of their guest rooms. We go there to change before each performance. And then, I stayed up there until the concert was over and Jian and I went home."

"Do you think you left it there?" Logan asked.

"No, no, I definitely had it because I remember later that night, Adam called me, all excited, saying he wanted to see me. That was around nine thirty, something like that. It was not cold, but I wore it when I walked down. It is not far—there is a little path across the street that goes down to the harbor."

"Adam liked that sweater," she said, smiling briefly.

"What time did you leave his boat?" Logan asked.

"I only stayed about forty-five minutes," Meiling said, looking shyly down at her hands. "I wanted to stay with Adam that night, but he wanted to start doing things right, now that we were making it official by telling his parents the next day. I was home in bed by ten o'clock."

"Do you think you left your sweater there?"

"I must have," Meiling said. "It is not here and I have not worn it since. Until you told me, I have been too upset to even notice it was gone."

"Okay," Logan said.

Although she thought she knew the answer, Logan asked, "Have you told anyone you saw Adam that night?"

Logan knew the police would have questioned Meiling if they'd known about their affair or that she may have been the last person to see him that night. Or the second to the last, if she was telling the truth and left before Adam was killed.

"No," she said, so quietly Logan almost couldn't hear her. "I didn't tell anyone. They might have told Mr. and Mrs. Hosteler about me and Adam, and I just couldn't."

"Besides," she added simply, looking up, "nothing I do or say now will bring Adam back."

Logan reached over to squeeze her hand. Grief she understood.

"What can I do?" Meiling asked.

Scooping up her car keys off the table as she stood to leave, Logan made a decision. If Meiling wanted to help, why not? Maybe she'd remember something after letting her subconscious work on it during the night.

"What are you doing tomorrow?" Logan asked.

"Nothing, all the workshops are over," Meiling said. "Jian and I usually pack and rest up for the next concert. We don't leave until Monday."

"Good," Logan said, "I really need to go get a phone now, since the police aren't giving me mine back anytime soon. How about if we think about it tonight and get together in the morning?"

"Thank you," Meiling said, walking her to the front door. "I practice in the morning, so I will be up early. You can come anytime."

Before the police arrived at Vivi's door Tuesday, delivering the awful news of Adam's death, the two women had talked about their instruments and their mutual love of the violin.

"Playing always helps me think," Meiling said. "Is it the same for you?"

"Absolutely," Logan said, "My mind empties. Sometimes only through music does the world make sense. There were several years I didn't play, but now I never travel anywhere without Bella."

Logan walked down the steps toward her car, turned back and said, "Don't forget to ask Jian if he remembers you wearing your sweater after Monday. Probably not, but good to check all the bases."

Meiling nodded and waved, staying on the front porch steps until Logan got into her car, then went back inside. She would like to have her as a friend. She hadn't had time to make many friends. Until Adam—and now he was gone.

Starting the engine, Logan checked her watch and realized she'd better get a move on if she was going to make it to Lincoln City to pick out a new phone, stop in and say hi to Rose—she'd skip lunch this time—and still get back before anyone wondered why she was gone so long. Ben and the kids were leaving tomorrow for Portland, so they were all looking forward to one last family afternoon at Little Whale Cove.

Ian enjoyed splashing in the warm, shallow water and Ben was putting together a 'simple' picnic that Logan knew would include plenty of leftovers she could live on for days. Which was a good thing. Left to her own devices, she'd be eating peanut butter and jelly sandwiches for a week.

Whatever thinking she had to do about Adam's murder she'd do after everyone left in the morning. That's what she told herself, anyway. There was too much time to think on the drive to Lincoln City. She tried to sort things out in her brain.

The police knew about her phone. They knew someone had messaged Adam from her phone Monday night. They knew, or would know soon, about Meiling and Adam's relationship and plans to marry. Which meant they would move Debra up on the suspect list. And maybe put Meiling on it.

Rick was always bugging her to keep her phone locked, but she never had. It was just one extra step to take before she could check her email or make a call. Kept life simple, and Logan liked simple.

But what about Chris? He argued with Adam. He had a violent past. And what did she really know about Meiling and Adam's relationship? So far, all she knew was what Meiling had told her. Could he have decided to stay with his wife and break things off with Meiling?

The very thought made Logan feel sick. What if she was trusting the wrong person? Both women seemed innocent, but was she refusing to see one of them as capable of murder because they were women? After all, it was a woman who killed the talented, young glassblower, Elizabeth, several years ago back at the arts festival in Jasper. That murder had been about jealousy, too.

45

Checking out the MAX route again on his phone, Jian pressed his ankles firmly together—trying to do so nonchalantly—securing the now full duffel bag between his legs. He wanted to clutch it to his breast, but that would be too obvious. He tried to act as if it contained old workout clothes, maybe a toiletry bag, and tennis shoes—not the $63,207 it actually held. Minus the four dollars for a triple espresso . . . and six hundred for the gun.

Surprisingly, Bergen's Coins didn't try to bump up their over-the-phone estimate. After an exacting inspection of the coin, which took much longer than he planned, they hadn't tried to bargain him down. They gave him the cash, he handed over the coin. Done.

He'd been so nervous about walking around town with that much money, he'd stopped into the pawnshop next door to Bergen's. There were only two people in the shop—an old man, presumably the owner, who pushed himself up out of a squeaky, old banker's swivel chair to see what he wanted, and a young man with a bad case of acne, straightening merchandise on the shelves.

Jian asked if he had any handguns. Said he wanted to buy one for personal protection—there were so many homeless people here. The owner didn't comment, but pulled out a couple for him to look at. When he mentioned they required a background check, Jian pretended not to like any of the offerings and turned to leave.

When the owner went back to his chair and started reading his book again, the young sales clerk silently signaled Jian to meet him outside.

Jian wasn't sure how this worked, but finally got the idea. When he didn't show up on the sidewalk in the front of the pawnshop, Jian walked around to the back where an alley connected several of the shops.

The clerk pulled out a gun.

"Thirty-eight, police special, six shots. Three hundred dollars. For another three hundred, you can skip the background check and I'll throw in some ammunition. You want hollow point or full metal jacket?"

Jian had no idea, so let him pick. They quickly concluded their business and the clerk went back inside. He couldn't believe it was that easy, but he felt better having it.

Taking a cautious drink of his coffee, which had cooled from lava to simply boiling, Jian consulted the directions on his phone again, trying to calculate the time it would take him to reach the airport, where the shuttle stop was located. He almost got on the blue line, but it was the red line that went to the terminal. Most American cities didn't have good public transportation, but Portland was the exception. Not like Brussels or Paris, but not bad.

It would be close, but he'd make it. Coastal Shuttle had only one trip to the coast daily. He couldn't miss it.

With ten minutes to spare, Jian, gripping the duffel bag, exited the MAX and started walking toward the pickup location. Skirting a woman pulling a large roller bag, talking on her cell phone, he tossed the empty coffee cup in a trash receptacle and looked for the van he'd taken this morning. Seeing it over the heads of people waiting in the taxi line, what he saw made panic rise and close off his throat.

Jian let out a strangled cry, "Wait!"

A dark blue mini-van with white waves painted on the side, proclaiming itself to be 'Coastal Shuttle: We'll get you to the beach and back!' was pulling away from the curb.

Shoving several people aside, Jian sprinted, but had to watch as his ride smoothly crossed three lanes of traffic and, picking up speed, melded into exiting traffic, oblivious to his shouts. All he could see now were the taillights.

Jian swore, then tried to calm his racing heart. Sweat popped out on his forehead and instantly, it seemed, his armpits were damp. He had to get a grip. He could not draw attention to himself. He'd just have to handle it from here. Things happened. They would just have to understand. Sitting on one of the metal, backless benches, he pulled out his phone and dialed the only number he had. The one he was supposed to use when he arrived in Depoe Bay with the money.

"Hello?"

"You're early. Are you here?" said a male voice. He hadn't told Jian his name.

"No, but I have the money," Jian said as quietly as he could into the phone, "I have it with me, but I am still in Portland. The shuttle left early, I will get there, I just have to find a ride. I am positive I can be there tonight, it just may not be by 5:00, as we agreed."

"You're going to be late," the man said.

"Yes, I mean no, I may not be. Let me make some calls. There must be a car I can hire to get me there sometime tonight," Jian said, looking desperately around for the taxi line, wondering if any of them would take him out to the coast, or if they only worked locally. "If not tonight, then I can meet you early in the morning."

"We will be in touch," the man said.

That didn't sound too bad. They weren't happy, but they knew he was coming with the cash. Damn that shuttle service, why did they have to leave early? He hadn't made a reservation, but he didn't think he needed to. They weren't supposed to leave until two o'clock.

It didn't matter. These guys were businessmen. He'd find a ride. He'd get there. It would all be okay.

46

Ben finished showing her where all the goodies were. Her favorite chocolate ice cream, the granola bars, cleaned and stored fresh berries in the fridge, next to some whipped cream and a good selection of yogurts.

"I cleaned some lettuce and made you some lamb and veggie kabobs from what was left of the farmer's market stuff," he said. "Promise me you'll cook these, okay?"

Doing her best bored teen impression, Logan rolled her eyes and pushed him out the door. He'd left detailed instructions for how to broil the kabobs if she couldn't figure out the BBQ. If she screwed up the kabobs, there were a couple of cans of tuna in the cupboard. She could throw that on top of the lettuce, squirt some ranch dressing on it and call it a salad. It was only for a few days. She'd be fine.

Kissing Ian on the top of his head before handing him over to Liam, she pulled Amy in for a hug and walked everyone out to the car. Visually, she checked they all had their bags and jackets.

"Chargers?"

"Yes, mom!"

Someone always forgot something.

Liam shut the door after making sure Ian was secured in his seat, full bottle and teething rings within reach, then walked around and got in the back seat next to him. Amy was riding shotgun in front.

"Don't forget to email that woman from the aquarium in Newport, sounds interesting," Logan said, shouting across the roof of the SUV.

"Def, Mom, will do," Amy said, "Did she say what it was about?"

"Not in detail, sounded impressed with what you told her about the Sea Otter Center in Jasper," Logan said. "She wants to know more about it, maybe they want to start something like that up here."

"But there aren't any sea otters in Oregon," Amy said. "At least, not anymore."

"I don't know, hon," Logan said. "It wasn't a long email. She just contacted me because that was the email I left for the photos to be sent. Maybe you can answer her from the airport while you're waiting for your flight. I forwarded you the email and it has her number."

"Okay!" Amy said, buckling herself in.

Giving Ben a grownup goodbye before he got into the driver's seat, Logan smiled into his blue eyes and wished for a moment he could stay or she was going home with him.

What was that Robert Frost poem . . . "But I have promises to keep, and miles to go before I sleep . . ." That was her. She had shit to do.

Vivi had offered to loan her one of their cars for the next couple of days, which was a good thing. Logan was due at

Meiling's soon. They hadn't set a specific time, just sometime after breakfast.

She'd done a lot of thinking last night and realized she needed to keep an open mind. She'd talked with Debra, she'd talked with Meiling, but she hadn't talked with Jian yet. How much did he know about what was going on? She really didn't want to talk to him—something about Meiling's brother rubbed her the wrong way, but she wanted to be thorough. Maybe he saw or heard something that would help. Logan hoped he would be there this morning.

◦ ◦ ◦ ◦ ◦

By the time Jian got home, it was after midnight and Meiling was asleep. Due to several simultaneous conventions and festivals in Portland that weekend, every taxi and limo service was booked. He finally found an Uber that would take him—unofficially—all the way out to the coast, but only for double the usual cost and for cash only. Luckily, cash was the one thing he hadn't been short of. He would have had trouble explaining such a large charge on the Chinese government-issued credit card he used for the few travel expenses not already prepaid.

Jian sent Meiling a text telling her not to worry and then ignored her questions. He hoped she'd just think his phone died.

It hadn't. He'd been smart enough to make sure it was fully charged. After the last text, he hadn't heard any more from the man. He'd half expected him to be waiting for him on the doorstep, but no one was there.

Finally, around two a.m., he fell asleep fully dressed, duffle bag tucked under his bed, phone set to vibrate so he wouldn't wake anyone when his contact called. When the phone finally did buzz, it took him a few seconds to find it. It had slipped off his chest onto the bed.

"Hello?" he whispered.

"Pirate Coffee, ten minutes."

Ten minutes?!

Checking that the money in the duffel bag was still there, Jian licked his palms and smoothed his hair. Almost free. He let himself out the sliding glass door onto the small deck off his bedroom. The sun was rising over the rooftops behind him. It was a beautiful day. In spite of yesterday's near disaster, he'd done it! He would be able to pay off the loan and be home before Meiling even got up.

And the cash he got for the coin, above and beyond what he needed to pay back his debt, would cushion their lives. He felt bad about the way things turned out with Adam. Meiling should never have gotten involved with him in the first place, but he'd make it up to her. Buy her something nice in Portland.

He had been dreading this meeting, but now he was actually looking forward to it. He couldn't wait to see their faces when he handed them payment in full. He wondered how they'd verify the cash was in there and how much. Probably take the duffel bag into the men's room. Yeah, just like in that movie with Brad Pitt!

◊ ◊ ◊ ◊ ◊

SATURDAY, AUGUST 18

Meiling dug into the Yoplait container for the last of the lemon filling, then licked the spoon. There was one left in the refrigerator for Logan in case she was hungry. Taking a sip of her coffee, she glanced at the clock. Logan would be here any minute.

She wished Jian were here. She needed to ask him about her sweater. She checked his room this morning, and it looked like he made it home safely last night, but she wished he would have waited until she got up before going out. The Andersons only had regular coffee. He preferred espresso.

Finally, there was a knock on the front door. Meiling set down her cup and got up to let Logan in. Instead of her new friend, two Asian men—Chinese as far as she could tell—stood on the porch. One stood right on the doorstep, too close for comfort. The other, a thick, short man, waited a few feet behind.

They weren't smiling. Maybe they were friends of Jian's. Before she could ask who they were or what they wanted, they pushed their way in, the first man zapping her in the stomach with a stun gun at the same time.

Immediately, Meiling's entire body seized and she lost her balance. She tried to get away, but had no control over her muscles. The tall man in front, arm extended, just kept coming, zapping her repeatedly, shoving her back into the room. Meiling crumpled to the floor. She couldn't understand what was happening. The pain was so intense, it felt like her spine was on fire.

Then the shorter man calmly stepped in . . . and shut the door.

47

When no one answered her knock, Logan rang the bell. It was eerily quiet. Maybe Meiling overslept. She looked around to see if maybe she or Jian were outside on one of the decks drinking coffee, but the deck was empty. The only people visible on the street were an older woman two houses down, trimming her roses, and a couple of men at the end of the street, walking into town.

Then she heard a muffled moan.

Not waiting for permission to enter, Logan tested the knob to see if the door was locked, then pushed it open and ran inside. At first, she couldn't see anything, so followed the sounds. Once her eyes adjusted to the dim interior, she spotted Meiling, lying on her side on the floor in the living room, between the coffee table and the couch. Her mouth had been duct-taped shut and her wrists were zip-tied tightly together behind her.

Whoever did this hadn't bothered to tie her feet. That's because they didn't need to. Her feet were a bloody mess. She couldn't have walked if she tried.

Logan shoved the coffee table out of the way and knelt down to help, rapidly dialing 911 on her new phone. She gave what she hoped were good directions and said yes, she would stay here with the injured young woman.

While she waited for help to arrive, Logan gently worked the duct tape off of Meiling's mouth. She was afraid to touch her feet. They were beyond her limited first aid skills. When she finally removed the last of the tape, Meiling started wailing.

She wanted to stay and comfort the girl, but needed something to free her hands. Logan ran into the kitchen and got a pair of scissors to cut off the zip ties, then gathered her in her arms.

"Shhhh . . . shhh . . . it's going to be all right," she said, stroking her hair, rocking her like an infant, "Everything's going to be all right. An ambulance is on its way."

As she held her, she looked down at Meiling's damaged feet. The blood wasn't gushing, but several of her toes looked broken. Meiling buried her face in Logan's shoulder, sobbing. The pain must have been unbearable.

"What happened, Meiling?" Logan whispered. "Who did this to you? Do you know who did this to you?"

❖ ❖ ❖ ❖ ❖

On the other end of town, Jian shifted nervously in his seat. He was on his third double espresso and they still weren't here. He checked the sign outside. Pirate Coffee. Yes, he was at the right place. He looked at his phone to make sure he had the correct time.

Good, there was a text. Maybe they'd been held up. He tapped the screen to read it.

Wednesday. Portland airport. $100,000. We're rounding up. Don't be late.

Next time it will be her hands.

SAFE HARBOR

The last line turned Jian's bowels to water. What had they done? He almost didn't make it to the coffee shop restroom. When he emerged, pale and sweaty, he grabbed his bag and bolted out the door, almost knocking a couple down as he pushed past them, sprinting across Highway 101 for home.

Meiling!

When Jian arrived, an ambulance was parked outside and two EMTs were bringing his sister out through the front door on a stretcher. Her friend, Logan, was holding the door open for them. He rushed to Meiling's side, taking her hand in his, but the attendant gently but firmly pushed him away.

"I'm her brother!"

"We're taking your sister to get some help, sir. You can meet us at the hospital, sir," he said. "She'll be at Samaritan Pacific in Newport."

All Jian could do was watch helplessly as they loaded Meiling into the ambulance. She was covered with a blanket, so he couldn't see anything, but her feet had been wrapped in something bulky. A wave of nausea overtook him. He turned and vomited in the bushes, then just stood there, hands on his knees, wiping the back of his mouth on his sleeve as the ambulance drove away, lights flashing, siren wailing. The duffel bag lay at his feet.

A woman was walking toward him, saying something. Still in a daze, he stared at her until her words started making sense.

"Jian? You're Jian, right?" she said, "Meiling's brother?"

"Yes," he managed to say.

"I'm Logan. Logan McKenna," she said, "We met briefly, the night of the concert, but you may not remember me."

She waited until he nodded. "I have my car here. I was coming to see Meiling and found her. I can give you a ride to the hospital in Newport if you want. They gave me directions."

Jian nodded again, mutely accepting Logan's offer of a ride. While she went to get the car, Jian said, "I will be right back. I need to get Meiling's passport in case she needed it at the hospital."

'Okay, I'll be here when you get back," Logan said.

Once inside the house, Jian went to Meiling's room and grabbed her passport. Next, he went to his own room to shove the duffel bag under his bed, then changed his mind.

Hesitating only a second, he reached under his pillow and removed the revolver he'd quickly stored there before he left that morning. Making sure the safety was still on like the guy showed him, Jian slipped it into the waistband of his jeans under his sweatshirt. This game had definitely changed. He wanted to be prepared in case Li Wei's men were waiting for him at the hospital.

He felt sick again. Not at all like Brad Pitt in Ocean's Eleven. He hurried outside where Logan was waiting, engine running. Tossing the duffel bag onto the floor first, he got into the passenger seat and closed his eyes to concentrate as Logan sped south on Highway 101.

He didn't understand any of this. Why had they attacked Meiling? They kept changing the rules! He'd *talked* to them. They *knew* he had the money. There was no reason to do what they did! Now they said they'd meet him Wednesday. Presumably they wouldn't do anything more until then, but he didn't trust them. He no longer believed anything they said.

All the way to the hospital, he remained silent, his mind whirling. Luckily, Meiling's friend didn't try to make small talk.

He needed to talk to Meiling. He didn't know what she knew or what they had told her, if anything. He had to make sure she didn't say anything to anyone about San Francisco or

Adam or any of their family business. He needed time to fix this—to figure out what to do.

How was he going to get that much money by Wednesday? They were supposed to fly out tomorrow, Monday. He could push back their flights a couple of days and still keep to their tour schedule, but would Meiling be well enough to travel by then? How badly had they hurt her? If he didn't get the money by Wednesday, he knew they'd follow through on their threat. If Meiling's hands were damaged, it was over. She would never play again. No more touring America. Their lives would be over.

How was he going to explain all this to Beijing?

That, he realized, was the least of his worries. Li Wei's men meant business. And then there was the little matter of murder. It was only a matter of time before the police discovered Meiling's relationship with Adam Hosteler and connected the dots. Once they did, they would almost certainly detain both of them for questioning, which would prevent him from meeting the Wednesday deadline in Portland. Everything was closing in.

How had everything gotten so out of control? He'd just wanted to have some fun. Li Wei seemed so kind, helping him out, making him feel at home in a foreign land, showing him respect when others so often dismissed him. Yes, he'd gotten himself into some trouble. But he had solved the problem. He'd figured out a way to pay off his debt. He'd done the impossible. Got the coin, sold the coin, brought the money back. But that wasn't enough. Nothing he did was ever enough.

And through all this, he had done his job. He'd protected Meiling, kept her from making a huge mistake, They were almost home free, but then, he realized bitterly, his face crumpling, he hadn't been able to protect her from Li Wei.

48

Five days. Chris had made it through the worst of the withdrawals and thought he'd be done, but according to his counselor, if he wanted this time to be the last time, this was just the beginning. The real work started now.

Now that it wasn't clouded with drugs, his mind was unfortunately crystal clear. For hours last night he kept replaying the awful scene at the harbor over and over in his mind. Anxiety mounting, since he wasn't sleeping anyway, he decided to get up and take a walk.

He used to love this time of day when no one else was up. But that was before. Before drugs, before every morning was a wall of pain to climb. He thought of all the time he'd wasted. Every minute of the last year at least had been taken up in figuring out how to score, how not to get caught, how to blame it on others, and to convince yourself—above all, yourself—that you weren't an addict. It was exhausting.

A light was on in the kitchen. A pot of water was boiling on the stove. Very homey, but no one home. The back door to the garden was open, though, so he went outside. He liked it out here. A slim man with wiry, dark blonde hair was already there, kneeling on the path. Probably the cook. Chris watched as the man pinched off a bit of a low, green plant, rubbing the leaf between his fingers, breathing in the aroma before gathering a bunch to place in the small basket on the ground.

Seeing Chris watching him, the man held one up for him to smell, "You like it?"

Chris held it up to his nose. "Yeah," he said. He recognized the pungent, soothing smell, but couldn't place it.

"Silver sage. I use it in the breakfast sausage, but it's also one of the teas we keep out in the common room. It's almost as good as ginger for nausea. I'll make you a cup when we get inside."

He stuck out his hand, "Symon. Symon Lutre."

"Chris Larsen, nice to meet you, Symon."

The man looked into eyes. "You're up early. How long?"

"I'm only on day five," Chris said.

"Congratulations!"

"I don't think they give chips for five days," Chris said.

"Ahh . . . give yourself credit. Any day without drugs is a cause for celebration, my friend."

Symon stood, brushing the dirt off his pants.

"And you?"

Chris had discovered almost everyone who worked here was a former addict of one kind or another who had successfully gone through the program.

"Fifteen years, seven months, and twenty-one days," Symon replied.

"Wow," Chris said.

"You'll get there." Symon looked at Chris again. "What's on your mind, son?"

At that moment, with the sun streaming through the garden, warming his body, the smell of the sage drifting up from Symon's basket, and the kind look in this man's eyes, something broke inside. Chris knew this burden was one he couldn't carry alone. Gratefully, tearfully, he stopped trying to control everything, and he told him.

All of it. Everything that had happened, up to and including what he could remember of that horrible night. Adam was dead. That much he knew for certain. He saw it clearly in his mind. Every time he shut his eyes. But the truth was, he'd been so wasted, Chris didn't know if he was the one who killed him.

There was only one thing to do. Symon let him use the phone to make the call.

9:12 A.M.

Monson sat back in his chair. It was Sunday, so he was the only one here.

He didn't know what to think.

Last night, he'd finished breaking down most of the room over the fire station and come home to his apartment in Newport to crash. All his stuff was in his car. A couple other members of the crime team were going to pick up their things tomorrow. His plan had been to sleep in, then maybe catch a game on TV.

Monday he'd start assembling the murder book. And deal with the pile of work he knew would be waiting for him on his desk. New cases. Hopefully mundane. Unrelated to charter boat captains being killed.

But at six this morning, while he was still deeply asleep, the phone rang. The deputy apologized for calling him this early, but said he knew the Detective would want to be notified right away. He had a visitor. Chris Larsen.

They'd been looking for Chris Larsen for a week, and suddenly, he shows up at the jail, turning himself in on a silver platter.

All this was good news, but even after going in and questioning Chris for two hours, Monson was none the wiser. Chris admitted he was there. Said he saw Adam Hosteler, but his memory was spotty. He'd been very drunk and very high at the time. They'd narrowed down the time somewhat. Chris said he left the bar when it closed. He remembered that much and Monson could verify that easily when the restaurant opened.

What Monson didn't know for sure was whether or not Chris had killed Adam. Chris remembered seeing him dead. That seemed to be a vivid memory, but he couldn't remember what happened before that. Wasn't sure if they'd argued or even if he had hit him—or if he was already dead when he got there.

Oh, he'd locked him up. Monson wasn't going to look a gift horse in the mouth, but for now, he just had Chris in a holding cell.

Monson knew he should have been celebrating. He could put him right there. His prints were all over the boat. He had a beef with Adam—Adam fired him. He *admitted* to being there. His description of the scene was spot on. He'd been there. That part of his story rang true.

And he ran. He hadn't come forward for days. Looked guilty as sin. He'd conveniently checked himself into drug rehab the morning of the murder, but did that make him a killer? Did seeing a dead body scare him into rehab, or committing murder? Adam had two head wounds—one fatal, one not. Which, if either, had Chris Larsen delivered? Or was he just in the wrong place at the wrong time?

Monson queued up the CCTV footage on his computer one more time, just in case he'd missed anything the first thousand times he watched it. Then he rummaged through some papers until he found his notes on the interview he and Grant took with Karen, the young woman camping out on the neighboring boat—their only witness.

She described the person she saw running from the scene early Tuesday morning as being of average height, slight build. Just like Chris. Could have been him. Could have been almost anyone—male or female. And what about the wife? Could have been her. She could have argued with her husband, like Karen said, earlier that night, then come back for more after Karen settled into her sleeping bag on the other boat.

There was just no way of knowing who had come and gone that night for sure. There were several ways down to the docks, and not all of them ran past the cameras at the Coast Guard station.

Monson rubbed his face with his hands to wake himself up. Time for another go.

49

Frank Waller packed up the last of his things and looked around his temporary work area for anything he'd missed. Now that most of the tables and computer equipment had been picked up, the large room looked forlorn and deserted, like an unwanted orphan.

Last night, he received the text they'd all been expecting, disbanding the LC Major Crimes Team, dumping the case back into the sheriff's lap.

Monson got them a one-day extension, but no new leads had come in during the last twenty-four hours, so they were pulling the plug. When he got back to the FBI office in Salem, Frank planned on writing up the last of his reports and sending what he had to Monson.

He wouldn't make it home in time for church, or even lunch, but he'd be there for dinner. Wrapping things up today would allow him to hit the ground running Monday morning when he got to his office. Work had been piling up in his absence.

It was a shame the victim's phone records hadn't come in yet. Maybe Monson would find something in them when they eventually pushed their way through the bureaucracy and landed on his desk in a few days.

Frank lifted his bulging workbag off the table. He was across the room and halfway down the stairs when his cell phone rang.

"Waller," he said, slowing down but not stopping.

"Tim Grumley, Frank. Financial Crime, San Francisco," he said, "You still out in Depoe Bay?"

"Yes," Frank said, "but I'm on my way back to the office, now. Why? You have something cooking in Salem I need to know about? I should be home in an hour and twenty minutes."

"No," Grumley said, "not in Salem. But something's happening where you are on the coast. That case you're working on connects to an operation of ours up here I think you can help us with."

"I'm listening," Frank said, stopping at the bottom of the stairs.

Grumley took a minute to answer.

"I'll fill you in when I get there. Flew in this morning—be there in twenty. Where's a good place to eat?"

Frank called his wife and let her know he'd be late. Again. Then he locked his gear in his car and walked the three blocks to Gracie's Sea Hag. They served breakfast until eleven thirty.

He wanted to run back upstairs and grab Monson—he was still in the building—but he valued his career enough to hear Grumley out first. Fellow FBI agent and all that. He'd argue for interagency cooperation if he had anything that would help their case.

An hour later, taking one last bite of a huge crab omelet, Special Agent Grumley set his plate aside, wiped his mouth, and flipped a file open onto the table, pushing it across the table to Frank. He tapped on the photo.

"This is him. Li Wei. We've been after this guy for over two years," he said. "Gambling, loan sharking, extortion . . ."

The photo showed a relaxed, well-groomed Chinese man with a dusting of gray in his hair. Fashionably dressed. Glass of red wine in hand. Smiling at something his companion said. He was at a party.

"This isn't a mug shot, so I assume he's never been arrested," Frank said.

"Yep. Slippery guy," Grumley said.

He flipped a page.

"But these two have—many times," he said. "We call 'em Laurel and Hardy. Their real names are Yi and Yun—the Wong brothers. The tall one is Yi. He's the alpha. Yun just tags along. More muscles than brains. Yi isn't any Rhodes scholar, though. He knows just enough to do whatever Wei tells them to do. They're Wei's enforcers."

"How does all this connect with our case? What's a dead, white, charter boat captain in Depoe Bay, Oregon got to do with Chinese gangsters?" Frank asked. "Hosteler had no connection to gambling, San Francisco, or criminal activity of any kind that we know of."

"Ahhh . . . but he *was* connected to a young, Chinese woman named Meiling Zhang. Very personally connected."

This was news to Frank, but he was still confused.

Grumley continued, "This morning, Yi and Yun paid her a visit—just blocks from here—put her in the hospital."

Frank had heard sirens earlier, but just figured it was an accident on Highway 101.

"Is this Meiling related to your guy, Li Wei?" Frank asked.

"No, but she is the sister of a Chinese national we've been watching, Jian Zhang."

Grumley pulled a paper out from the back of the file. On it was a copy of the front page of a music program showing a smiling, young woman playing the violin, and next to it, a headshot of a man he assumed was her brother, Jian.

"They're both musicians. He plays piano for her. Been on tour in America a few times. This trip, Zhang got in debt with these guys—but here's the kicker . . . Meiling was the lover—and according to the texts and calls we found on his phone—the next *wife* of your murder victim, Mr. Adam Hosteler."

So that's why the phone company hadn't forwarded Hosteler's phone records to the LC Major Crimes Team yet. The FBI always got first dibs. Frank wasn't sure how he felt about that. Frank was FBI, but he respected Monson and felt bad he'd been left out of the loop. Maybe if he'd had this information, they wouldn't have suspended the team yet and they'd have a chance to solve their case.

Reading his mind, Grumley reassured him that Adam's phone records were on their way to the sheriff's department. Monson would have them first thing in the morning if he didn't already. As a courtesy to local law enforcement, the Lincoln County Sheriff's department would receive copies of their reports, redacted if necessary and slightly delayed.

Frank knew enough not to comment. He just nodded as if he agreed. This guy had seniority and a lot more pull.

Grumley then laid out his plan, which included putting both Meiling and Jian into protective custody. Being Chinese nationals, the FBI had jurisdiction. He'd offer Jian a deal.

"We have someone on their way to the hospital now," he said. "His sister's about to go into surgery. We can pick him up there."

SAFE HARBOR

He didn't care about the local murder connection—it had nothing to do with his case. Monson was welcome to that once he had what he wanted. Grumley was only interested in using Jian to help him take down Li Wei's organization. He kept his eye on the prize—using a little fish to catch a big one. He heaved himself out of the booth, leaving Frank to pay the bill.

Next stop, Samaritan Pacific Hospital, Newport, Oregon.

50

By the time Logan got to the hospital and parked, Meiling had already been taken back. The only other people in the ER waiting room were a pregnant woman reading a magazine and a boy around ten or eleven with bandages on his chin and elbows, presumably her son. He didn't look badly injured, but was fidgeting in his seat, craning his neck to look past his mother through the glass doors to the beautiful, sunny day. He was clearly annoyed at having to be stuck in here.

"Ethan!" she said, frowning at the boy. "Settle down."

Looking over at Logan she said, "Skateboard."

They each took one of the uncomfortable, plastic bucket seats. Jian spent the time scrolling through his phone, which gave Logan the opportunity to observe him. She hadn't gotten a good look at him at the concert, and he had ditched his reception line duties after the concert as soon as possible. There was a family resemblance, but where Meiling's features all came together in a delicate balance, Jian's seemed oddly arranged. Wide, unruly brows. Tiny, feminine mouth—seashell pink and bowed, like a silent film star. Gelled black hair, shaved close on the sides.

She couldn't put her finger on it, but something bothered her about him. She knew it wasn't fair, but she couldn't help but compare him to her own brother, Rick. True, Rick was her little brother, but he was always there for her. Jian was here now, but something about his concern for Meiling didn't ring true. Yes, he was there. It was obvious he was upset about her being attacked, but somehow, he seemed more concerned with himself and whatever was on his phone than his sister. He wasn't anxiously awaiting news about Meiling. He didn't go ask the nurse when they could go back and see her. It was Logan who kept doing that.

But that didn't matter. Whatever their relationship was, it was. What mattered was Meiling. Why had she been attacked? Who did this to her? And was she going to be okay?

As they sat there, waiting for the nurse to give them permission to go back and see Meiling, Logan stood up and stretched. Her sciatica was mild these days, but she still had to remember to not sit too long.

When she got up to stretch, she looked over at Jian and noticed a two-inch gap between his jeans and his sweatshirt.

Oh my god. Jian had a gun!

She only saw it for a minute before looking away, but that was definitely a gun. What else was gray, shiny, and stuffed into the back of one's pants? What was Jian doing with a gun?

Before she could process this information, the emergency nurse called them over. By a stroke of luck, an orthopedic surgeon was available. He was on his way. The patient was in X-ray now. The nurse would notify them as soon as Meiling was either taken up for surgery or treated and sent home. Logan had seen Meiling's feet. This wasn't something a few bandages would fix. They were going to be here a while.

While Jian filled out paperwork, Logan went to scrounge up some coffee and something to eat. She had no idea what to say or do about the fact that Meiling's brother had a gun in his pants. Was this a normal thing? A cultural thing? Maybe he always carried one. What was going on?

Where had Jian gone that morning? What did he know about Meiling's attack? Logan's mind was spinning.

Not wanting to get out of hearing range of the nurse's station, Logan decided to wait until she could figure this out. For now, she'd just act like everything was normal. If Jian was dangerous for any reason, she didn't want to confront him in the middle of a hospital waiting room. What could she do anyway? She looked around for a security guard but saw no one. Apparently, anyone could walk into a hospital with a loaded gun. Was it loaded? She assumed it was, but she wasn't going to test that theory just now.

She found a vending machine around the corner and brought back some chips and two coffees. Aiming for nonchalant, Logan offered Jian one of the coffees. He accepted the java but turned down the food. Logan stuffed the rest in her purse, trying to bring her heart rate down from a zillion beats a second and keep her face from giving her panic away.

Thirty minutes later, the nurse said they could go back, where Meiling was back from radiology, waiting for an OR to open up.

They were directed to the third bed on the left. Technically, they were gurneys that could wheel the patients in and out efficiently as needed.

The first was occupied by an older man, propped up on pillows, accompanied by a weary-looking woman, probably his wife. She was seated next to him, absentmindedly holding his hand, scrolling through her phone.

Rolling, aluminum frames of thin, blue fabric separated the bays, creating a modicum of privacy for each patient. At the head of each patient's gurney was a wall of medical equipment Logan remembered with a shudder from her own trip to the ER years ago.

The second bed was empty. Then they got to Meiling's. None of the others were occupied. Meiling looked frail against the white sheets. Hooked up to an IV, she was no longer thrashing around in pain and panic. She managed a weak smile when they arrived.

"We're giving her something to relax her and ease the pain," the nurse said. "Just fifteen minutes. We'll be prepping her for surgery soon."

She checked the IV bag then left.

Jian hung back, staring at the bulky lumps at the end of the bed, presumably Meiling's feet, encased in some kind of protective coverings until surgery. He started to back away.

"No," Meiling said weakly, "Wait!"

Jian came back in.

Logan stepped to the foot of the bed, making room for him. The gun was no longer obvious in the back of Jian's jeans, but she knew it was there. It was all she could see.

The last thing she wanted to do was intrude on a private, family moment, but she needn't have worried. The siblings were staring at each other, ignoring her completely. Jian stood at the side of his sister's bed.

"Why, Jian?" Meiling whispered. "They kept saying it was your fault—that you owed them money."

Jian's eyes filled with tears, but he said nothing.

"The short one had a small hammer," she continued. "It was in his jacket, I think. He was so calm. The other one held me. That hammer just kept coming down. They would not stop! I could not get away!"

Logan didn't want to hear this.

Meiling began shaking, obviously traumatized by the memory of what the men had done to her. She kept her voice low, but was on the verge of losing control.

"They said that was for the original debt. If you do not pay them, Jian, the tall one said they would be back . . . and this time, they take it out of my hands! My *hands*, Jian! They cannot do this to my hands!"

Lifting her head off the pillow, she held her hands up in front of his face, almost pulling out the IV needle. She looked at him imploringly.

"Why did you borrow money? We have everything we need!" she cried.

Jian's mouth twisted angrily, his pity turned to fury. He leaned in close to keep the nurses from hearing. He didn't seem to remember or care that Logan was in the room.

"*You* have everything, Meiling—*you*, not me. The tours, the fame. I have nothing. All I do is take care of you!"

Meiling fell back, looking as if she'd been slapped.

Jian stepped away as if to leave, then came back. "One time I went to have some fun—one time! To do something besides play the piano for the famous Chinese wonder woman, Meiling Zhang! Yes, I made a mistake. But you . . . getting involved with that American. You ruined both our lives! You didn't care what happened to your family . . . to me. Did you think Beijing would let you go that easily once they found out?"

"I am responsible for you. That could not happen." Jian paused, looking at the ceiling. Meiling just stared at him, her eyes wide and her mouth slack.

"Who do you think took care of that for you, Meiling? I kept you from making the biggest mistake of your life, from throwing it all away. Your job, your family, me! I cleaned up your mess. You made me do it.

"You were so stupid, leaving your sweater on the boat. If I did not see it, the police would have found out about you and Adam . . . and now this! Don't worry about your sweater, I got rid of it. Now, I'm stuck here taking care of you again . . . and they will return, Meiling, all of them! The police will figure it out . . . they will find Adam's phone . . . if they haven't already . . ."

"You were on the boat?" Meiling said slowly, "the night Adam was killed . . . you were there?"

Jian began pacing up and down beside the bed. "I just wanted him to stop seeing you, but he wouldn't listen . . . he started yelling. I had to shut him up. I had no choice!"

Meiling shrunk back into her pillows, a look of horror on her face. Logan couldn't believe what she just heard. The man standing two feet away from her just admitted to killing Adam Hosteler. She kept as still as possible. He seemed to have forgotten she was in the room and she wanted to keep it that way.

Then, as suddenly as Jian's anger ignited, it seemed to dissipate. Letting all the breath out of his body until his chest sunk and his shoulders rounded, he stood still, looking at the floor.

"I'm sorry, Meiling," he said softly. "about everything."

Logan wanted to leave, to go get the police, but she didn't dare move. Jian was too close.

Then, Jian straightened up.

"I need to leave now," he said calmly, turning to go. Then added, ". . . but I'm not leaving alone."

The next few seconds played out in slow motion. Jian grabbed Logan's left arm and before she could fight back, pulled her in front of him, pressing a gun into the small of her back.

He slipped it under her t-shirt and she felt the cold steel of the barrel against her skin. She stood absolutely still, hyperaware of her surroundings, waiting for any opportunity to escape. She wished a doctor or nurse would come in right now, and at the same time, fervently hoped no one would. Any small movement might set him off. Logan didn't want anyone getting shot, including herself.

Growling in Logan's ear, Jian whispered, "We will walk out of here, just you and me. If anyone asks, we are going to collect Meiling's passport and things from the car."

He transferred the gun to his pocket, but kept it pointing at Logan.

"Do not doubt I will shoot you."

Afraid to move or speak, Logan could only nod in agreement. She'd never been so scared in her life. She'd fought hand-to-hand with a killer once, but this one had a gun and there was no dark forest nearby to run to or hide in. No hope of escape.

"And you," he looked back at Meiling. "You already cost me my life. Stay quiet and you might save hers."

51

Chris Larsen had nothing new to say, but Monson trusted his instincts. After another hour and a half of questioning, his gut told him this man wasn't a killer. A drug addict, yes, but not a killer. But he couldn't prove it either way. That was good news for Chris, but not for the investigation. It put them right back to square one.

Monson sighed. Might as well kick the guy loose. He was going straight back to rehab. They knew where to find him if new evidence pointed in Chris's direction. Might as well get this over with. On his way out to the jail, he noticed some papers had spilled out of the fax machine and landed on the floor. He bent over and picked them up.

Adam's phone records.

It was about time. Then he noticed the agency. Forwarded from the FBI? What did the FBI want with his murder victim's phone records? Frank hadn't said anything to him about it yesterday. Monson looked at the source office. San Francisco. He'd give Frank the benefit of the doubt. Maybe he didn't know.

After skimming through the records, though, Monson felt

a jolt of adrenaline. Finally, a crack in the case. By virtue of being male, Adam Hosteler had given two people good reason to be angry enough to kill him. The motive was as old as time. Jealousy. He now had two new murder suspects: the wife, Debra Hosteler, and the girlfriend, one Meiling Zhang. It was probably one of them.

According to the numerous phone calls and detailed texts, Adam had a relationship going back at least a year with Meiling—so not just a one-night stand. Either the wife found out and confronted him, accidentally killing him, or killed him in cold blood before he could divorce her.

Money could have played a role, too. If Adam divorced her, Debra would only get half. If she killed him, she'd get it all. Charter boat fishermen didn't make all that much, but he'd known people to kill for less.

Or it was the girlfriend. Maybe Adam Hosteler started thinking with his head instead of his dick. If he left his wife, he'd lose too much—including his kids and half of whatever equity they'd accumulated in the business and house—if they owned one.

At this moment, Monson was glad he didn't have a wife to answer to. His former wife always gave him grief for being late, and he'd be working late tonight.

As far as he knew from the interviews he and Grant conducted with Debra Hosteler, she had no alibi. Time to see if Meiling Zhang had one. See what her story was. Then he'd circle back to the wife.

Monson grabbed his coat and headed for his car, then checked himself. Better let them know to release Chris Larsen.

He had to admire the man. Barely detoxed off some really strong drugs, he'd come in to do the right thing—report what he'd seen—what he could remember. Left himself wide open to arrest for murder. Wasn't even sure if he'd done it or not.

SAFE HARBOR

Monson didn't usually cut druggies any slack, but this one seemed different. He'd have one of the deputies drive him back to Safe Harbor. He'd never heard of the place before—it was a private facility—but it sounded like a good place. He hoped Chris made it.

God knows most of them didn't.

○ ○ ○ ○ ○

He'd talk with them one at a time. First up, the girlfriend.

Calling Adam's parents for Meiling's address was out of the question. They probably didn't even know about their son's affair, but at the last minute he remembered they'd collected the young woman's contact information at the Hosteler's house, along with Logan McKenna, the woman who had driven her home the day they did the death notification. He remembered that Meiling and her brother, Jian, were visiting musicians from China. The concert was a week ago. He wasn't even sure they'd still be in town.

He had Meiling's number, but didn't want to call. No sense in scaring her off if she had a reason to run. He'd take his chances and show up unannounced.

When he arrived, a chunky, blonde woman in her fifties opened the door. She was out on the porch and halfway down the stairs before he even got out of his car.

"Wow, I just called," she said, looking at the cell phone in her hand, then started waving him in. "You got here fast! In here. We haven't touched anything . . ."

Monson didn't bother to correct her—he wasn't responding to a call—but followed her inside the house. Once there, he understood. A coffee table had been pushed to the side and a significant amount of blood was drying in large splotches on the carpet in front of the couch.

"That's blood, isn't it?" she asked, gesturing toward the scene with her phone. "It was like this when we got home. We've been at my sister's in Bend and decided to cut our visit short, my brother-in-law can be a jerk sometimes . . ."

Monson surveyed the scene quickly and told them they did the right thing by not touching anything, then pulled out a small notebook and got their names—Judy and Zeke Andersen.

"Meiling and Jian should be here, but we didn't see them anywhere," she said.

"They didn't go with you?" he asked.

"No, no they stayed here. They always give workshops at the schools the week after their concert and they were keeping an eye on the house for us. We weren't supposed to be home until Tuesday. We've looked in the house and there's no sign of them anywhere. I'll show you their rooms."

Monson followed the woman through the hall to the two guest rooms. Just like she said, Meiling and her brother were not there, but their luggage was.

He walked the woman back down the hall, where her husband was waiting. To keep them occupied and out of the way, he asked them to go into the kitchen and start writing out a timeline of events—they'd get full statements from them later. He went out onto the porch. He called in and put out an All Points Bulletin on one Meiling Zhang and her brother, Jian. Victim or perpetrator, he needed to find Adam's girlfriend as soon as possible.

52

Frank tucked the tip under the saltshaker and followed Grumley outside. It was a beautiful day. Sun was shining. Happy visitors milling around, going in and out of shops, collecting souvenirs. He'd have to bring his family out here when all this was over. They'd gone clamming one year up in Lincoln City. Kids loved it.

Grumley's rental was parked at the south end of the block, in one of the narrow spaces angled in front of the shops and restaurants lining Highway 101 on the east side.

A man on a mission, Grumley got in and started the car, waiting impatiently for Frank to catch up. Frank felt like crap. He hated being caught in the middle. They should notify the locals—at least Monson. He should know what was going on, particularly as it connected with their case. He'd just have to wait until they got to the hospital and hooked up Jian. Then he'd call Monson.

Grudgingly, Frank got in and buckled up. The parking spaces were tight. They'd have to back out directly into oncoming, northbound traffic first, then do a u-turn back to Newport. Grumley began inching back.

"Clear?" he asked.

Frank looked over his shoulder.

"Not yet, but the light's changing . . ." he said, then "Wait . . . don't look, just go back in."

Grumley put it in drive and slid back into the space, but left the engine running.

"What?"

"It's him," Frank said. "Your guy. At the light. Black Hyundai."

Grumley rotated the passenger-side mirror with the power button until they could see the vehicle.

Idling at the light, first in line, was a black, Hyundai Tucson. Driver and passenger clearly illuminated by the bright, noonday sun. Maybe he was imagining it, but Jian looked sweaty and nervous. He kept looking back and forth between the road in front and at the long-haired woman driving, like he didn't want to lose sight of her.

"Got him. Who's the driver?" Grumley asked. "We know her?"

"Logan McKenna," Frank said. He explained he recognized her from her smiling driver's license photo on Monson's white board in the command center. She wasn't smiling today. Gripping the steering wheel at ten and two, today the woman looked terrified.

"Suspect?"

"Person of interest," Frank said. "Her phone was used to call the murder victim, but she says she lost it."

Grumley made up his mind and had Frank call it in as a

possible hostage situation. They'd follow discretely until backup arrived. Hopefully, there'd be an OSP unit nearby, and they could contain the situation and make the felony stop in a less-populated area, before reaching Lincoln City, ten miles away.

When the light changed and the Hyundai passed by, Grumley backed out and merged into traffic—staying two cars behind. Until help arrived, there was nothing more they could do.

❍ ❍ ❍ ❍ ❍

Loading up his car with the last of the equipment, Detective Grant pushed down on the lid of a cardboard banker box full of extension cords until the trunk would close. The OSP Officer, Rob Clancey, had just helped him carry out the heavier computers already. Dinosaur desktop units, Grant hated them. He sort of wished he'd drop his so he could get a laptop. He had his eyes on a MacBook Air.

Rob had just gotten to his unit when the radio squawked. He leaned in to answer.

"Bravo12," he said.

"Bravo12, Tag12 FBI requests assistance. Proceed Caution Code Two to northbound Highway 101 outside Depoe Bay. Tag12 in green Mercury, following suspect in black, Hyundai Tucson, license plate 930 KKM. Two occupants. Passenger Jian Zhang, Chinese national 36, 5' 8", medium build, black hair, black eyes, wanted in connection with felony. Driver and possible hostage, Logan McKenna, 46, 5' 9", medium build, brown hair, green eyes. Situation unknown but suspect considered armed and dangerous. Tag12 requests you make a felony stop north of Depoe Bay when units are in position."

"Copy Dispatch. Bravo12 en route to northbound Highway

101. Code Two. Detective Grant, Newport PD with me in the car. Negative on the felony stop, Tag12, if there's a hostage."

"Do you copy, Tag12?"

53

Logan felt the engine idling smoothly beneath her. She and Jian had just crossed over the Depoe Bay Bridge and were waiting at the light. Hard to believe that just a few days ago, she and Ben sailed out under that bridge with Adam on the *Mary Ann* for a fun half-day of fishing. Another lifetime.

Naturally she had to be in a reliable car. The last twenty miles had seemed an eternity and according to the GPS, they had a hundred and two miles to go. The stop for gas at the Shell station had been nerve-wracking, but they'd survived without incident.

Jian had taken her phone and somehow managed to plug in a route while keeping his gun trained on her the whole time, then propped it up in the cup holder where he could see it. This model Hyundai didn't come with navigation. Her phone informed them . . .

You will arrive at your destination in two hours and thirty-eight minutes. Traffic is light, as usual.

Not in Depoe Bay it wasn't. Summer tourist season was in full swing here.

Logan wasn't sure what their destination was, but she had to assume someplace in Portland. This was the route they'd taken to get down here, and besides McMinnville and a few other small towns, there wasn't much else between here and there. What Jian was going to do with her when they got there she didn't know.

Whether Meiling called the police or not, Logan couldn't think of a scenario in which this was going to end well. Every possibility she could think of ended with her or innocent bystanders getting shot.

He kept his gun below the dashboard, pointed right at her side. He was already a bundle of edgy nerves, so she'd been scrupulously avoiding potholes or sudden lane changes. She doubted Chinese pianists were experienced with firearms.

She kept thinking of Amy, Ben, and Ian. She just wanted to survive. She had to survive. Amy had already lost her father, she couldn't lose her mother, too.

Logan pulled her mind into focus. Desperately running from both the police and Meiling's attackers, Jian wasn't a man with very many options left. She'd have to think of at least one. One that included letting her go. She only needed one. If she could just catch a break—a weak moment—maybe she could get away.

Logan looked around. This was a very long light. The sidewalks along the shops were full if not packed. Families entering and exiting Gracie's Sea Hag and the gift shops, or just strolling along. Clumps of humanity, children, couples, a group of teens—some with coffee, packages, or ice cream. Across the highway, standing on the sea wall, a little boy jumped up and down, tugging on his mother's hand, shouting and pointing with delight at what was probably a whale spout out in the ocean.

When the light turned green, she eased forward slowly.

"Why are you driving so slow? Go!" Jian said.

"I can't. It's only twenty-five miles-an-hour through here. Do you want me to get pulled over?" Logan said.

No, Jian didn't want that. Switching his gun from his left hand to his right, he wiped his palms on his pants, then after checked back to make sure Logan's hands stayed on the wheel.

Great. He's sweating.

Just outside of town, the speed limit increased to forty-five. Navigation lady was right. Traffic was light as usual. There were a few cars behind them, but no one was honking their horn and trying to get around them as they would have in California. Things were more laid back here.

Logan decided to try to establish a rapport with this guy. Isn't that what they did in the movies? Couldn't hurt at this point. As long as she was driving, she didn't think he'd shoot her, or else he'd be risking his own life. She tried to think of something positive to say.

"I know you didn't mean for Meiling to get hurt," she said. "Or mean to hurt anyone else."

Jian didn't reply.

"It sounds like you've been a good brother," Logan tried again. "How long have you played the piano for her?"

Silence. She sounded inane, even to herself.

The scenery was beautiful. Any other day, Logan would have enjoyed the deep, green trees and the dramatic, ocean vistas. They passed a small sign for Moss Creek Pottery. It couldn't be too much farther and they'd be in Lincoln City. If she could just get Jian to turn himself in—there must be a police station there. She didn't have much time left.

"Look, Jian, I don't know all the facts. I don't know who the men are who attacked your sister. I don't know what happened that night with Adam on the boat, but if there are extenuating circumstances . . . you're safer with the police than with whoever those guys were who attacked Meiling."

"Stop talking. Only drive!" Jian said.

Several fat raindrops hit the windshield. A blanket of gray clouds slid over the sun.

"I will, but you must know that whether Meiling tells them or not, the police will find out. They're probably already on their way. If you let me go now, I'll tell them you didn't mean me any harm. I'm a mother, Jian. I have a daughter, Amy, and a grandson. His name is Ian. I know you don't want to hurt me."

"Shut up!"

"You can take my car. Just pull over and let me out. You have my phone. I can't call anyone. You can get away . . . I know you're not a bad person."

❂ ❂ ❂ ❂ ❂

Jian looked at her, considering what she said. He'd been curling in on himself for some time, tightening every muscle, feeling more and more desperate. But this tendril of hope. This lifeline she was throwing him. Could it be possible?

She didn't know where he was going. He could make it to the train station. He'd stay off the main roads. GPS worked like that. He could take alternate routes. So, even if someone picked her up and loaned her their phone and she called the police, they might not find him.

He'd seen the train station right off the freeway on their way in from Portland. He'd take a train. Pay cash. He didn't think he'd have to show any ID at a train station. Not like all that security at the airport.

And where would he go? He couldn't go home. Not to China. Ever again. And he didn't trust Li Wei. Even if Beijing forgave him and he paid Li Wei back, he'd killed an American.

No. He needed to get lost. America was a very big country. With the cash in his bag, he could go a very long way. He might still have a chance.

"Up here," Jian said.

54

Was he going to let her go? Logan couldn't believe it. She'd never been that lucky. But she did as she was told, putting her blinker on, slowing down, trying not to hold her breath in case she passed out.

There was a bridge up ahead and a road, but there was nothing but people and houses beyond that, so Logan took a chance and braked now, easing off the highway onto the widest spot she could find on the very narrow shoulder. She left the engine running. There was a generous turnout and plenty of room for parking across the highway on the other side, but not here. On this side, a wall of green rose forty feet straight up a steep hill, forming an impenetrable barrier.

"Put your window down, then keep hands on the wheel," Jian said, letting himself out of the car.

There was barely enough room for him to open his door. The dense matt of tangled branches and brush almost made it impossible.

Logan did as instructed. A gust of cool wind blew in from the ocean. She smelled rain. Heard the seagulls.

Just another few minutes.

This is going to happen.

He's going to get in and drive away.

He's going to let me go.

I'll be stranded, but I'll be alive.

Logan suddenly noticed how quiet it was.

Where were all the cars?

As he came around the front of the car, Jian paused. He must have noticed the same thing. On the other side of the bridge, a police car blocked the highway, stopping all traffic from that direction.

As this registered, another car came up behind them, coming to a full stop, positioned slightly to the left, so Logan could see them plainly in her side mirror. One more car pulled in right behind the first one. There were no other vehicles on the road. She couldn't see, but someone farther back must be blocking traffic coming up from the south.

Jian had taken full advantage of the last few seconds. Holding the gun up so the cops could see it, he pointed it through the open window—aimed at Logan. His hair and shoulders were wet. If she had had anything to eat, she would have lost it. Abject fear left no room for dignity.

"Don't move until I say," he said.

As if she had a choice.

Every sound was magnified. The mechanical clunk of the car door as he pulled it open wide enough for Logan to get out. Like they were on a date. Her feet hitting the ground, gravel crunching as he swiveled her into position in front, shielding him, hand gripping the back of her neck, the muzzle of the gun up against her spine.

Out of the corner of her left eye, Logan could see a man she assumed was a police officer—even though he wasn't in uniform—crouched in a shooter's stance behind an open door on the passenger's side—gun clutched in both hands, aimed directly at them. Rick had once demonstrated this move to her.

Logan didn't see how they could shoot Jian without shooting her. Unless they were very good shots, and Rick said even trained police officers who qualified frequently missed more than half the time. And that was at the shooting range. Not in a hostage situation with adrenaline pumping through their veins.

"Police! Drop your weapon!"

In answer, Jian pressed the gun harder into Logan's back and edged her forward, across the highway, moving in lockstep with her.

A large Oregon History sign, informing visitors about the Great Tsunami of 1700, rose above a low, wooden fence running along a strip of untrimmed brush. Twenty feet below, a vast expanse of muddy flat sand stretched into a bank of fog and mist. Across a finger of water on the north, a small group of people were digging in the sand—probably clamming. Too far away to see what was happening here. They'd better hurry—the tide was coming in.

Right in front of them, about eighty yards away, rose several solitary sea stacks—little more than jagged chunks of rock and dirt—with a single, gnarled pine clinging to the top of the tallest one.

A survivor.

Jian stopped when they got to the edge, looking for a way down. She had to try something.

"Jian, you don't have to do this. Let's turn around. I'll walk in front of you. You can put your hand up with the gun in it, show them you're not going to use it," she said. "Otherwise there's a good chance we're *both* going to die, Jian . . . Please!"

She hated hearing the desperation in her own voice. Unbidden, tears filled her eyes. Panic rose in her chest. There had to be a way out of this. The thought of losing everything now, now that she had so much to live for . . . she couldn't let this happen.

A different voice now boomed, cutting through the fog. A much calmer one.

55

"Jian Zhang, this is Steve Grumley, FBI. No one is coming any closer. Let's take a break here. I know you don't want anyone to get hurt."

Logan felt Jian tense. They stopped.

"I spoke with your sister. Meiling, right? She's worried about you, Jian. Meiling is in surgery now. She's going to be okay. I know you care about your sister, Jian. We can get the men who did this to her, but we need your help."

Jian didn't answer, but he remained in the middle of the now empty highway.

The FBI man seemed encouraged by this.

"These are some very bad men, Jian. But you can help us bring them down—stop them from ever hurting anyone ever again. It's not too late, Jian. I have some pull here if you give me a chance. Helping us will go a long way in solving your problems with the police. But first you need to put your weapon down. Let the woman go. Think about it, Jian. Let's all relax here. Nothing will happen until you say so. Take all the time you need."

In answer, Jian pressed Logan forward, keeping her in front of him. Along one section of the fence, a single board barricaded a small, unofficial footpath made by visitors looking for a shortcut down to the flats. Jian instructed her to duck under it. She did, then reached her foot out, tapping the ground for a good spot, tentatively taking a step. Occasional patches of loose gravel made her unsure of her footing, but she kept going. Maybe if Jian felt safer, less exposed, he'd listen to the FBI.

She felt her heart beat against the hard steel of the gun. For a minute, her vision blurred from her tears, then she blinked her eyes furiously, forcing herself to concentrate. There'd be time to cry later.

She hoped.

They reached the bottom, Jian hugging them close to the earth wall they'd just come down, keeping them out of sight. She could no longer see the police or the FBI and had no idea what they were doing.

There was nowhere to go. Then Logan saw the head and shoulders of an officer running low toward them along the highway from the south—crouching down to keep from being seen.

So much for waiting for Jian to give himself up. What were they thinking?

They were trapped. All that lay before them was the bay. Only the first sea stack was visible, but just barely. And the tide was almost in. Logan didn't have time to make a plan. Things were happening too fast. All she knew was she wanted to get away—to put as much space as possible between herself and Jian. Give the cops a chance to take him down.

What was it they said? The lack of options clears the mind marvelously.

Using the one self-defense move she could remember, Logan raised her left foot and brought it down and back with as much force as she could, directly on the top of Jian's foot.

She wished she'd been wearing her boots. Tennis shoes didn't provide as much power. Bone didn't crunch, but he let out a yell and released his hold on her for a second.

A second was all she needed.

Launching herself away from Jian like a horse out of the starting gate at Churchill Downs, Logan, churning up sand and mud, sprinted for the first sea stack. All she could think about was getting something solid between her and Jian's gun. The foot of the first stack was only yards away.

A loud *BANG* split the air, followed rapidly by another, more muffled one. Terror seized Logan, but she didn't look back or wait to feel a bullet. Hurdling over a clump of rock and dirt, Logan landed on her bad ankle and almost fell. Regaining her balance, she could hear running footsteps, so if those sounds came from the cop's gun, he'd missed.

Quickly assessing her situation, she scanned what she could see. There wasn't much to shield her, but she had to take what she had. A bushy pine clung to the stack halfway up the side. Scrabbling until her feet got purchase, looking for handholds of rock or brush along the way, Logan began to climb.

She strained to hear the FBI guy on the megaphone, but if he was still talking, they couldn't hear him out here. Hopefully, the cavalry were on their way.

If the pathway down to the flats was narrow, the path up to the top of the island was non-existent. Raining in earnest now, the loose rock, dirt and sand was quickly turning to mud, causing Logan to slide back several times, but she had no choice but to keep going. Someone had made it before her. She'd seen people standing at the top, taking selfies. There had to be a way up.

"Stop!"

Jian's voice rang up from below. He was right behind her.

With every second, Logan wondered why he didn't just shoot, and then she realized why. He still needed her. The only chance Jian had was to get back to the car with her as his hostage. That's if he was thinking straight. In this situation, she couldn't be sure.

Nearing the top, Logan looked desperately for a final hand hold, something she could use to pull herself up onto the top. The smell of salt and wet earth filled her nostrils. The rock and dirt she clung to was turning into a mudslide.

If she could just make it to the other side, she had a chance. The cop she'd seen running toward them could stop Jian before he reached her. It was her only chance. If Jian got her back under his control again . . . .

Nope. That is not going to happen!

Logan spotted an exposed root twisting out and back into the rock and dirt several feet above her head—almost out of reach. Tightening her core, she gathered her body. Using every ounce of strength she had, pushed off the fragile foothold she was on. If she missed, she'd go crashing down the side into the water, which was now licking the base of the sea stack she was on.

Cold wind and rain lashed Logan's face, cutting her hair into her eyes. Jian's hand closed around her ankle, pulling her back. Grabbing onto the tree root, Logan caught herself, but lost her foothold. Frantically she searched for something, anything, to support her weight, stabbing her toe into every crack in the dirt and rock she could find. She couldn't afford to be choosy. When she found one she thought might hold, she pushed herself up, gripping the tree root harder. *Finally!* Using all her strength, she managed to pull herself up and over, crawling onto the flat surface of the stack.

In full force here, the rain pelted her back as she crawled, squashing herself against the rock and dirt, trying to disappear into the surface. Jian was right behind her. In seconds, he was up and over the edge, throwing himself on top of her, pinning her to the rock.

Pushing back with all her might, Logan twisted to the left and rolled out from under his body. A blast of cold air hit her chest and she tasted freedom.

But as she instinctively scrabbled to gather her feet under her, she heard another loud BANG, a deafening crack this time, momentarily stunning her. Something like a searing poker stabbed the back of her calf. Unable to stop the momentum propelling her toward the edge, Logan grabbed for anything to hold onto, but only succeeded in scratching and scraping her fingernails across loose stones. In one agonizing second, she realized she had lost.

Thrust into the air, for a moment, she felt nothing at all.

56

The day dawned warm and sunny, and had remained so, even though the weatherman had predicted rain. Colored light streamed into the chapel, painting the mourners in deep reds, blues, yellows, and an occasional splash of green. A solitary casket rested in the center aisle. Closed.

One of the last to arrive, Ben whispered an apology, but the usher waved it off. He'd been expecting him. He was to be seated in front, with family. The usher whispered directions and Ben pushed the wheelchair up the outside aisle, positioning it next to him at the end of the first pew, securing the brakes before he sat down.

He'd flown in on a red-eye Tuesday and hadn't gotten much sleep since. There was a surprising amount of work to do to prepare for a funeral. Between running errands and visits to the hospital, it had been a full week.

Vivi Hosteler spotted his arrival. Leaning forward in her seat, she reached across her husband to pat Ben's hand.

Then seeing his companion, Vivi got up, made her way past both men's knees and gave the woman in the wheel chair a long, tearful hug.

"And you," she said, "I'm so glad you could make it."

"Me, too," Logan said.

Thanks to Jian, she almost hadn't.

Logan remembered almost nothing after she blacked out, but sometime during her harrowing battle for survival on the top of the sea stack, she'd been shot. Adding insult to injury, she'd rolled over the side and fell thirty feet straight down. Although she felt like she'd broken every bone in her body when she came to, she'd landed in shallow water, missing a rocky outcropping—just barely.

No one would ever know what thoughts went through Jian's mind during those final seconds. Did he intend to shoot Logan, or did his gun simply discharge by accident in the struggle? No one would ever know. As soon as he had a clear shot, the deputy she'd seen running along the highway took it.

Jian's bullet had nicked Logan's shin bone, but hadn't shatter it. The surgeon who repaired her calf muscle said she was damn lucky it was a copper jacket and not a hollow point. With time and diligent physical therapy, she should heal well. It'd never be 100 percent, but close. Her leg might look funny, but all her toes would wiggle and yes, she'd be running on the beach again hopefully in the not-too-distant future.

As the service began, Logan looked around. She was pleased for the Hostelers to see so many people there. It was obvious Adam had been a respected member of the local community. After the eulogy, the minister invited people to come up and share their memories of Adam. In addition to his deckhand, Eric, quite a few charter boat captains got up to speak about how much they appreciated Adam's mentoring of them and how much he always helped others. Whatever the man's flaws, he'd obviously garnered many friends.

One admirer was conspicuously absent. Meiling. She had elected not to attend Adam's funeral. Logan assumed local law enforcement knew everything by now, but didn't know if Adam's family had been informed privately that it was Jian who'd killed their son or why. Due to the United States' current rocky relationship with China, the FBI had so far been able to keep the news of a Chinese national murdering an American on American soil out of the press.

After her own surgery, Logan had asked Ben to wheel her into Meiling's room, where she was still recovering. Meiling's injuries were far more serious. She faced a long rehabilitation period to regain the use of her feet, but as soon as she was able to travel, she said she planned on returning home to China.

Meiling said she couldn't face Adam's parents—it was her brother who'd killed their son, and she did not want to add to the family's grief. Let his memory rest in peace. Besides, she was grieving herself—not only for Adam, but also for her brother. She would do both privately.

Even though Jian had killed Adam and was responsible for her own injuries, he had been her brother. She even felt somewhat responsible for Adam getting killed, and for Jian being in America.

"I put Jian here. He was not ready. My actions led to this. I should have seen the signs," Meiling said.

Logan comforted her as best she could, but knew Meiling would have to battle her personal demons alone. She hoped she'd make it through to the other side, to a place of peace.

Vivi insisted they come back to the house and again thanked Ben for his help. Later, after most everyone had left, she took Logan aside, wheeling her into the office. Pulling a small package out of a desk drawer, she paused, holding it against her body for a minute, then handed it to Logan.

"I want you to give this to Meiling," she said. "Adam would have wanted her to have it."

So she did know. At least about their affair.

"It's pictures, mostly, of the two of them, some personal items. I found them on the *Mary Ann* when we starting going through it," she said. "I knew he and Debra weren't . . . weren't happy. They were never well matched. Adam didn't come right out and say so, but I knew. Looking back, I think I always knew. The first time he saw Meiling—whenever she was in the room, he came alive again."

For a moment, she looked lost, the pain still new and fresh, then met Logan's gaze evenly.

"Detective Monson came by. He wanted us to hear it from him before the whole story came out in the news—that Jian killed Adam. He also told me what happened to Meiling. The attack. It was just awful. I can't believe Jian got himself into so much trouble—borrowing money from some criminals in San Francisco and then stealing that coin from Stan to pay them back. From a receipt in his duffle bag, the police retraced Jian's steps back to a cash-for-gold place in Portland. That's where he got all that cash.

We didn't know Jian well. He kept in the background, but he seemed like such a nice young man. How could one man bring so much pain and destruction down on everyone around him?

"I wanted to go to the hospital, to see Meiling, but when the time came, I just couldn't.

"I hope she understands. But I want her to know we don't think what Jian did was her fault. I know she must be suffering—physically and emotionally. First Adam, then her brother. Both gone. And dealing with her injuries will take a long time.

"Please tell her for me . . . tell her she's a lovely, talented young woman. Her brother's sins are not hers. Tell her . . ." Vivi gathered herself together and looked up, ". . . tell her I would have approved," she said simply.

This was a message Logan was happy to deliver. Thanking Vivi for trusting her with such an important package, she tucked it into her purse and Vivi wheeled her out to the front door, where Ben was waiting.

Logan was impressed that Vivi looked beyond her own grief to alleviate the pain of another. It would have so easy to blame and wallow in hate. Even if Vivi couldn't bring herself to deliver the message in person, those simple, kind words would go a long way toward healing a young woman's guilt and grief. Logan hoped she would do the same given similar circumstances.

57

The flight to Orange County was blissfully uneventful, if uncomfortable. They got the last two seats on Sunday's flight out. Logan graduated to crutches for the trip, but because they had last minute tickets, the front row seats were already taken. The best they could do was an aisle and a middle in the back of the plane. Logan couldn't believe how cramped the seats were. Her under-the-seat bag, which had always slid in easily, barely fit. She had to jam it in with her good leg. Ben had to put his in the overhead.

"Jeez, can they pack any more of us in here?" Logan whispered.

When the drink cart came rattling by, Ben ordered for both of them.

"Two vodka and cranberries," he said.

"Make that three," said Logan.

Couldn't hurt.

Logan took a long draw from hers and tried to relax.

On the drive out, Ben had to spend most of the time on the phone pacifying a client, then calling Taylor, directing the work from his cell. When the hospital had called, he'd dropped everything and caught the first flight out. Logan told him she was fine and he didn't have to come, but Ben insisted. He'd made sure he was listed on all her devices as the first to contact in an emergency.

While they waited to board, she'd filled Ben in on her conversation with Vivi. Now it was his turn.

"What were you and Stan talking about out there while I was in with Vivi?" she asked.

"He mostly told me about what Detective Monson shared with them," Ben said. "Which was a lot."

"Like what?"

"He said Meiling verified what you told them Jian said in the ER. It took some time, but that and other new information that came in helped them tie up some loose ends, clarify things—particularly something they hadn't been able to explain in the ME's autopsy report."

Ben took a sip of his drink, waiting for the drink cart to rattle by on its second pass.

"Apparently Adam had been hit twice that night. They had a witness of sorts—homeless girl camping out on one of the boats nearby. They had video and interviews. With Jian's quasi-confession in the ER, they finally were able to piece everything together. They verified it with the wife.

"Debra didn't want to admit it, but she got into it with Adam earlier that night and hit him, but not hard enough to kill him. She was holding back because she didn't think the police would have believed her that Adam was alive and well when she left him there that night."

"They probably wouldn't have," Logan said.

"Yeah, they found out it was Jian who contacted Adam and arranged to meet that night," he said.

"With my phone?"

"Yep, they didn't get any prints off your phone, but there was a partial on one of the pearl buttons on Meiling's sweater Jian used to wrap your phone in."

There didn't seem too much else to say, so both of them settled into their thoughts. Ben got out his iPad and started working, rearranging his schedule for next week.

Logan shifted two inches in her seat, trying to get comfortable. Her leg was beginning to throb, but she didn't want to take any of the pain pills they'd given her. She poured the second little bottle of vodka into their plastic cups, splitting it 50/50 with Ben.

The pilot's assuring, monotone voice came on the air.

"Ladies and Gentlemen, we have now reached our cruising altitude of thirty-seven thousand feet. We are going to turn the seatbelt light off, and you are free to get up and walk about the cabin. But we ask that you keep your seatbelt fastened when you are seated. Hope you are enjoying your flight. We should reach Orange County a few minutes ahead of schedule tonight, so please relax and enjoy the remainder of your flight. We know you have a choice of airlines, so we want to thank you for flying Alaska."

Logan closed her eyes, letting her thoughts wander.

Now that everything was over and she was safely tucked into her seat, going home, the unfinished business she'd left behind filled her mind. Front and center, now, demanding her attention, refusing to be ignored any longer.

Logan sighed.

She and Rick had talked a couple of times since she'd been gone, but nothing had been resolved. She did manage to convince him to wait until she got back. Logan was going to give their mother one more chance. If she stood her up again, that was it. Door closed. She'd call her tomorrow.

Amy and Liam were waiting for them at home, dinner ready—two large pizzas and a tossed green salad. Ian kissed her booboo, then scooted off her lap to play with Marmo, who'd come over for a play date with Purgatory. Amy helped her unpack and do a load of laundry, while Ben and Liam cleaned up.

It was good to be home.

The next morning, after making sure she had everything she needed, Ben got on the road early. He'd be working late tonight to get caught up on his jobs, so Bonnie said she'd check in on her later.

Once Ben left and Logan had answered all her emails, she picked up her phone and stared at it. No sense putting it off any longer.

o o o o o

"Hello?" Her mother answered on the first ring.

"Hello, Sofia," Logan said, deciding not to use the honorific.

Her mother hesitated, but did not object.

"I hope since you're calling, you've decided to see me," she said.

"Yes, but only briefly," Logan said. "Where shall I meet you? I'm free tonight or tomorrow if that works for you." The sooner she got this over with, the better.

"Yes, of course. How about Emeline's at 6:00 p.m.? Or we can go somewhere else— anyplace you'd like."

"Emeline's is fine. I'll be there at 6:00," Logan said, disconnecting the call before she changed her mind. She was getting pretty good with the crutches. Emeline's was only a few blocks away. If she couldn't manage Killer Hill's steep angle down, she'd have Bonnie give her a ride, drop her off on her way home. After dinner, she could make her way back. Uphill was easier.

SAFE HARBOR

She hadn't meant to let it show, but a vein of anger had pushed its way to the surface the minute she heard her mother's voice . . . and it refused to be pushed back down.

58

Bonnie offered to come along for moral support, but Logan decided this was something she had to do alone. She'd left a message for Ben, letting him know where she'd be in case he got home early.

After showering and towel-drying her hair, she perused her tiny closet.

What to wear?

She hated that she cared.

Luckily, there wasn't much of a selection. And she was limited because of her leg. Her normal jeans and boots wouldn't fit over the bandage.

She finally decided on a pair of loose-fitting hiking pants and a long sleeve t-shirt. At the last minute, she added a light jacket. Even in August, summer nights turned cool at the coast, and there'd be air conditioning in the restaurant.

Downstairs, Dimebox fed, back door left open a crack for his nightly wanderings, Logan turned out the kitchen lights and swung her way to the front door. Grabbing the keys off the hook, she checked her reflection in the hall mirror.

Reaching into her bag, she found some lip gloss and slid some on with her ring finger. Standing back for a final look, she fluffed her hair so it would dry faster, opened the door and stepped out into the long rays of the summer sun. Coastal sage and salt tinged the air and herbal aromas were released each time she stepped on the thyme she'd planted between the slate flagstones creating the walkway that meandered out her front door to her studio, Lola's former garage.

"Sorry, girl. Takin' the biped route tonight," she said, patting Lola's hood as she went by. "I'll make it up to you soon, with an early morning spin."

There was nothing Lola liked better than a pre-dawn drive down PCH, before traffic. Logan, too. Hair pulled back, baseball hat jammed on her head, sunglasses at the ready for the sun's appearance over the horizon, she loved those mornings. Even in the winter, she loved to feel the wind on her face. In her mind, every day was a top down day!

In spite of the crutches, Logan made it on time, giving herself a pep talk on the way.

You're a grown woman. With a job, a child of your own, and a man who loves you. And a grandson. Nothing this woman has to say is going to change anything. It's an hour out of your life. Let her say her piece, then send her on her way.

When she arrived, the *maitre d'* showed her to a table in the back, one with an ocean view, where Sofia was already seated. Logan had never eaten here. The menu was above her budget.

After explaining away the crutches as nothing more than a sprained ankle, Logan leaned them against the wall and lowered herself into her seat.

"I thought you might like French, since you so enjoyed your exchange student experience in Provence," she said.

Logan wondered how she knew about that. That was in high school, several years after Sofia left. She'd lived with a family in the south of France—one with both a mother and a father in residence.

"Yes, I did," was all she could think to say.

After the waiter took their order and Logan said yes to wine, her mother ordered a bottle of something white. If you could go by the depth of the waiter's bow and the dollar signs in his eyes as he went to fetch it, it must have been expensive.

Whatever. Might as well let the woman spend her money.

Wine arrived and poured, Logan settled back and took a sip. It was very good. She settled back into the booth, subconsciously distancing herself, and looked at the woman sitting across from her. Silk dress. Perfect hair and makeup. Very chic.

"You must have a lot of questions," Sofia began.

A set of readers lay by her plate. Must have needed them to read the menu. Again, Logan was struck by how much her mother had aged. The setting sun streaming in the window threw her smoker's lines into relief and she could see now the stylish cut was an attempt to hide her thinning hair.

Logan felt no obligation to start the conversation. This was her mother's show. It wasn't her job to make this any easier for her. She looked at her evenly over her glass, then took another sip of the delicious wine. Waiting.

"Okay. You're right. Probably the best way to do this is for me to just tell you. Then if you have any questions, you can ask them."

59

"Your father and I were happy. Deliriously so. We met at Stanford and when we graduated, like many young couples, we packed up our car and moved to wherever the jobs were. Orange County, in our case, so your father could take an engineering position, as you probably know."

Logan nodded. She knew all this.

"I wanted to live in New York, near our parents—it turns out we grew up just blocks apart, but never knew each other back then, or San Francisco, even—but we had to go where the work was. I was a CPA, so I could work anywhere," she said, pausing to take another drink of wine.

"We were fine for a while. Your father was happy here. He loved the hiking, the surfing, the laid back everything. When you came along, you were just like him. Not only did you look like your father's Scotch/Irish side of the family—tall and lean—you also had the same energy and temperament. If the two of you could have lived and slept out under the stars every night, I'm sure you would have. I didn't fit."

Sofia turned the stem of her wineglass clockwise, with perfectly manicured fingers and glanced out the window, watched a pigeon pecking at some breadcrumbs left on a railing outside.

"I managed to stay busy and if you remember, when you were very young, I went on the camping trips. I may not have gone on the hikes, but I was always there."

Logan did remember. Her mother was there, sitting at the picnic table, doing someone's books by lantern light, but didn't join in the fun. What she could not remember was ever seeing her mother smile.

"I know it's hard for you to understand, to understand how the things that made you and your father so happy didn't make everyone else happy, but they didn't," she said. "I felt more and more like I was living someone else's life. And more and more left out of yours."

"There was a conference I needed to attend. Well, I wanted to attend. It was being held in New York," she said. "It was rare for companies to pay for women to travel back then. It didn't take your father long to encourage me to go. We were hardly speaking by then. You'd just turned twelve."

Logan remembered a baseball-mitt-shaped birthday cake and an afternoon game with her dad. He got great seats, just behind home plate. She sat on his left and Rick sat on the other side. Her mother must have been there, too, but she couldn't place her.

"The next morning I flew to New York," she said. "After the conference, I decided to visit his parents. Mine had both passed away. They invited me to extend my stay, and since I knew I wouldn't be missed, I agreed."

Sofia's eyes lit up. "His mother and I had a wonderful time—museums, shopping, then out with both of them to see a show or meet friends for dinner."

Her voice raised a little and took on a slight pleading tone,

"I wanted to bring you out to New York, to see the city before school started, but you didn't want to leave the beach, or your father."

Logan didn't remember being asked, but it was a long time ago. She did remember her father making comments about it—how it was a crowded, dirty city so jammed with people and cars he couldn't breathe there.

"I came back a week before your first day back. Wanted to make sure you had your clothes and school supplies, but your father had already taken you," Sofia looked sadly up at Logan. "You didn't need me even for that. He'd taken over everything. The cooking—such as it was, neither one of us were very good cooks—your homework, the bedtime stories . . ."

The waiter cleared his throat to announce his arrival.

"*Cassoulet*," he said, placing Logan's dinner, an aromatic, comfort food dish her French foreign-exchange mother often made in the winter, in front of her. "And for you, Madame," he said, delivering what looked like a vegetable quiche to Sofia, "the *Flamiche*."

"*Bon Appetit!*"

They turned down the offer of another bottle of wine, although they'd made a good dent in this one. Sofia suggested they eat first, then finish their talk. Not that Logan was saying anything. They covered the weather and other safe small talk, but, for the most part it, was an awkward, mostly silent meal.

After the waiter removed their dinner plates and discreetly brushed the crumbs from the white, linen tablecloth, Sofia asked for coffee and continued.

"Just before Thanksgiving, we had a huge fight. The next day, I left," she said.

Logan sat stunned. She couldn't imagine any scenario in which she would give up Amy.

"Your children—one thirteen year old daughter and a nine year old son, weren't worth more than a few lunches and museums?"

"That's not why I left," Sofia said quietly.

"Then why?" Logan asked.

Apparently she did want to know.

"I discovered I was pregnant," she breathed, "and the child—the child wasn't your father's."

Logan took a moment to absorb this surprising bit of news. Her mother sat up straighter in her chair.

"I met someone in New York, an older man, Peter Landers. I offered to end it, of course. I already had, in a way, by coming home to California. But I would not get rid of the baby." She took a breath. "That was a deal breaker for your father.

"He insisted I get an abortion. That was the deal. In order to be with you and Rick, I would have to get rid of my unborn child. And he wasn't offering forgiveness even if I had the abortion."

Sofia took a drink of courage and looked Logan directly in the eyes. "My life would have been hell if I'd stayed."

Logan couldn't imagine her father being so cruel. On the other hand, she couldn't imagine raising a child that your spouse had with another person while still married to you. What a mess.

Sofia continued, "We fought until we were too tired to fight anymore. He slept on the couch that night. I never did get back to sleep. I'm Catholic, but I don't know how much that had to do with my decision. It would have gone against everything I'd been taught if I'd had an abortion."

"But adultery was okay?" Logan said.

Her mother didn't answer.

"I was exhausted, probably not thinking straight, but I had a life with a man who understood me and loved me waiting for me in New York, and his child on the way. I took it . . . and paid a very high price."

Just then, the waiter arrived with their coffee. He started to tell them about tonight's desserts, but taking a look at the two women's faces, thought better of it.

Smart man.

60

LABOR DAY

Labor Day may have marked the official end of summer, but you couldn't tell by the thermometer. Temperatures were still in the eighties and nineties. Southern California had no winter to speak of, and fall didn't make its first cool foray until sometime around Thanksgiving, if then.

In spite of her injury, Logan had put in full days working with her leaders the last ten days, getting Fractals up and running for the school year. For once, they were fully funded and staffed. As Logan spent more and more time fundraising and up in Oregon at the New School, Mavis Washington had been taking on increasing responsibilities here. With Mavis as her second in command, Logan was hardly needed. Hiring her was the best decision Logan had ever made. Unlike Logan, Mavis was an experienced educator, with thirty years of teaching under her belt—twenty in the classroom and ten as an administrator. Mavis deftly navigated the school district's political waters better than Logan ever could.

Although Amy didn't work as a teacher, her job at Jasper's Sea Otter Center was tied to the school calendar. Amy was in charge of educational programs and field trips. She, Liam, and Ian had come early to help set up. Liam always threatened to bring the *haggis*, but never followed through.

Usually Bonnie and Mike and their kids came, but they were going to his folks this year. So, it would just be family.

After long and hard consideration and a marathon phone call with Bonnie, Logan had decided family included Sofia. She still couldn't bring herself to call her Mom, but couldn't deny Rick that opportunity, or deprive Amy of a grandmother and Ian of a great-grandmother.

And there was more family in their future. Logan was still wrapping her head around the fact that she had a half-sister out there. Madison Olivia Landers, a thirty-three-year old New Yorker—single, no kids. Sofia had wisely made the call not to bring her daughter or her husband along on this trip. One step at a time.

Logan still didn't know what made Sofia reach out to her now and not during all the years that had gone before, but she supposed the woman had her reasons. Weird how your own mother could be a stranger in so many ways. It would take time to get to know her again.

Right now, Ian was showing Sofia his favorite toy, a stack of different colored, plastic rings that lit up when he got them in the right order. To her credit, Logan thought, Sofia hadn't shown up with a truckload of expensive gifts to win him over, but sat quietly playing with him. She'd even dressed down to capris and flats, probably didn't own a pair of jeans.

Watching them now, Logan felt a fierce wave of protectiveness. Her first instinct was to whisk them all away—Rick, Amy, Ian—wrap them in bubble wrap in case Sofia let them down again. But she let the feeling roll over her and pass. Not only would it be impossible, but withholding love or trying to control everything wouldn't really protect anyone.

If she hadn't let go of her hurt and anger toward Jack, if she'd continued to live in fear, she'd never have let Ben into her life. Yes, love was always a risk, but better than being locked in a prison of your own making.

Rick and Paula brought Portuguese beans, a recipe from Paula's Aunt Marilyn. And Charlie, Rick's K-9 partner. Entering the back yard gracefully, Charlie made his way over to the newcomer, sniffed her tentatively, then lay at her feet, nosing Ian playfully.

Traitor.

Ben assuaged her feelings with a shoulder rub and a fresh glass of wine.

After everyone left, Ben helped Logan up the stairs to the rooftop deck to enjoy the stars and listen to the sibilant shushing of the ocean gently caressing the shore. She still kept her crutches handy, but relied on them less and less. Lying back, they took in the view. Reaching over, Logan took Ben's hand in hers, grateful for his presence.

Her mind drifted back to her moments of terror on the sea stacks, not knowing if she was going to live or die. Life was so tenuous. It could easily have gone either way.

Life was also short. Logan looked over at Ben and grinned. She'd have to make an honest man out of him someday.

61

Logan's leg was healing well, so she kept the reservations for her regularly scheduled October trip to the New School. Huey was going to show her some upgrades he'd made to his animated computer math program.

But before that, Ben joined her for a three-day romantic getaway in her favorite city, Portland. They had reservations at the Sentinel and Jake's Grill the first night for a true Pacific Northwest dinner of fried oysters and ribeye steaks, Logan's favorite.

They wandered through the never-ending book stacks at Powell's, took in a play, and ended their stay with a trip to the Japanese gardens. Ben was always looking for new ideas, and Logan just loved the calm and peace that surrounded her there.

The night before, they'd met Huey, Than, and her new husband, Tamim, for dinner. Logan recognized Tamim as the handsome owner of the food truck next to Than's, Damascus Dining. After all Than had been through, Logan was glad to see her so relaxed and happy.

After dinner they'd walked down to a club Rheanna was

playing at. A dispatcher with Portland PD as well as a musician, Rheanna was also Rick's fiancee's old roommate. Logan had stayed with her briefly a few years ago when she first started working with the New School.

Logan didn't have Bella with her, but Rheanna loaned her a violin and she sat in for a set. When she got back, a man Logan recognized joined them at the table. Sometime in the last two years, Detective Keenan had graduated from Rheanna's boyfriend to her husband. Ben pulled out a chair for Logan at the increasingly crowded table.

Amy, Than, Rheanna, Rick . . . was everybody getting married?

⊙ ⊙ ⊙ ⊙ ⊙

The next day, Ben took the MAX to the airport and Huey gave Logan a ride out to the New School, where she put in a full week before taking up Rita's offer to spend a few days at her place in Little Whale Cove.

Rita said she'd understand if she didn't want to go back so soon, given her recent ordeal, but Logan found herself accepting her offer immediately.

Something about the Oregon coast kept drawing her back. Besides, she looked forward to visiting with Vivi, who'd been keeping in touch the last few months. She said she'd been spending a lot of time with Debra and the girls. She hadn't been very close with her daughter-in-law, but now that Adam was gone, their relationship had improved. In her last email, she'd shared that Meiling had flown back to China and probably would not be returning. She had finally gone to the hospital to visit her. Meiling told her she'd accepted a job teaching at the music academy in Beijing.

She also told her that when the police tracked down the money in Jian's duffel bag, they discovered the theft and subsequent sale of Stan's coin. Stan had noticed it was missing, but had assumed he'd misplaced it in his hurry to get downstairs and help Vivi with the concert preparations. And then of course, the news of his son's death pushed such unimportant concerns from his mind.

As soon as all the paperwork was completed, Detective Monson said the funds would be deposited into their account. They'd decided against the cruise, starting a college fund for the girls and a Safe Harbor scholarship in Adam's memory instead.

Also, according to Monson, they didn't need to worry about any more violence from San Francisco. With Jian dead and his sister back in China, Li Wei had no one to collect from. The only arrests the FBI had been able to make were the two goons who's attacked Meiling. Grumley was hoping they'd turn on their boss, but it wasn't a done deal. So far, they hadn't.

With no agenda, Logan spent most of her time taking long, meandering walks through the forest and along the ocean path that ran along the bluffs. This afternoon, she'd walked into Depoe Bay. Just like in Jasper, her favorite time of year was when the tourists were gone. Stopping for some coffee first, she crossed the highway and sat on the bench anchored on the edge of a small grassy area behind the sea wall.

She loved it here.

The Oregon coast was such a unique and beautiful place. On this trip, she'd gotten a better sense of the people who anchored these towns sprinkled along Highway 101. The tenacious, hard-working families who sank down roots, clung to the rocks and weathered the storms, making their living in one way or another from the wild, open sea. The residents of Newport, Depoe Bay, and Lincoln City, Oregon.

The more she got to know these people, the more she respected them.

Jasper would always be her hometown, an oasis of beauty in Southern California, rare in that it had not been overdeveloped like every other square inch of Orange County. But drive five miles in any direction from Jasper and you slammed into either a stucco subdivision, a shopping mall, or bumper to bumper traffic that crawled in the baking heat almost twenty-four seven.

In contrast, the Oregon coast's cool, rugged beauty stretched for miles, interrupted every ten miles or so by small towns not much more than wide spots on the 101. These were real towns, grown from the original fishing and logging families who worked forest and sea, not artificial suburban communities with street names of ivy-league schools back east.

Amy & Liam like it, too, and Ben felt the same way.

Her phone burred, so she pulled it out and retrieved a text from Ben. She smiled. He'd already been looking online and sent her several properties to check out while she was there.

She didn't know how they'd swing it, but if they pooled their money, they just might have enough. She'd never thought of herself as a woman who could afford a second home, but why not? They'd run the numbers and with a large enough down payment, it was doable. She traveled up here for work several times a year anyway. Neither of them had any debt and Ben had saved a good chunk over the years. Of course, this meant her relationship with Ben would take a significant move forward.

Surprisingly, the thought didn't scare her.

Looking out to sea, she reflected on all that had happened over the last few years. Jack's death, the new life she'd built for herself and loved—her house, her rediscovered joy and passion for music, changing careers, getting Fractals off the ground and bringing music to so many more children. Ben.

Of course there had been other deaths besides Jack's. Young

lives cut off. Families forever changed. She was beginning to realize she could feel the full force of those tragedies without letting them overwhelm and devastate her. Facing these losses makes you realize how precarious life was, but also, how precious. We're not guaranteed the next second, let alone the next decade.

She didn't want to waste any of it—this fragile, wonderful life. Whatever number of years she had left on the planet, she wanted to live them fully with those she loved.

Just then, a big *whoosh* startled her, followed by a vertical spout of water just yards away. Logan looked down in time to see the back of one of the resident gray whales slide by, then slowly sink back under the surface as it continued on its way. She loved that it came this close, surfacing to breathe as it scratched its barnacled back along the rocks or fed in the kelp beds nearby.

"Hey there, big guy," she said.

Just knowing the gentle leviathans were still out there, doing their thing, in spite of the challenges they faced, gave weight to Logan's world.

As long as there are whales, we'll be okay.

ACKNOWLEDGMENTS

I rely, as Blanche Dubois said in *A Streetcar Named Desire*, 'on the kindness of strangers'. At least in regards to occupations, law enforcement procedures, settings, historical events, and the many other topics I need to understand in order to write my books. If I have, or can obtain first-hand experience, I do, but if I don't know something, I'm not afraid to ask.

I'm often calling people I don't know and asking them to take time out of their day to tell me about their jobs. For this book, whether I wanted to learn about charter boats, whales, fisheries, the Coast Guard, or the Lincoln County Major Crimes Team, everyone I asked stepped up to the plate and generously shared their expertise with me. I tried my best, within the realms and demands of fiction, to represent the knowledge they shared with me authentically. All remaining errors are mine.

Captain Frank Boersma, Retired, and Chief Pettey Officer Seehagen, Boatswains Mate, USCG shared their knowledge of Coast Guard personnel and procedures. Living on the coast, we really get to see how much everyone here relies on their service.

Linda Snow, Retired Lead Legal Assistant, Deschutes County, Oregon, who currently works cold cases for the Lincoln County District Attorney's office, and Ron Benson, Lincoln County Investigator and member of the Lincoln County Major Crimes Team helped me understand the way homicide investigations work in the Lincoln County area covering Lincoln City, Depoe Bay, Toledo, and Newport, Oregon. I wish I could have used some of the real stories they shared—they were much more amazing than anything a fiction writer could have dreamed up! Truth is indeed stranger than fiction.

When I wanted to understand more about my new community, including the fishing industries and local history here, several people provided assistance. Stuart Cory, NOAA Special Agent (retired), taught me about fisheries, law enforcement, and Interpol. Michele Eder Longo, author of Salt in Our Blood: The Memoir of a Fisherman's Wife, introduced me to the beauty and hazards of the lives of commercial fishermen. I'm a lot more aware and appreciative of every piece of fish I buy and eat, now that I know how it gets to my store and onto my plate.

I was also lucky enough to meet the Depoe Bay twins, Lizbeth Robison Martin and Lars Robison, who shared their lifelong knowledge of charter boat fishing in the area. Lars is also the co-owner of Dockside Charters and Captain of the Samson. Although we didn't know it at the time, by serendipitous good fortune, the image selected for the cover turned out to be one of his earlier boats going into the harbor under the Depoe Bay Bridge. I'd also like to thank the photographer, Bob Poole of Salem, Oregon, for the photo.

Jeremy Burke, Publisher of the News Times in Newport, Oregon, generously provided access to his reporters, Madeline Shannon, Stephanie Blair, and Steve Card, Executive Editor.

My fictional reporter, Samantha Badger, will probably find her way into future novels.

It wouldn't be an acknowledgments page without thanking my hard-working Alpha and Beta readers, who plow through earlier drafts to help me strengthen the story before it goes to editing: Michelle Montclaire, Maurice Davisson, Alisha Henry, Lois Oestrich, Sue Levy, and Mickey Boersma.

Cover, interior design, and editing were provided by the very talented and hard-working Kimberly Peticolas. She is also responsible for the powerful new cover and interior designs of the second editions of the first four books of my Logan McKenna series.

The writing community, both online and in person, is full of generous and sharing people. Orange County Writers, Author Support Network, Teresa Burrell, Indy Quillen, Julie Davis, and many others provide ongoing mutual support and fun in all aspects of this profession. Many people I've met at conferences, book fairs, and library events have become close friends.

Last, but not least, I want to thank my readers for their enthusiasm and loyalty. So glad they love reading about Logan McKenna and friends as much as I enjoy writing about them.

ABOUT THE AUTHOR

A self-admitted book addict, Valerie Davisson was the kid with the flashlight under her pillow, reading long after lights out. After a life of travel, she now lives on the Oregon coast with her husband, John, and their new puppy, Finn. When not working on her latest book, she's probably in the kitchen, cooking up a storm for family and friends.

Enjoyed the Book?

If you enjoyed *Safe Harbor*, please consider leaving a review on Amazon or Goodreads. And be sure to check out the rest of the Logan McKenna series.

Shattered (Book 1)

Forest Park (Book 2)

Devil's Claw (Book 3)

Vanishing Day (Book 4)

Want to know more about Valerie Davisson or her next book? Make sure to visit www.valeriedavisson.com and sign up for her newsletter.